HAWKE'S REVENGE

Historical Adventure on the Western Frontier

A.T. BUTLER

CHAPTER ONE

Raucous laughter from the group of men at the bar distracted him. When he looked up, the edge of the table jabbed into his ribs. Matthew Hawke sucked in his breath sharply, and he brought his gaze back to the man across from him, his rage building. Standing abruptly, Matt deliberately pushed the table back into the other man.

Matt had always had a problem with his temper. He wasn't proud of it, but now that he was out west in the territories, among men who reveled in their lawlessness, he found that there were more and more occasions for him to lose it. This land was so far from being settled that basic politeness was disregarded by many, and all Matt seemed to find were frustrations. Men who cheated. Men who lied. Men who didn't respect women the way they should.

And now this man in particular, trying to intimidate him by pushing the poker table into him.

"Look, mister," Matt said, balling his hands into fists.

"You've already relieved me of my horse. I got nothing left. I don't even know where I'm gonna sleep tonight. I don't have anything else you want. Let's call this quits before I get really angry and do something I shouldn't."

"You? Angry? Is that supposed to scare me?"

Matt's adversary stood up to match him, glaring over the expanse of table littered with cards and poker chips. The four other players merely watched, not involving themselves. One avoided Matt's eyes deliberately. Each was trying to stay out of the confrontation and let the older man do what he needed to do.

"I'm gonna go," Matt insisted, "before this gets messy."

He stepped to the side and stumbled a bit, tripping over the leg of the chair in his attempt to extricate himself. Matt had been in situations like this before. If he stayed much longer, he'd be slugging the man in the jaw before he even realized his fist was in the air. He needed to put distance between them.

"You're gonna sit back down and finish," the older man said, pointing emphatically at the chair.

Matt shook his head. The man—Bud, he thought his name was. Bud Humphrey—had bullied him into taking the game in the first place, bullied him into raising his bets, and, now that Matt was down to a single greenback and his pistol, was attempting to bully him into handing those over as well. It was time for Matt to stand up for himself. No more showing deference to his elder.

Bud didn't deserve that respect.

He had intended to say his say, and leave the saloon as calmly as he could, but one glance at Bud's fury and Matt knew it wouldn't be that easy. But if he stayed,

Matt's temper would get him in trouble. All he wanted to do was wipe that smirk off the other man's face, to make him pay for his bullying. As he tried to back away from the table, Bud rushed him. He pushed past two men standing nearby and was in Matt's face in an instant.

Matt was tall; he was used to towering over other men, having reached his full height of six feet when he was only fourteen years old. But Bud was just as tall. His bushy, tobacco-stained mustache was only inches from Matt's own mouth. The man glared at him, eye to eye. As he continued to back up, away from Bud, Matt struggled to contain his temper. He clenched his teeth, willing himself to be the more mature one. He didn't owe Bud a thing. And if the man kept pushing him, he'd get more than he was looking for. But such thoughts were interrupted, as Matt backed into the row of drinkers leaning against the bar.

Just after sunset as it was, the Golden Eagle Saloon had filled quickly. All the ranch hands and cowboys from the surrounding country were blowing off steam and finding refreshment after a long day. Juniper Falls, Wyoming, was home to two churches and a few hundred folks finding their fortunes in the rising beef prices. Most of the town was dedicated to their work, and the Golden Eagle Saloon was their only option for a drink, if they didn't want to ride the three hours to Laramie.

It was right into two of these hard-working, whiskey-deserving ranch hands that Matt stumbled backwards. He hardly had realized what happened when he was roughly shoved forward, back into Bud. There was a short pause, the space of a breath, as Bud realized what had happened, before he shoved Matt right back.

Soon four different men were shoving Matt off of them; he couldn't keep his feet underneath him, and not a single one seemed to hear him calling for them to stop. All the while, his anger rose. He may not be as experienced a card player as these boys, but surely he had a right to decide when his game was done. For not the first time in the past few weeks, Matt wondered if coming west had been a mistake.

Getting one final kick to the knee, Matt dropped to the dusty wooden floor under their feet. His hat fell from his head. He had gone too long without a haircut, and his dirty blond hair fell into his face as he groped along the floor.

Matt's knee burned with pain, but the kicks kept coming. Somehow, barely, he clawed his way between the legs of the men surrounding him. No longer caring who he offended, Matt pushed men aside as he lurched to his feet. At least one of them was knocked to the ground next to him, but Matt didn't have time to see if he was also getting kicked.

"Hey!" he heard from behind him.

Matt didn't stop in his scramble. He left his hat in the chaos—maybe it would remain unnoticed and trip up one of his pursuers—and staggered the few feet between himself and the front door. Around him echoed more shouts of protests, rough laughter and even a couple gunshots, but all he wanted was to get out. He had a faint hope that Bud wouldn't consider him worth the effort. Maybe once he reached the road he could relax.

Matt pushed open the door to the saloon, almost falling the few steps across the boardwalk and into the dirt road of Juniper Falls. He inhaled deeply of the spring evening air. He was out. He was free. He still needed to figure out how he was going to pay for his bed that night. Matt stuck his hand in his pocket and fingered the only dollar he had left.

That thought was jolted from his mind as he heard another shout close behind him.

"You!" Bud roared. "You get back here!"

Matt glanced briefly over his shoulder, startled that the man was even closer than he thought, before he took off running down the street, limping slightly as his right knee still ached. It infuriated him that he couldn't stand and fight this man, but Matt didn't get this far on his own by being reckless. It was hard enough to keep his temper from getting in his way. He'd have to wait, bide his time, and get his revenge another day.

He ran, first to the right then back to the left and down a dark, narrow alley between buildings, hoping to lose the man still cursing and panting behind him.

A heavy thud told Matt that Bud had followed him into the alley, ricocheting against the side of a building as he curved around the corner.

"Blast it," Matt whispered to himself.

He couldn't catch a break. What had he done to warrant this? It was just a poker game. A poker game that Matt hadn't even won.

The alley ended and Matt darted around another corner to run up still another street, all the while hearing Bud's footsteps and increasingly heavier breathing behind him. He glanced briefly over his shoulder and noticed with a burst of relief that he had managed to increase the distance between them. Just as he was about to push a little harder into a sprint, a shot rang out against the quiet night.

Almost immediately, Matt felt a searing pain in his right calf. He lost all strength in that leg and tumbled to the ground, rolling several feet in the dirt as he reached for the pain. His pant leg was quickly becoming drenched, and when Matt pulled his hand back up to his face, the fingers were stained with blood.

He had been shot.

Shot!

The pain blurred his vision momentarily. He couldn't see Bud stalking toward him, but he heard him. Heavy steps. A low, triumphant chuckle.

"You shot me," he said weakly.

"I told you, boy. You don't walk away from me or my game."

"Look," Matt groaned out as he marshaled his strength. "I don't know—"

"What is this?" a third voice said. "Back away from the boy, Humphrey."

Matt was sitting up in the dirt, hunched over his injured leg, and it took all his power just to turn his head to see who the new speaker was. The dim light coming from nearby windows illuminated the street. An older, white-haired man with a full gray beard and attire refreshingly free of dust stood about a dozen feet behind him, with his hand resting casually on the butt of his gun.

Matt had not seen this man in the mere week he had been in Juniper Falls. There was no reason he could guess why he was coming to Matt's aid. In spite of the kindness of the man, Matt couldn't help but flush with embarrassment. He was no boy. He was twenty years old. He had been on his own for almost six years. Who did this man think he was?

"Back off, Conway," Bud was saying when Matt was able to focus again. "This ain't your business. Why don't you move along and let me finish up here?"

The man called Conway stepped closer, almost to Matt's side. "Bud Humphrey. Looks like this boy could use a doctor."

Bud chuckled. "Maybe. Not my problem."

"It will be your problem if he bleeds out and dies. I'll see to that."

"You think Sheriff Vance gives a—"

"Murder is murder, Humphrey. No matter who is investigating." Conway squatted in the dirt next to Matt and handed him a handkerchief. "Tie that around the wound. Tie it tight, now. I'll see that you're all stitched up, but for now we have to stop the bleeding."

Matt took the worn blue sliver of fabric and mumbled thank you. His pride still burned from being treated like a child, but if wishes were horses, then beggars would ride and he didn't like to think about the possibility this man was right. Any injury could kill a man if it wasn't seen to properly.

After he had seen to Matt, Conway continued walking forward, straight toward Bud and stood between them.

"Go on then, Humphrey," Conway said with a nod. "You won. You shot this kid from behind, injured him beyond escape, and, if I know you, have already taken all the money he has. What are you even doing here?"

"He left the game before I was done with him. I won't be disrespected. He's gotta learn how things are around here."

Matt scowled. That was a problem? When he had played poker with the boys at Hamilton Prep, that had never been a rule. He sighed, shaking his head, frustrated with himself. He'd learn, eventually. Hopefully before he got himself shot again.

Conway was chuckling. "Humphrey, if you cleaned him out, what good would him staying in the game do?"

Bud frowned, darting his eyes to Matt sitting on the ground. "He still got his pistol."

"That's right. I do. And I'll—"

"Son. Believe me. He's not worth it. Bud, you let him alone," Conway insisted, this time drawing his gun casually on the other man. "Enough."

"Bud! You coming?"

Matt vaguely recognized one of the other card players pop his head around the street corner and yell for his friend. He held his breath, barely daring to hope that the cranky man would give up his quarry. But, he must have had enough. Or he was more afraid of Conway than he let on. With a huff, followed by a self-conscious laugh, Bud backed away.

"I'll leave it. But only because this boy is all but lying in a puddle of his own blood. I don't want to see your face there again, you hear?" he concluded, shouting threats at Matt.

Matt nodded, gulped, and held his tongue. If he hadn't been shot he could hold his own; he could fight this man with fists or words. But, the fact that the pool of blood under his leg was only getting bigger kept him grounded.

Conway and Matt stayed silent, not even looking at each other as Bud headed on down the road and turned the corner to go back to the Golden Eagle Saloon. Once he was surely out of ear shot, Matt spoke up.

"Thanks a lot, mister." He started to pull himself to his feet.

"Whoa there." Conway squatted in the dirt next to him again. "You just hold on now a minute. I didn't go through all that just to have you faint on me."

"I ain't going to faint," Matt protested, but paused in his attempt to stand as he adjusted to a wave of dizziness. "I'm not. I'm fine."

"You're not."

"Yeah. I am. I just need—"

"Stop." Conway put a big hand on Matt's shoulder, holding him gently but firmly on the ground. The warmth in his deep gravelly voice was comforting, and made Matt more inclined to listen, in spite of his frustration at being treated like a child. "You don't have to get up just yet. Why don't I re-tie this handkerchief," the older man deftly bandaged up his leg with what he had, "and you can tell me what you have planned. You got a place to stay tonight?"

"Well, I—"

Matt stopped himself. He had been staying in a cramped boarding house near the outskirts of town. He could probably talk his way into one more night before Mrs. Bennett realized he was out of money, but that wouldn't be fair to her. He supposed he could probably find a barn or stable to bed down in for a night, but eventually he would need a way to make more money. It didn't seem as though cards would be the way to do it.

"I'll figure it out," he told Conway stubbornly.

"Hmph." The older man stood. His gun had been holstered, and he pulled out second handkerchief that he used to wipe the little bit of Matt's blood off his hands. "No, that won't do at all. You're coming with me."

"What?" Matt spluttered, trying again to get to his feet. The bandage around his calf was much stronger now; he was losing less blood but he still hadn't quite recovered his strength. Conway watched silently as Matt struggled. "I ain't coming with you. That is ... I'm not. Thank you, sir, but—"

"Son, my ranch isn't that far outside of town. I have the medical supplies necessary to help you heal, and I won't charge you the way Dr. Gilpin would. I can offer you a warm meal and a heavy blanket for tonight at least. What else are you going to do? Come with me. My wife would never let me hear the end of it if I didn't offer you simple Christian charity. Do it for her, at least."

"I can figure it out, I said."

"Like you figured out how to beat those boys at poker?"

Matt could tell the man was teasing him. Conway's bushy white mustache twitched, even as it hid his smile.

"I'm not a child," Matt said, too late realizing how petulant he sounded.

"Of course you're not," Conway answered soothingly. "You're an injured man. And there's nothing wrong with taking help now and again."

Matt sighed. He was losing the energy to argue any

further with this man, this stranger. Should he be suspi-cious of his motives? Matt noticed a dull gold ring on his left hand. So, Conway was married. He wasn't lying about that. Maybe he was telling the truth about the rest too.

"Well," Matt began, hesitant to give in too quickly. "Thanks, but, I lost my horse too. I don't have any way to get out there."

Conway beamed, bent down to grab Matt's upper arm and help him to standing. "That's no trouble, son. It just so happens I brought my wagon to town this morn-ing. Come with me and we'll get you fixed up."

Matt winced as he put weight on his injured leg. Even with Conway's help this wouldn't be easy. In spite of his reservations, he was grateful he didn't have to do this alone.

"My name's Matt, by the way. Matthew Hawke."

Conway nodded, his face close to Matt's as he bore some of his weight. "Richard Conway. Pleased to meet you, Matt."

CHAPTER TWO

The ride from Juniper Falls to Conway's ranch was easy and comfortable, even after dark. Conway asked Matt questions, peppered by small anecdotes and observations, but didn't press him. It was too dark out for Matt to see much of the countryside, but the road they traveled seemed well maintained and as they passed through the gate to Conway's Circle C Ranch, he felt a wave of peace come over him.

The lamps inside the house were all lit. As they drew closer, Matt noticed the silhouette of a woman in the doorway. Someone was looking for them. Someone had waited and worried about them, eager for their return. Or, Conway's return, at least.

"Stay put," Conway told him, as he hopped down out of the wagon and over to Matt's side. The older man was even stronger than he looked, all but lifting Matt bodily to the ground.

The younger man leaned on the wagon as long as possible, to keep weight off his leg.

"Where have you been, Richard?" a worried voice called.

"We have a guest, Susan."

"Oh?" The woman came down off the porch toward them. Matt hobbled on his feet, trying to make his way closer to the house and his host. "Why— Goodness, what's wrong?"

"He'll be all right, Susan," Conway said soothingly as he wrapped his arm around Matt's waist to help him to the house. "He's just been shot."

"Shot?" The horror in her voice was apparent. "Shot? You didn't bring trouble home, did you?"

"No, no, nothing like that. Just Bud Humphrey flexing his muscle. It's nothing. But Matt here does have a hole in his leg that will need stitching up."

"Oh, well ..."

"After supper will do, Susan." Conway and Matt had reached the porch and made their way carefully up the couple steps. "I know I've kept you waiting and twenty more minutes won't make any difference. It's stopped bleeding anyhow."

"Oh, I'm so sorry. Matt, is it?" He nodded. "We'll see you get what you need."

She pulled him into a hug and he relaxed into the embrace. She smelled like cinnamon and butter. It wasn't his home, but it was the closest thing to a real loving home Matt had been to in a long time.

"We've been holding supper for you," she scolded gently. "It's not much, but— oh, it's fine." She took Matt's arm, patted it kindly and helped him to one of the chairs. "You sit here. Rest that leg. Michael!"

A twelve-year-old boy, still sporting baby fat around

his face and likely just shy of a growth spurt, came bounding in from the hallway. "Yes?"

"Can you bring in an extra chair, please? And ask Violet to come set an extra place? We have a guest."

The boy bounded out again without response. Mrs. Conway bustled around the stove behind Matt, while Mr. Conway had disappeared, presumably to take care of the horses and wagon. Matt was adrift, left alone in the middle of an unfamiliar place with unfamiliar people and unknown expectations.

He folded his hands into his lap. He noticed the dirt under his fingernails for the first time and wished he had the use of both his legs so he could offer help or wash his hands at least.

"I thought you might like this," a gentle voice beside him said as a bowl of warm water was placed on the table in front of him.

"What? I—" Matt looked up to see a tall, slim, blonde young woman smiling at him.

"Pa told me you'd been hurt, and I know washing up before supper always makes me feel better about things. A fresh start, you know?" She had a distracting, shallow dimple on her left cheek.

Matt realized his mouth was hanging open and closed it abruptly. "Thank you," he stammered.

"I'll leave these here for you," the angel said, placing a towel and small knot of soap on the table next to him. "Take your time."

She turned her back to him then, pulling dishes out of a nearby cupboard. Matt was stunned. She had practically read his mind. This must be the Violet that Mrs. Conway had mentioned.

Matt glanced over his shoulder at the back of Violet one last time before he focused his efforts on washing his hands. He was determined to get them good and clean, to scrub away the dirt and dried blood that had smeared nearly down to his wrist. If Violet thought washing his hands would make him feel better, then wash his hands is what he would do.

She returned to the table and began setting out plates, forks and cups all around, glancing at him with a smile periodically.

He opened his mouth to say something, but Mrs. Conway reached the table at the same time.

"Oh! Violet, did you do this?" she asked, gesturing to the bowl in front of Matt now filled with dingy water. "How thoughtful. But move it aside, please."

Matt dried his hands hastily on the towel, so Violet could clear the space in front of him. He didn't want to be a reason she was scolded again.

"I'm sorry I can't help, ma'am," he said to Mrs. Conway.

"Oh, heavens. Never fear, dear. It's nothing. We're happy to help."

Michael, the boy, appeared in that moment, struggling valiantly under the weight of the heavy wooden chair he had procured from some other room.

"Here, dear," Mrs. Conway instructed, moving aside one of the chairs opposite Matt. "And, Violet—? Oh, thank you."

The family continued to arrange and scurry all around Matt as he sat uselessly. Violet arranged the last place setting. Michael sat in the chair directly across from Matt and stared openly, but said nothing. Mrs.

Conway brought a second pan to the table—cast iron cornbread to go with the large steaming pot of chili. It all smelled amazingly. Matt felt a lump in his throat, wondering what he had done to deserve such kindness.

Conway appeared in the doorway, hung his hat and coat on pegs nearby and grabbed his wife for a kiss as she passed by quickly.

"Go wash your hands, Richard Conway," she teased. "Supper is just waiting on you now."

Five minutes later, Matt was bowing his head as Conway said grace over his family's humble dinner, thanking the Lord for his abundance so they could host this young man, Matthew Hawke. Matt swallowed and peeked up at Violet. It was embarrassing to be called out as a charity case in front of her like this, but what could he do?

"In Jesus's name, amen."

"Amen," the others echoed all around him.

Matt cleared his throat, but didn't say anything. He didn't pick up a fork. He just waited, watched, unsure of what was expected of him. In moments his plate was full of rich, hearty chili and he was being urged to try a bite.

"The best in Wyoming," Conway said, smiling.

"The best anywhere, I should think," Mrs. Conway said, with playful indignation. "But seeing as you'll only be in Wyoming tonight, that seems sufficient."

"Did you shoot the other fella back?" Michael asked through a mouthful of cornbread.

"What? I ... uh." Matt was surprised. He had never shot at another person in his life. "No. No, I didn't."

"Don't worry about the shot, Michael," Conway said. "Matt got mixed up with a man without scruples, and sometimes there's a price to pay for that. His leg will heal, and I'd like to think it won't happen again."

Matt flushed, glancing at Violet to see how she responded to her father treating him like a child again. If only his leg was healed. If only he had a horse, or more than a dollar in his pocket, he wouldn't have to take this charity.

Perhaps Mrs. Conway sensed his uneasiness. She changed the subject, to tell her husband all about the church bazaar that was scheduled for the following week. Though occasional comments and questions were directed to Matt, primarily he was left to himself. He ate quietly, listening and wondering what he would do next.

As Michael used a hunk of cornbread to sop up the last of his second helping of chili, Mrs. Conway sighed happily. "Finish up, please, Michael. We shouldn't leave Matt's wound untended any longer than necessary, and I won't have you eating at the same table."

Michael widened his eyes, looked at Matt in wonder, and chewed more quickly.

"Violet," Mrs. Conway said. "Please go to my room to get the bandages. I'll clean up in here, but we need to get Matt's leg dressed."

Violet rose, and pushed her chair back in to the table. Her hand rested lightly on Matt's shoulder for a brief moment, and he wondered if it was deliberate. Once again, Matt found himself sitting uselessly while the Conway family bustled around him. As the women cleaned up, Michael was sent out to the well to collect more clean water and Conway added fuel to the fire. Matt sat awkwardly, inspecting his wound in the low light. The pant leg around his calf was now stiff from the dried blood, and he was hesitant to remove the handkerchief that had stopped the bleeding.

"Here, let me do that."

Violet set a lit lamp on the table, and pulled out the chair on the other side of Matt and guided his leg to straighten and rest his ankle on her knee. He blushed, embarrassed again to have such a lovely young woman touching him, embarrassed to be so helpless. Embarrassed that he might get blood on her lovely dress. He cleared his throat.

"I'm sorry, you don't need to worry about this. I think it's probably okay," he mumbled as she untied the makeshift bandage.

She laughed, kindly. "It's not okay, not yet. But it will be soon."

Violet produced a pair of scissors and cut up the side of his pant leg to expose his calf to the air. "I'm so sorry about this. You'll have to get a new pair of pants."

Matt didn't say anything. He had no money for a new pair of pants, but that wasn't something that Violet needed to know. He winced as she applied a warm wet rag to his calf, gently rubbing the area surrounding the wound first, cleaning off as much of the dried blood as she could before she touched the bullet hole itself.

"This looks like a clean wound," she said as she inspected both sides of his leg. "The bullet seems to have gone out the other side."

"That's good, right?"

She nodded, but didn't look at him. "This is going to hurt," she said in a whisper. "I'm sorry."

Matt clenched his teeth, readying himself. Miraculously, he didn't let out any sound as Violet applied the wet cloth to the wound. He wanted her to think he was tough, and that he endured wounds such as this and worse all the time because he was constantly doing brave deeds and taking on enormous adventures.

But he couldn't maintain it. As she continued to clean the wound, he let out a tiny squeak of pain when she poured whiskey on it. Matt clenched his teeth and screwed his eyes shut, not wanting to watch.

Violet must have been focusing intently on her task —or perhaps she sensed his unease—because she didn't try to engage him in conversation any further until the wound was completely cleaned and bandaged up tightly.

"There." She patted him gently on the ankle. "You're all done. You'll want to change the bandage again in a few days. I can show you, or—"

"No, I'll probably be gone by then," Matt said, lowering his foot gently to the floor. "I appreciate this, Miss Conway."

"You can call me Violet," she said.

Matt realized that the rest of the family was sitting only a few feet away, able to hear every word he and Violet said to each other. Even if he felt brave enough to talk to this beautiful girl, he wasn't brave enough to do it right under the nose of her mother. He cleared his throat again, awkward in the silence.

"How do you feel, son?" Conway asked from where he sat by the wood stove. He had a Bible open on one knee and was reading quietly by the firelight. "Did my girl get you all fixed up?"

"Yes, sir. She did. Thank you, kindly, all of you, really. I don't know how to thank you."

"Oh, my dear, it's nothing." Mrs. Conway rose from

her seat near her husband and came over to check her daughter's work. "We're always happy to help a neighbor in need."

"Are you a neighbor?" Violet asked, leaning forward toward him. "Do you live in Juniper Falls? I don't think I've seen you around anywhere before."

"Oh, I, uh ... I don't know. I've been here only about a week or so. I hadn't decided yet if I was going to stay, or keep moving west."

"I think you should stay," Michael said loudly from his spot on the floor where he was lining up a row of toy wooden soldiers. "Juniper Falls is swell."

"Well, he doesn't have to decide this instant," Mrs. Conway said, smiling. "First let's worry about tonight. Now, Matt. I know it's a little bit chilly tonight, but if I give you a couple blankets, will you be all right in the barn? I'm sorry, but we just don't have the space in here for a guest."

"Of course. Yes. Thank you, thank you. Yes." Matt got to his feet, leaning much of his weight on the table. "That's more than generous."

"Oh, you don't have to go now," she said. "It's early yet."

Matt felt as though he could fall asleep right there on the floor. "I think I'd like to, ma'am, if that's okay. I don't mean to be rude, but I'd like to rest this leg. And get out of your hair. It's been a long day, and you've already been so kind to me." He glanced at Violet shyly, but looked away.

"I'll just go get the blankets," Mrs. Conway said.

"You won't leave first thing tomorrow, right?" Violet asked. "You'll be here for breakfast?"

"Oh, I'm not sure—"

"Yes, stay," Conway said. "I'd like to talk to you more, but tonight is not the time. Come to breakfast at the house and we'll chat."

"That sounds lovely," Mrs. Conway said as she returned with an arm full of quilts. "Violet, dear, I'd like to start the dishes. Could you show Matt where he'll be sleeping and then come back and help me?"

"Yes, Mother." Violet took the pile of blankets from her and led the way to the door. "This way, Matt."

He followed her silently across the yard to the barn, stifling a yawn. As they walked, he tried out several questions and beginnings of conversations in his head before rejecting them all. When he had been younger, a teenager in Boston, he had had no trouble talking to girls. He was always quick with a compliment to turn their head or a joke to make them laugh. But this girl. This... woman. This... Violet. He couldn't come up with a single phrase that wouldn't make him sound ridiculous.

"Here we are," she said brightly as they reached the door to the out building.

They had walked slowly enough to accommodate Matt's injury, but the time together had to end sometime.

"I'm glad you're here, Matthew Hawke," she said. She held the door open for him, but didn't go inside.

"Thank you for your help."

"I'm happy to. And tomorrow I'll show you how to do it yourself."

"All right."

"Good." She grinned, flashing that dimple again. "Until tomorrow."

After pressing the folded blankets into his arms, she left the lantern with him and returned to the house. Matt stayed in the doorway to the barn, watching her walk back through the dark yard to the house, all lit from the inside and welcoming. As he went to find a spot of clean hay to bed down in for the night, he thought about what Conway wanted to say to him the next day and wondered if it would mean staying near Violet.

CHAPTER THREE

The following morning, Matt was woken before the sun when a sharp boot nudged into his ribs and rolled him several inches, scattering hay across the barn floor. He had slept heavily, exhausted from the fight, and for a few moments upon waking he was uncertain where he was.

"You, hey. You. Get up."

Matt blinked, rubbing his eyes and looking up at the man towering over him. From what he could see at this angle, they seemed to be about the same age, and the man had a messy shock of red hair that fell down over his eyes. He was a complete stranger, which only added to Matt's confusion. He had a fleeting moment of wondering how he had missed meeting this additional Conway the previous evening.

"Get up. You don't belong here. I'm taking you to Uncle Richard."

"Uncle Richard? You mean ... Mr. Conway?" Matt was having trouble understanding what was happening. He rubbed his eyes again, trying to clear the fog. He only just remembered why he was sleeping on the floor of a barn in the first place when he felt the pain in his calf again.

"Circle C is Uncle Richard's ranch, and he wouldn't just let anyone on the property. Get up. You're going to have to explain yourself."

"But, I..." Matt wasn't sure how to even start. "But, Violet told me this is where I should sleep. Look, she even gave me a blanket." He pointed, but the quilt he had been using was half-buried under hay.

"*Miss Conway*, you mean? I know you don't have permission to use her Christian name." The other man's eyebrows shot up. "You say Miss Conway told you to sleep here? Then we are *definitely* taking you to see her father. Up, I say."

At that, the man bent down to grab Matt by the arm and yank him to his feet. He couldn't help but let out a surprised yelp when forced to put weight on his injured leg, but he didn't complain. Clearly this man knew the Conways and the ranch far better than Matt did. Was it possible he had somehow misunderstood what the Conway family was offering him? Did they expect him to leave in the night? But now he was being hauled bodily out of the barn by a stranger who claimed Matt shouldn't be there at all.

So much for the Christian charity Mr. Conway had promised. Matt's temper flared, indignant of his treatment, but he was too much in pain and too confused to stoke that anger.

This stranger dragged Matt across the yard to the Conways' house. With trying to avoid using his injured leg, Matt couldn't get the other one underneath him for long enough to maintain his balance. He stumbled, at times dragging one foot then the other, biting his lip to keep from crying out at the pain. This stranger didn't seem to care or notice, however, finally dropping him abruptly on the farmhouse steps.

"Stay there."

He knocked loudly; Matt cringed. It was barely sunrise. This kind family had invited him to eat breakfast with them, sure, but not come pounding on the door immediately after waking.

The door opened. Mr. Conway stood in the opening, pulling on his coat, the room behind him still dark. Matt could see from his expression that whatever the older man had been expecting at the door, this red-headed stranger was not it.

"Silas," he said. "Is something wrong?" He frowned, looking between Matt and Silas, but waited for further explanation.

"Found this one in your barn, sir." He grabbed Matt's shoulder and shook him. "Want me to just run him off the property, or take him all the way into town to Sheriff Vance?"

"No, that won't be necessary," Conway was saying, when Violet appeared behind him.

"Matt!" she said, smoothing down her hair. "How are you feeling?"

"You see, Uncle Richard?" Silas exclaimed. "He's already influenced your daughter. Just say the word, sir, and I'll take care of him."

"No, no, Silas. This is Matthew Hawke. He is a guest of ours. He came in from town with me last night."

"A guest?" Silas said derisively, turning to look at Matt. "A guest? Where did he come from?"

Matt stood listening, as he leaned against the porch rail. His leg ached after all the jostling and he was trying to keep as much weight off his injury as possible.

"Why don't you come inside and sit, Matt?" Violet offered, nudging her father to step out of the doorway.

Silas grumbled.

"Thank you." Matt limped into the house, past Silas, past Mr. Conway, past Violet and sat in the same chair he had inhabited the previous night. "Who is that?" he asked Violet in a whisper.

"Oh, that's just Silas. He's my cousin that moved west with us after his parents died, but he doesn't live here anymore. He just comes to work every morning and leaves before dinner. I guess Pa didn't think about what it would look like to him to find you in the barn when he arrived this morning. He's harmless. Just a little protective."

"I guess." Matt tried to smooth down his unruly hair. As he ran his fingers through, a piece of straw fell down into his lap. He couldn't imagine how he must look to Violet since he had been so roughly dragged out of his sleep. "He's probably right, though. I should likely get going. I can't be taking advantage of your family's hospitality, and I don't want your cousin to think any worse of me than he already does."

When he glanced at Violet, where she was standing at the stove, she looked stricken, though she tried to cover it quickly, nodding before turning back to the coffee.

"We'll see what Pa says. At least he can give you a

ride back into town. How will you walk all the way back with your leg like that?" Her smile was tentative.

Matt was spared having to answer by Conway entering the house, alone.

"Well, son, how are you feeling? I imagine that leg is a mite stiff. Sorry about my nephew, but I think I've straightened him out."

Matt sat up straight, still trying to make himself look presentable. As the older man sat down at the table next to him, Violet brought over a cup of coffee for each of them. Matt smiled is thanks at her, while trying to figure out what to say.

"I'm feeling much better, sir. Thank you. In fact, I was just telling your daughter that I thought it was about time I got on my way. Wouldn't want to trouble you folks anymore."

As he spoke, Matt's mind whirred searching for possibilities of what his next step would be. How would he pay for food or lodging, or even new trousers? This pair was torn to bits and blood-stained. It would be near impossible for him to find work with this injury. He had left the eastern states after getting caught stealing, and while he could do that again, the whole point of coming west was to give himself a fresh start.

Though he was looking down at his hands twisting in his lap, Matt's expression must have revealed his hopelessness. The next thing he heard was Mr. Conway assuring him he shouldn't worry.

"We're happy to host you as long as you like, Matt," he said gently, as he sipped his coffee. "We have the space, and you know the Good Book calls us to be generous to our neighbors. If you're worried about it, we can find some work for you to do. There's plenty. But mostly I'd like to just give you a chance to rest."

"I'm not a charity case," Matt mumbled, painfully aware of how much he had already accepted from the Conways.

At that auspicious moment, Mrs. Conway entered the room, tied an apron over her dress, then said, "Matt, how do you take your eggs?"

That did it. The shame Matt felt for having to be waited on and taken care of became too much for him. He stood—or tried to—and ended up leaning on the table again for support.

"Thanks much, ma'am, but I really must be going. I don't want to put you folks out. You've already done so much for me."

He avoided looking directly at Mrs. Conway, afraid of what hurt he might see in her face. Instead, Matt made his way toward the front door, limping and wondering if he could find a walking stick between here and town. Before he reached the threshold, Silas appeared again, letting himself into the house without knocking.

"Uncle Richard. If you're not busy, sir ... Come quickly, as soon as you can, please. I'm trying to lift the beams up to the top of the structure, but I can't seem to get enough leverage on my own. I need another pair of hands."

When Matt turned back to see the rancher's reaction, he was greeted with a smile.

"Well, we just happen to have an extra pair of hands. This sure is fortunate. You'll help out, won't you, Matt?"

"I don't see—"

"It's easy," Silas said impatiently. "Your leg won't be a bother at all. Come with me."

"But, I—"

"How do you like your eggs, dear? I'll have them waiting when you boys get done."

"Well, I, don't—"

"It's just breakfast, Matt," Conway said quietly. "Breakfast is barely payment for what Silas needs your help with. Let us help you the way you are helping us."

Matt sighed. He couldn't argue with that. As long as he was being helpful, he could allow himself to accept a meal. He nodded and limped his way to the door where he followed Silas out.

The sun was now risen over the far hills and the warm light cast long shadows across the yard. The ranch hand walked quickly, a good four or five strides ahead of Matt. He had a bounce in his walk that made him even faster and at times turned to walk backward as he addressed Matt.

"Like I said, I just need an extra pair of hands. Don't think you're doing all that much. We'll get this new crossbeam situated, and then I can finish the frame."

"Crossbeam for what?" Matt asked. He had come from Boston and never worked on a ranch, so some of the details confused him.

Silas made an exasperated face. "It's eventually going to be a small barn. The Conways are looking toward the future and might want to invest in some dairy cows. But improving the land like this gives him a better chance of keeping it. The bank has been cagey about his loan lately. He had to take a second mortgage to expand the herd, recently, and I'm not sure that's going well. Uncle Richard thinks one of his competitors in Juniper Falls is trying to buy him out. So, the more permanent structures we put on Circle C, the better it looks to the bank and the better for the Conways."

"Do you know who might be doing that?"

Silas shrugged. "Could be anyone, I guess. Not everyone around here has the work ethic to build their own little piece. They'd rather just take it from someone else."

"That's terrible."

Silas nodded. "I might suspect Sheriff Vance, even, but I don't think he wants anything to do with running a ranch. Could be one of the neighboring property owners, wanting to expand. Could be the fellow who holds the biggest beef contract, wanting to get his hands on Uncle Richard's herd too. I don't know. Doesn't make much difference to me. The work is the same either way."

Matt nodded, as though this all made sense. As though he knew the first thing about a beef contract or a mortgage. He had no experience with land-owning or business at all. His father had tried to teach him when he was growing up; Matt was the youngest of three brothers, and their father owned a small neighborhood dry goods store. But Matt was out on the street by the time he was fourteen. Fending for himself and resorting to stealing food to survive.

The ramifications of taking out a second mortgage to buy a business asset, and then having that very asset be at risk was beyond him. Even just the idea of having the means to take out a loan at all was beyond him.

Matt was still wearing trousers with a cut up one pant leg, after all.

"How do you know all this?" he asked.

Silas turned back and shrugged. "Uncle Richard trusts me, I guess. We're a family here. He always says we'll be all right as long as we're together. We're all in this, so it works in his favor to have more folks working on the problem. Here we are!"

Matt set aside the idea that a family all works together to mull over later. That had not been his experience with his own family, but so far he had only seen such a concept in practice at the Conways' ranch. Silas had changed the subject when they arrived at the sparse wooden frame some thirty yards from the house. Even without any real mechanical experience, at a glance Matt could see how this beam could be lifted through leverage. Both ends had a rope tied, which then was cast over the top of one of the other existing beams and dangled down the other side.

"You see?" Silas said, as he moved to take up the loose end of rope. "We just pull on it here, and the wood should lift roughly into place. You can probably do the whole thing without even putting weight on your injured leg."

"Right. Great, I can do that," Matt said, as he limped into place beside Silas.

The redhead handed him the rope, positioned himself in front of Matt and grabbed on to the rope himself.

"You got a good grip? All right. On three," he said. "Steady... One, two, three!"

Matt pulled hard, heaved, leaning his weight back to

leverage the wooden beam as high as he could. Hand over hand, Silas and he hauled it up higher and higher until it just reached the apex of the frame.

"Okay, hold it there," Silas commanded over his shoulder. "Hold it. Just hold your ground right there. Don't move."

Matt nodded, but Silas's back was to him. The ranch hand didn't even wait to hear an assent, before he had let go of the rope and began scrambling up the side of the frame. Matt clenched his teeth and held tight. He anchored his good leg into the dirt, pressing the heel of his boot down hard to keep from moving. Once the beam was in the air, all it took was focus to keep it at the right height. And Silas had been right: he didn't need to use his injured leg at all.

In the time it took Matt to have all these thoughts, Silas had scrambled to the top of the structure and maneuvered the crossbeam into position.

"Okay! Now slowly—I mean, SLOWLY—lower it down!" he shouted to Matt.

Matt held his breath and did as instructed. Hand over hand, letting the rope go little by little. He watched as Silas held on to the structure with one hand, and reached for the new beam with the other. Maneuvering the long piece into place, Silas exhibited remarkable balance. Matt didn't know if he could do the same thing. There wasn't far for the beam to move; just releasing a small foot or two of rope landed it exactly where it was meant to be.

"Perfect! That's exactly right, Matt."

Matt watched Silas make a few other adjustments and checks before he scrambled down again. His hands were a little raw from the rope; his inexperience with physical labor was showing. But he had loved it. Every moment. Being part of a project that required his muscle, a project that resulted in a visible effect. It was exhilarating. Far better and more satisfying than the time and effort he had been devoting to learning poker, hoping for luck to swing his way.

"What else do you need done?" he asked Silas as the other man reached him.

Silas looked around the space, hands on his hips as he considered. "Oh, I'm sure there's plenty. I'd have to do some thinking to see what you can do with the bum leg, though."

Matt stammered out, "Of— of course. Right. Whatever you need."

"That's done, though. Let's head back. I bet breakfast is ready by now."

This time, on the walk across the yard, Silas stayed at Matt's side instead of loping on ahead. All it took was Matt asking one question about Circle C Ranch for Silas to talk away without pausing. How big the herd was, when they would be driving to market, what Silas's daily chores looked like, how much the younger boy, Michael, helped. It seems that running a ranch of this size was a constant workload, and after listening to Silas, Matt could identify a few places he could fit in to help, even with his lack of experience.

He, too, could be part of this team, all working to make the enterprise successful. The small sliver of hope scared him, but Matt could see his way to fit into this family.

They reached the farmhouse, where the front door

stood open and the sounds and smells of a big meal wafted out toward them.

"This is perfect timing," Mrs. Conway said to the young men when they entered. "Wash your hands," she nodded to the wash basin on the other side of the room, "and come have a seat."

Matt followed Silas, taking care to leave his weight off his injured leg as much as possible as he limped across the room. He needed rest, as much for this family as for himself. The sooner he was at full health, the sooner he could make himself the most useful to Circle C ranch and maybe repay some of their generosity.

Once his hands were clean, Matt took a deep breath and sat. The smell of bacon made his mouth water, and the fried edges of his egg white looked crisped to perfection. He couldn't help but give the Conways a small smile and settled in to the meal with them.

CHAPTER FOUR

After breakfast, Matt dropped all talk of leaving Circle C Ranch. Instead, he followed Silas back to the barn and was put to work mucking out stalls. It required him to be on his feet, not resting his leg, but he could lean against the walls or even the shovel as much as possible. No one expected more of him. His bandage was sound and Matt thought it better that he start helping as quickly as possible than sitting around waiting to heal.

The day passed quickly, and Matt continued to be amazed at how good he felt just putting in the physical labor, even with his injury. The burn of his muscles doing what they were supposed to do exhilarated him. He forgot the pain in his leg for hours at a time. When the men went back to the house for lunch, Violet scolded him gently about resting and needing to replace his bandage later, but Matt thought he saw admiration in her eyes.

He wasn't sure if it was Silas's natural chattiness, the

gorgeous weather, or something else that helped him feel welcomed so quickly, but before Matt knew it, he found himself mentally making plans to stay at Circle C long-term. He hadn't even been invited beyond Conway wanting to make sure his leg healed, but Matt could visualize himself working alongside Silas every day. Building a life here. Becoming part of what they were all working toward.

Matt heard his name and pulled himself out of his reverie.

"You'll be here tomorrow, won't you, Matt?" Silas said, as they reached the barn for afternoon chores.

"I think so. That is, it'll be up to Mr. Conway, won't it?"

"Sure." Silas nodded. "But seeing as tomorrow night is the church dance, I would think you'd be welcome. Aunt Susan would love to see you at church, I'm sure, even if it is a social event."

Matt grinned. He immediately conjured an image of himself asking Violet to dance, sweeping her around the dance floor, impressing her with his wit and grace—before the pain in his leg twinged again and that image disintegrated.

"Will you be going?"

"Me? I've already asked Uncle Richard if I can be off a bit early, so I can go home and get clean. I got me a girl, you know." He looked at Matt meaningfully.

"Do you?"

"Yep. Miss Mary Ann Whitaker. Her sister's the schoolteacher in Juniper Falls. She's just the prettiest thing, Matt." Silas looked off into the horizon wistfully.

"The prettiest dark brown hair and eyes that would sparkle in the dark."

Silas had thawed remarkably from just a few hours earlier when he had kicked Matt awake. Now he was chattering on about his girl and Matt smiled at his friend's daydreaming. He listened and let him talk about this Mary Ann Whitaker while they brushed down the horse Mr. Conway had been riding that day. Silas had only met Mary Ann a few weeks earlier, but was already smitten, planning how he would save his money to buy them a place and how they would be the most successful cattle ranchers in Wyoming.

"So, like I say, Matt. You've got to stick around tomorrow and go to the dance with us. You can meet Mary Ann."

"But I can't dance."

"Oh." Silas's mouth hung open. It evidently hadn't occurred to him, and Matt's injury didn't factor into his daydreams. "Well. Still. You should come. The whole family will be there."

Matt shot Silas a sharp glance, but the other man didn't seem to have meant anything particular by that last comment. He was too focused on his task at hand. Matt allowed himself to fantasize some more, as they worked in silence side by side. Even with his leg useless, they could sit and talk. They could get to know each other. He might even be able to limp around the dance floor if Violet was willing.

But would she be willing, he wondered. Maybe what he perceived to be a magical connection was only one-sided. He hadn't really had much chance to talk with her.

Sure, she dressed his wound, but was that enough for her to be interested in him? Would she be able to see past his inexperience and injury to the man he really was?

The considerations of attending a social dance with Violet Conway ate up all of Matt's thoughts through the day.

About midafternoon, when Matt and Silas were in the nearest part of the Circle C pasture digging holes for fence posts, Silas stopped mid-sentence and asked, "Do you hear that?"

Both men paused in their movements to listen.

Matt heard it then.

Hooves.

And voices. Men's voices. From this distance it was impossible to hear what they were saying, but it was apparent that a small group of men had ridden onto Circle C Ranch and were calling back and forth to each other.

"Who is that?" Matt asked, with a frown. "Was Mr. Conway expecting someone?"

"Not that I know of," Silas said, darkly. "We should go see if he needs us."

Matt nodded, set his jaw, and started off behind Silas as quickly as he could. The other man didn't wait for him before he hurried to his uncle's side—just as it should be. Mr. Conway may need them sooner rather than later, and Matt would be mortified if his own injury got in the way of Silas helping.

The yelling and calling grew louder as he reached the crowd. The closer he got the more Matt heard the derision and cruelty in the shouts. Mr. Conway stood on the porch of the house, while Silas stood nearby at the foot of the steps. The rest of the Conways hovered inside the open door. Whatever greeting or pleasantries might have occurred, that was all over by the time Matt reached the crowd.

As Matt limped his way to stand by Silas's side, he noticed the Juniper Falls sheriff near the front of the crowd, his badge prominent on his chest. He was younger than Matt would have expected, with a round face and a bored, blank expression, as though whatever hassle he had been dragged out of his office to deal with wasn't worth the effort.

Immediately to the sheriff's right was an older man, wiry, muscular, with grizzled hair and broad shoulders. His eyes were cold and when he opened his mouth to talk, the venom in his words made Matt almost wanted to draw back physically away from him. What kind of man came to visit his neighbors with such animosity?

Matt had so many questions he wanted to ask Silas, but he dared not interrupt.

"If you would just accept my position," the cold man was saying, "we could put all this aside."

"Is that right?" Mr. Conway said indulgently. "I do that and you'd just walk away, no harm, no questions? Somehow I don't believe that, Mr. Addison."

Addison chuckled, and the men all around him echoed. He had brought a posse of sorts, half a dozen hard, dirty men holding their guns carelessly, spitting tobacco into the dirt and eyeing Violet as she stood half hidden behind her mother. A flash of anger tore through Matt when he recognized the hungry, entitled look in many of the men's eyes.

That anger surged when he realized one of the men

in Addison's party was none other than Bud Humphrey, the gambling man who had shot Matt just the night before.

"What is *he* doing here?" Matt whispered.

"Shh." Silas elbowed him.

"Well, now," Addison said. "I don't expect you to just take my word for it, of course, Conway. But this telegram from the governor might convince you."

He nodded at Sheriff Vance, who absentmindedly patted his coat pockets until he found what he was looking for. A wrinkled, thin piece of paper was plucked from within the coat. Vance glanced at it, nodded almost imperceptibly and handed it over to Addison.

Matt took this small moment to watch Mr. Conway and try to interpret his reaction. Though he hadn't known the man long, his entire impression of the rancher had been to marvel at and be grateful for his equanimity. In the face of Matt's injury, family dynamics, and all the pressing work on Circle C, Mr. Conway had taken everything in stride. Now, though, as Addison prepared to read out the telegram purportedly from the governor of the Wyoming Territory, Matt could see the muscles in Mr. Conway's neck tighten, as though he was tensing for a blow.

"Let's see." Addison cleared his throat. "Can confirm price discussed. Take control immediately."

There was a short pause as Mr. Conway blinked, as though confused, and then grinned. "That's it? That's what it says? Why, Mr. Addison, you must think I'm stupid, sir. That telegram confirms absolutely nothing for me. You all could be chatting about the price of lace, for all I know, and the governor is asking you to get a sample. You can't expect me to roll over based on that, surely."

The smile that Addison shot back was even colder than his eyes; Matt didn't see how that was possible. This man must have no scruples, no honor at all.

"Suit yourself," he said. "The longer you hold out, the worse it will be for you. The sheriff will have every legal right to seize your property once you miss the next payment. And I have the power on my side. The governor himself supports my taking control of Circle C." He waved the telegram in the air.

"I will not be missing a payment," Mr. Conway said quietly. He stood up even straighter, squaring his shoulders.

"Look, Mr. Conway," Sheriff Vance drawled, "we're all gentlemen here, aren't we? This man is just looking out for his own family and fortunes. Surely we can't begrudge him that." He nudged his horse to take the couple steps closer to the house. "And, I have to be honest with you. He does have a claim. He has filed the necessary legal paperwork, he has the cash to invest, and as you've seen, he also has the backing of the most powerful man in the territory."

"I will not be missing a payment," Mr. Conway repeated.

"But, sir, you already have, haven't you? That's why we're about to come up on the third missed payment." Sheriff Vance lowered his voice, as though relaying a secret. "Does your wife know? Do your hands here?" He gestured to Silas and Matt.

"They know enough."

Matt noticed Silas frown slightly and wondered if the man had known the full extent of Conway's troubles.

"Richard." Mrs. Conway spoke quietly and put her hand on her husband's arm. "Why don't we thank these men for bringing this to our attention and go back inside? We have plenty to do around here. Especially with the deadline that Mr. Addison so kindly alerted us to."

Matt caught Violet's eye as they both listened. The young woman's expression was worried, that was certain, but he also detected in her an air of defiance. This was no shrinking violet, no matter her name. This daughter would fight for her family and her home. Violet looked away, again watching their visitors intently, and Matt followed suit.

Suddenly, one of Addison's men began laughing manically for no apparent reason. Even Sheriff Vance revealed his surprise in glancing at the tough. It was Bud Humphrey, Matt's attacker. And he was laughing and pointing right at Matt.

"You?" Several of the other men looked at Matt as well. "You're here? Well." He laughed even harder.

"Is there something the matter, Mr. Humphrey?" Addison asked pointedly. "Would you care to share the joke with the rest of us?"

"Oh, just this one is useless. Harmless. See that bandage around his leg? That's my doing," he said proudly, never taking his eyes off Matt. "If this is the kind of help Conway is running his ranch with, the land is as good as yours."

"Is that so?" Addison appraised Matt, looking him up

and down and not bothering to hide the disdain on his face. "How fortunate."

"How can you live with yourself?" Matt shot back. "Taking a man's hard-earned livelihood from him? Taking this family's home? Is this really the legacy you want to leave? What kind of man does that?"

He stopped himself. He wanted to yell. He wanted to threaten. He wanted to promise Bud Humphrey that he'd get what was coming to him. Matt had never had much luck keeping his temper, but knowing Violet was watching, knowing Mr. Conway and the rest of his family would suffer if Matt brought a fight to their door, he held his tongue. But only just. He knew he must look furious. He could feel the flush of anger creeping across his cheeks, only worsening as Bud watched and continued to laugh at his ineffectiveness.

His emotions were checked by a new voice.

"You get out of here!" Michael shouted from behind his mother, his voice cracking with fear. "You leave my father alone!"

Silas nodded, elbowed Matt again and took a step forward toward Addison and his gang. Matt didn't see how the two of them would be able to run off this many men, with them on horses and himself limping, but he gamely followed after.

Addison chuckled at the sight. His gang of toughs laughed along with him.

"All right. You have until the third," Addison said. "But we all know you can't come up with those three payments in that short of time. And then this ranch will be mine."

With that bold declaration, he gave a shout and rode off the property, his muscle riding shortly behind him.

Sheriff Vance stayed long enough to tip his hat. "Mr. Conway. Mrs. Conway. Always a pleasure."

CHAPTER FIVE

The rest of the day passed by in unnatural silence. Each member of the family focused only on the tasks in front of them and paid little attention to anything else. The spring afternoon was crisp, green buds sprouting from trees that had been bare for months, but even that tiny glimpse of hope did nothing to alter the mood on the ranch. Matt followed instructions set for him by Mr. Conway and Silas, stewing in his frustration all the while. The more he considered the situation he found himself in, the angrier he got.

Yes, he was frustrated for the Conways, that such men held leverage over them and that they had their very livelihoods at risk. But as he continued to think on it, Matt was also frustrated *with* Conway himself. If he were in such straits, how could he offer charity to Matt? It was just irresponsible, from what he could see. For a brief few hours, Conway had let Matt believe that he might have a home here, that he might have found his career. But now, knowing that the Conways had foreclo-sure looming over their heads, he felt that all torn away.

Just as his father had disappointed him. Just as his older brothers had left him on his own when he got into trouble during his tumultuous teen years. Just as his first travel partner had deserted him on their way west not six months ago. Matt had been abandoned by every man he had put his faith in, and now it seemed as though Mr. Conway was doing it too.

As the sun set, Silas and Matt finished up their chores and said good-bye. Though, apparently, Silas occasionally stayed for supper with the Conways, tonight was not one of those nights. He headed back into Juniper Falls, while Matt made his way into the family home on his own. The scent of hearty gravy filled the house, Michael was lighting the lamps scattered throughout the main room, and Violet absentmindedly directed Matt to the basin to wash his hands.

He did so in silence, carefully watching the move-ments of the family all around him. The previous night he had been distracted by the pain in his leg and thoughts of hopelessness, but tonight he could just observe. Michael again brought in the extra chair from another room. Violet again set the table. And Mr. Conway, again, came in at the very end just in time to eat.

Matt watched as the older man kissed his wife's cheek and patted his daughter's shoulder, thanking them both for the meal they had prepared, before he sat. He hadn't seen this man since their visitors earlier in the day, and Matt ached to question him about how he planned to come up with the money needed. The uncertainty, the not knowing if he would even have a corner on the floor of the barn to sleep in worried him. Something had to be done, but Matt had no idea what.

Matt felt his temper bubble up within him again. As much as he tried to be patient and understanding, he just couldn't fathom the thought of this kind family being turned out on their heels. Where was this man's responsibility to his family? Even though Matt knew he had benefitted from the older man's help, he still resented Mr. Conway for diverting himself to take care of a stranger rather than his own family.

Violet didn't deserve this.

When he finally came to his seat at the table, Matt knew he was sulking. He remained silent as Mr. Conway said grace. He only muttered thanks when Mrs. Conway served the shepherd's pie. He felt Violet's inquiring eyes on him, but would not look at her. Matt felt as though he hung on to a very delicate balance, certain that if he made any kind of contact with any member of the family his temper would blow up. He was clear-headed enough to guard against such volatility.

Conversation was stilted; each member of the family seemed lost in their own thoughts. Just when Matt was beginning to think he might be able to get through the meal with his temper in check, Mr. Conway cleared his throat. The attention of the rest of the Conways turned toward him.

"I'm sorry you had to witness that earlier, my dears," he said. "That wasn't how... That is... I had hoped it would never come to that. I apologize if the episode was upsetting."

Mrs. Conway clucked sympathetically and reached across the table to pat his hand.

That tiny gesture was too much for Matt to witness without reacting.

"So, you just were going to keep it all to yourself?" he asked.

The shock and hurt on all the Conways' faces when they turned to him almost made him pause. In the back of his mind, a small voice warned him he was speaking out of turn, that he had only known the Conways a day, that this was not his problem to solve. But Matt abhorred a bully, and had been holding his frustration in too long.

"Matt—" Mr. Conway began sorrowfully.

"You asked me to stay." Matt heard his voice crack with emotion, but that just made him angrier. "You brought me here, offered me food, lodging, even bandaging up my wound and promising me all sorts of things. You gave me hope. Maybe that wasn't your intention, but I believed this could be my home, after not having one for years. How could you, when you knew you couldn't see it through? How could you bring the rest of your family to this?"

"I can—"

"You can't do anything," Matt yelled, pounding his fist on the table. Next to him, Violet's silverware bounced. "You shouldn't be promising anything. Silas told me that there was some trouble, but I don't think even he knew the full extent of it. Did *anyone*? You could lose this whole place. Did you just think it would blow over?"

"Matt," Violet said quietly.

He paused in his tirade to give her his attention, breathing heavily. When he looked at her, though, his heart broke at the sight of tears in her eyes. She looked at him with a pleading, sorrowful expression, seemingly begging him to calm down. Matt huffed. His temper had been unleashed. The last thing he wanted was to hurt Violet—his indignation was on her behalf if nothing else —but he was too far in his rage to pull it back.

"I just— I can't—" Matt stood, pushing his chair back so abruptly that it fell over. "I can't be here," he said finally.

No one said a word as he limped the few feet to the front door, yanked it open and exited into the night air. His heart pounded. His face was hot. Matthew Hawke was more incensed than he had been in a long time. He hadn't realized how much hope he had put into the small offer of a home until he was at risk of losing it.

He knew he should sit and rest; his leg was never going to heal with all the labor and pacing he was doing. But he couldn't be still. His muscles twitched, taunting him into taking action. He limbs felt tingly and charged somehow. Matt felt like he could cut down the largest tree or climb the highest building, anything to keep him from punching the face of the man who had so angered and disappointed him.

"Matt?"

He whirled around at the sound of his name. Mr. Conway stood on the dark porch, backlit by the open doorway. He faced the yard, toward where Matt had been pacing back and forth. Neither man said anything further, as the rancher closed the front door and came down off the steps to walk to him.

Matt forced himself to take several deep breaths, focusing on the cool air filling his lungs to keep himself from thinking about his fury. He leaned his weight on to his injured leg and grimaced, hoping the pain would distract him further.

"Matt," Mr. Conway said again. "I can see that you're angry."

Matt snorted derisively.

"I understand why you might be ... frustrated."

"Do you?" Matt shot back. "How can you? You have your land and your family and you've been safe and secure in this life for how long? Years. Decades. I—" Matt stopped himself, shook his head, took a deep breath and tried again. He was starting to see more clearly now. "I know I have a temper. It doesn't matter what I think about it, and I should have held my tongue. I'm sorry. I should go."

"I wish you wouldn't."

"Why?" he demanded. "Why not? You don't even know me. You lured me here with all sorts of promises and now you're letting me down just like everyone else has. Why do you care if I stay or go? Wouldn't you all be better off without another mouth to feed anyway?"

"It's not as simple as that."

"Of course it is!" Matt threw up his hands in frustration. "It's always been as simple as that. For everyone I have ever trusted. Why don't you see that?"

Mr. Conway paused before responding, watching Matt thoughtfully. "I wonder if you might tell me more about what you mean. What do you mean that 'everyone' has let you down?"

"Why, just ... *Everyone*. I don't know how else to

explain it. Everyone means everyone. Every person I have ever known looks out for themselves first. My parents. My brothers. My travel companion coming out west. Every landlady I've ever had. Every copper I've had to tussle with. Not one person my whole life has ever done something for someone else first. You're no different."

"That may be." Mr. Conway nodded. "That seems like a hard lesson to learn, certainly. I'm very sorry."

Matt could feel his temper ebbing. It was often like this: a flash of fury, followed quickly by a peaceful understanding, and often regret. "I shouldn't have gotten so mad, I suppose. I should have expected this. That's my fault."

"I hate to be yet another example of how men have failed you.

Matt shrugged. "It doesn't matter. I'll just be on my way, and neither of us will trouble the other."

"Or," Mr. Conway suggested hesitantly. "Would you give me a chance to try to change your mind, Mr. Hawke? To show you that not everyone will let you down."

Matt looked at him in surprised. He thought it was the first time he had addressed him as Mr. Hawke, as though they were on the same level. He felt a surge of pride, in spite of himself. "I don't know... Waiting might just make things worse."

"You won't get far on that leg." The older man nodded to Matt's injury. "And I could use a man of your passion by my side. I would hate for you to find yourself in a bind on your own when we could both help each other."

"Well..." Matt sighed, and looked down at the bandage, bleeding through now with all his exertion. He did need a place to stay, but more than that Matt desperately wanted to believe that there were good, reliable folks in the world, in spite of all the evidence he had seen. Maybe it was naïve, he thought, but he did not want to give up that idealism just yet. "I ... I suppose I don't have to leave this second. What did you have in mind?"

A smile broke across the older man's face. "Come with me."

He turned and headed back into the house, Matt following as quickly as he could with his limp. Both men strode through the open door; Mr. Conway didn't even pause when both his wife and his daughter called after him. Matt looked at them, puzzled at the rancher's behavior, but also a bit embarrassed about his own. He smiled apologetically and kept following, almost through the next doorway.

When Matt reached the threshold, he hesitated. This was the Conways' bedroom. That was their marriage bed. This seemed too private and too sacred a place for Matt to enter, so he waited in the doorway until Mr. Conway turned his attention back to him.

The older man had knelt on the floor, in front of a large wooden trunk that stood against the far wall under the window. Holding the lid open with one hand, Mr. Conway searched through the contents with the other, occasionally pulling out items to set aside and out of his way. A worn quilt, a tissue-wrapped package, a handheld mirror all joined the pile next to his knees before he finally let out a triumphant 'ha!' and withdrew a small wooden box.

Returning to standing with box in hand, Mr. Conway finally noticed that Matt hadn't followed him all the way in. Not only was the younger man still standing in the doorway, but now the rest of the Conways were gathered around him, watching as well. Mr. Conway smiled at the sight.

"Well, now, Mr. Hawke. I want to tell you again how sorry I am that you've had such disappointments in your life. My own father died when I was just eleven, so I know what it's like to lose someone. Though I would venture your loss has been more painful for different reasons."

Matt nodded solemnly. He almost hesitated to breathe, not wanting to miss a word the older man said. There was a magic about this moment that made him feel as though he was about to be part of something big, something that he would remember the rest of his life.

"You're a good man, Matt. I can see that already just in the little time we have had together. The way you stand up for others and the way you pitch in immediately to help. Even the way you tried to avoid a fight with Bud Humphrey in town speaks well of your character. I admire your attempt to hold your temper, even if you don't always succeed. Your decision to leave the room when you found yourself unable to impresses me even more."

Matt blinked in surprise. As after every time he had lost his temper, Matt was embarrassed by how he had handled his anger. Everything he thought he had been doing wrong, Mr. Conway was now finding as a reason to admire him. Maybe this older man was not going to be the disappointment Matt anticipated.

"If you have no objection, Mr. Hawke, I'd be proud to call you a friend."

"Oh, well. Um. Of course. Yes." He ventured a glance at Violet who stood to his right in the doorway and smiled at him.

"I'm glad. A man can always use another friend. And in a case like this, when, as you know, we have enemies all around us, friends are even more valuable."

"Yeah," Matt ventured. "I'm really sorry about that..."

"Thank you. To be honest, this crisis has reminded me of what I have. And what I stand to lose. A man gets complacent when things go too well for too long, and if nothing else Addison and his bullying has shaken me out of that." He took a couple steps closer to Matt, holding out the wooden box. "Your passion for what is right, as well as your willingness to stand up to those who are doing wrong is precisely what I look for in a friend. You've proven to me that you are a man of integrity, a man we can trust. You don't owe my family anything, Mr. Hawke, but I would be honored if you stayed here at Circle C with us. We can discuss lodging and payment. We can talk about how to help you work toward your future. And, as a bonus, I'd like you to have this."

He handed the wooden box to Matt, who accepted it hesitatingly.

"Richard, are you sure?" Mrs. Conway asked.

"I am."

She looked uncertain but didn't say anything, instead

trusting her husband's choice. She nodded slightly at Matt.

He opened the lid of the box to find a silver pocket watch and chain resting gently nestled in gray silk interior.

"Wow," he said under his breath.

Lifting it carefully out of the box, Matt examined the delicate etchings that decorated the edge of the watch. Curling lines swirled around the outer border of the silver, framing the quote within: "No amount of money or success can take the place of time spent with your family."

"Why...? I can't accept this," Matt said, protesting. "Isn't this a family heirloom? Shouldn't it go to one of your children?" He gestured helplessly at Michael, watching from his mother's side.

"I'd like it to go to the man who behaves as family even though he is not related and, Mr. Hawke, you are that man. Yes, Michael might have done the same had he been older, but he's my son. He does his duty, of course, but that just underscores the fact that you didn't have to do that."

"But, anyone would have."

"No. They wouldn't." At this, Mr. Conway finally permitted himself a smile. "Silas didn't, and he's family. He stood silently and waited. Only you were honorable and thoughtful enough to question the persecutors. This watch was a gift from my first employer, when I was about your age. It has a tradition of being passed through merit, not just blood. Please honor me by accepting it."

"I don't know ..." Matt still hesitated. The watch was

beautiful; the gesture was kind. But is this what he wanted for his life?

As that thought bounced around his brain, he became aware of Violet Conway standing close by his side.

Matt held his new pocket watch carefully in one hand and closed the lid of the box.

"Thank you, Mr. Conway. I can't tell you how much I appreciate this. I'll do my best to deserve it."

Without warning, the older man crossed the final couple steps and enveloped Matt in a hug, the other members of the family joining too.

"Wonderful," he said as he pulled back. "Mr. Hawke, I know this is the beginning of a promising partnership between us. Let us finish eating, and begin planning. With your help, I am certain that together we can come up with the money necessary for the next mortgage payment. Circle C Ranch will stay in the family. It must."

Matt rejoined the Conways at the supper table, each member of the family kindly not mentioning his earlier outburst. They carried on as though there had been no interruption. His plate and food had remained untouched at the chair—*his* chair. Matthew Hawke had a home again for the first time in years, and he wasn't about to let that go.

CHAPTER SIX

Silas was at Circle C Ranch early the following morning, and led Matt in another collection of chores that exhausted and thrilled him. But both young men were distracted by thoughts—hopes—of what would come that night. The evening after they had installed another ten feet of fence, Silas left the ranch early to go home.

"I still have at least a week before I need to bother with a bath," he said as the two men put away their tools, "but I'll make time tonight for Mary Ann."

Matt returned to the family home without him, ready to inquire about further chores or tasks that needed doing since it was still early, well before sunset. As soon as he opened the door, though, Mrs. Conway saw him and scolded.

"Why, Matthew. I completely forgot! You'll need a good scrub down and a clean shirt if you aim to go to the church social tonight. Oh! And you can't wear those pants with a cut up the leg, even if we could get out that blood stain. Wait right here. I'll go see what Richard has."

"Thank you, ma'am," he said with a grin.

On the opposite side of the big room, Michael was complaining.

"That's too hot!"

Matt watched Violet pour a pot full of steaming water over her younger brother as he sat crouched in a large tin tub by the stove. His otherwise lily-white shoulders were now a bright pink from the heat, and his hair was plastered to his forehead. It was bath night for someone else, not just Silas.

"Hush," she said indulgently, returning to the stove to heat up more water. "Scrub yourself, Michael. All of you." Violet caught Matt's eye and grinned, her dimple flashing. "Your turn next?"

Matt felt himself blush. "Oh, probably not."

But in due time, Mrs. Conway had him stripped down to his torn pants, had forced the wet, soapy towel into his hand, and got Matt all spruced up beyond what he thought possible. He could not remember the last time another person had bothered to look after him in this way, and though it was somewhat embarrassing to be mothered, Matt secretly relished the attention. She was a master at rustling her family, and they were out the door, on the road, and at the church social before Matt knew it. It was a whirlwind, and he was just along for the ride.

When they arrived at the field where the social was to be, Mr. Conway directed the wagon and horses to the far pasture where their neighbors had also come. The family climbed down to make their way to the tent.

Michael ran on ahead, while Mr. Conway helped his wife out of the wagon and Matt reached up to help Violet. She lost her balance momentarily when she touched the ground, falling into him. He was able to hold them both up, in spite of his injured leg.

"Careful," he said gently. "Are you all right?"

"Of course," she said straightening up. "Thank you for catching me."

"Come on, you two," Mrs. Conway called to them, leading the way into the tent that had been set up on the edge of a neighbor's field.

They could hear the lively, dancing music even from this distance. Matt had never been much of a dancer, but with the sounds emanating from the crowded tent, he wasn't sure he could help himself, injury or no. A crowd was gathering and streaming toward the tent alongside Matt and the Conways.

When the family reached the opening to the tent, Matt stood for a long moment just inside the doorway and watched. Michael, having rushed ahead of them, was already at the refreshments table, a cookie in each hand. Mrs. Conway spotted him the same moment Matt did and hurried over to take control of the child again. The band was set up on the far end of the tented space, already playing a lively song for the growing crowd.

Only three couples were on the dance floor this early in the evening, but Matt recognized one of the men as Silas. He grinned as he watched his friend lead his lovely dance partner around the floor, stumbling occasionally but oblivious to anything but her.

Matt wondered if he would get a chance to talk to

Silas at all that night, or if the young man would be too enamored by his date to notice anyone else.

The neighbors and church members that had come out for the social this evening represented a wide range of western settlers. Children like Michael and even younger ran around, weaving between the adults, and in and out of the tent but always back to the cookies. Matt remembered back to when he was that age, all the games and rough-housing he would get into with his friends. Michael was in the last true months of his childhood, before he would be expected to fulfill all the responsibilities of growing up.

Next were the young folk, in the first years of taking on more responsibilities or leaving school. They were gathered in gender-divided clusters on either side of the band. Even from this distance, Matt could see the way the fourteen, fifteen and sixteen-year-old girls were whispering as they watched their male counterparts. The boys, for their part, acted oblivious. Or, more likely, were actually oblivious. When Matt had been that age, he had very little exposure to the girls of his neighborhood. He had plenty of his own troubles to think of when it came to finding a place to sleep and food to eat, and it wouldn't have occurred to him that the next-door-neighbor of his entire life might be thinking he was cute. Matt grinned and made a bet with himself on whether or not any of those boys would ask a girl to dance.

Next, the sweethearts, the handful of neighbors all around Matt and Silas—and Violet's—age, flirting, dancing, finding private corners in which to sit and talk in these few stolen moments between chores. With as much work as each person did every day, it must be difficult to find any time at all to go courting. Matt wondered if that were a reason Silas didn't live at the ranch; living in town gave him slightly more time in which to see Mary Ann.

The married couples filled the rest of the space, ranging from the blond couple strolling arm in arm around the perimeter of the dance floor who couldn't be any older than Matt, to the octogenarian couple seated primly in spindly wooden chairs against the canvas tent wall farthest from the music.

All in all, Matt could see why the Conways were so eager to join their church community here tonight. The warmth of the families was contagious and Matt felt an unexpected urge to go introduce himself to strangers. He had never been shy, but neither did he voluntarily insert himself in someone's conversation.

No sooner had that thought crossed his mind, then he noticed Mr. Conway crossing to him.

"Matt, I'd like you to come with me, if you would. There's some folks I'd like you to meet."

Matt followed behind, intrigued, though surreptitiously looking around the tent for where Violet had gone. He still hoped to ask her for a dance, even if his leg was already beginning to twinge.

The small group of men Mr. Conway led him to were all much older than Matt, and, to a man, inspected him critically with their expressions.

"Gentlemen, this is the new ranch hand at Circle C. I met Mr. Hawke in town just a couple days ago and he has already proved to be even more helpful than I could have hoped. Mr. Hawke, please let me introduce you to Mr. Frye, Mr. Bullock and Mr. Demijon." The rancher indicated each of the three men in turn, and Matt committed their names to memory.

Mr. Frye was tall, thin and pale. He peered down at Matt with a flat face and rather reminded the younger man of a headstone. He pushed that uncharitable thought out of his mind and shook hands with the next man.

Mr. Bullock was large, but otherwise unremarkable in every way. If it weren't for the fact that the man accidentally stepped on Matt's foot, he wasn't sure he would remember him at all.

And Mr. Demijon was a tiny, round chipper man whose smile Matt found contagious. He smiled back at him.

"Pleasure," Matt said, shaking their hands.

"Another ranch hand? Why? Silas Denbow not doing enough for you?" Mr. Frye asked. "You know he's been seeing my sister-in-law, Conway. Is there something I need to know?"

"Your sister-in-law?" Matt asked, even though he knew it was likely rude to speak before addressed directly.

Mr. Frye nodded toward the dance floor. "Miss Whitaker is my wife's younger sister. Silas is calling on her sometimes up to three times a week, and if I should be concerned about his prospects, I wish you'd tell me now, Conway."

"No, no. Nothing like that. Silas is always more than satisfactory. It's just with the expanded herd comes expanded chores and we can never have too many hands around the place. I wanted to make sure you gentlemen met Mr. Hawke, in the event that either he or I can be of service to you. I trust him as I trust my own family."

Matt opened his mouth to ask a question, but closed it again after considering. It seemed as though Mr. Conway had a specific conversation topic in mind, a reason he had wanted to introduce Matt.

"I was actually hoping to talk to you, Mr. Bullock," the rancher said. "Wondering if we might talk privately about the matter."

"Oh, well. Now might not be the best time, Conway," Mr. Bullock said. "But on that subject, I take it Addison came around to the ranch yesterday?"

"I—" Mr. Conway stopped himself and smiled pleasantly. "You heard about that, did you?"

Mr. Bullock laughed. "Well, Bud Humphrey was there, wasn't he? Won't stop talking about it in the saloon. Seems like you've got quite the debacle on your hands."

"Well, you're right that it's not ideal. But, as I say, I've got Silas, and now Matt here, and we're handling it. Circle C will be just fine."

"Just as you say, Conway," Mr. Bullock said, looking distractedly at the dance floor now almost full.

"I've been meaning to ask you, Mr. Bullock. That ... financial matter we spoke about months ago—"

"Oh, yes. All taken care of. You can count on me, Conway."

"Thank you, sir."

"I'm happy to do whatever I can for you, look out for options and such. But as a rule, I don't like to get in the middle of business transaction like that, though. It all needs to be above board. See that you do handle it. The bank will of course honor the terms of the mortgage, and provided payments are made on time you shouldn't have anything to worry about. But if not ..."

He gestured with one hand, as if to say 'what can I do,' and kept his attention on the dance floor.

"You must excuse me, gentlemen," Mr. Bullock said. "I see my wife calling me over. I promised her I wouldn't spend this entire evening talking business."

"Good evening," the men murmured, shaking hands and nodding good-byes.

Matt stole a look at Mr. Conway and realized immediately that the conversation had not gone as he had hoped. Perhaps he had imagined the banker would grant leniency. Maybe even having Matt as a new asset, so to speak, would work in his favor. But now they were right back where they started, with that deadline looming overhead.

What else could they do? What other options were there?

"Are you gentlemen both ranchers?" Matt asked the other two.

"I am," Mr. Demijon said. "Mountain Shadow Ranch. Just on the other side of the hill behind Circle C, as a matter of fact. We share a small border. I'm surprised Mr. Conway didn't tell you." Mr. Demijon seemed vaguely insulted.

"Oh, please don't blame him," Matt assured him. "I've only been there for a couple days. I still have a lot to learn."

"I own the hardware store in Juniper Falls," Mr. Frye said. "And, as I mentioned, my wife is the schoolteacher in town as well. I've tried and tried to get her to give up her work, since we got married. But. Well, you know how women are."

The other men laughed, and Matt smiled to himself, noticing Violet across the room at that very moment. She didn't seem like the kind of woman who could be talked into anything she didn't want to do.

As he watched her, standing with several girlfriends not far from the refreshment table, Matt noticed another man watching her as well. The man appeared to be a bit older than Matt, but with his black hat pulled down low over his face, it was difficult to be certain. As Matt watched, the other men around him continued to talk, about the hardware store, about another new arrival to town, but Matt couldn't focus on the conversation. The black-hatted man leering at Violet was swaying on his feet, likely already drunk although the night had only just started.

Matt felt his anger rising, but checked it. He didn't know this man. Maybe this was a friend of Violet's. Maybe he wasn't drunk, only tired. Maybe he would just watch and not bother her.

Maybe Matt was overreacting.

The stranger stood near another seemingly inebriated man, who was talking at him incessantly. From this distance Matt couldn't hear what was being said, but both men now gaped openly at Violet.

And she had noticed.

Her girlfriends standing with her took the bold step to turn their backs completely to the men, blocking their view of any of the ladies' faces.

Those men did not take well to being shunned. The

black-hatted man Matt had noticed first took a couple lurching steps toward the circle of women.

That was Matt's cue to move.

Without even making his good-byes to the men he was ostensibly talking to—he had no clue where the conversation had led—Matt strode quickly to Violet's side. Or, rather, as quickly as he could while limping on his injured leg. As it happened, with that encumbrance, Matt was only just able to reach Miss Conway at the same time as the stranger.

The drunken man was using a shoulder to push his way between two of the young ladies.

"Well, now," Matt heard him say to Violet. "You must be lonely over here without any male company. It's a good thing I noticed, so I could come give you what you clearly need."

Violet shrank back, away from the looming man, and away from his alcohol-drenched breath. Though she was frightened, Matt could see a glimmer of defiance in her eyes. She wouldn't be cowed. She wouldn't give in to this man's demands. Matt reached forward, clasped onto the man's shoulder and spun him around.

"I don't think your company is what she needs," he said, seething. His temper had gotten him into trouble before, but now he cherished this rage. This fury was a guide. This righteous anger had led him to protecting Miss Conway and her friends from harassment, or worse.

"Nobody asked you, kid," the man spat into Matt's face. "Leave the lady and me alone."

In the short moment the man had turned his attention to Matt, Violet had taken the opportunity to leave the situation. Grasping the hand of one of her girl-friends, Violet darted onto the crowded dance floor, getting lost between the couples and vanishing from sight.

"You see?" Matt said, almost mockingly. "You're not wanted."

The man was slow to turn, as though he hadn't quite believed what he was seeing. But with Matt's help, Violet had extricated herself. She had saved herself. Matt would just need to keep an eye on this fellow the rest of the evening, to ensure he didn't bother her anymore.

Although, now that Violet was hidden within the crowd, Matt despaired of finding her again to claim his own dance. Maybe after this run-in with an unwanted suitor, all men would be despicable to her.

The drunk had finally turned to give Matt his attention.

"Why don't you just go on back to your friend over there?" Matt suggested.

The other man hauled back and landed his fist smack in the middle of Matt's cheek. If he had been less inebriated, or had better aim, that punch had enough power to break a bone. Fortunately, under the current circumstances it only stunned Matt. He was surprised—though he could tell this was a violent man, Matt didn't think he had done anything to warrant such abuse. But if it meant sparing Violet such attentions it was worth it.

He felt his temper rising again; this man deserved a whooping and Matt was just the person to give it to him. But just as he began to advance, he finally caught Violet's eye on the other side of the room. She was watching him, noticing how he handled himself and took care of the situation. He would make her proud.

With that final thought, Matt changed the trajectory of his blow. Rather than punching the drunk in return, he reached forward with both hands to seize the man's lapels.

"That's enough, I said. I won't have you causing a scene."

Even with his injured leg, Matt was able to over-power the drunk man and haul him to the entrance to the tent. Everyone he passed watched, some amused, some grateful, some sneered in disgust when they smelled the stranger. Matt didn't care. He knew this man would do worse as soon as he got any kind of leeway.

He dragged the man through the tent entrance and another twenty feet beyond it, well out of the way of the churchgoers and neighbors who had come to the social tonight for a calm, safe evening. Matt flung the man to the ground.

"You go home, now," he said. "Go take a bath. Drink some coffee. Sober up. I won't have you ruining the dance for any of these fine people."

When he turned back to the tent, he blushed when he noticed that Violet Conway had watched the whole thing.

CHAPTER SEVEN

After Matt had tossed the drunk, leering man out of the church dance tent into the dark night, he turned around to see Violet waiting for him at the entrance. Another family passed her on their way into the tent, but Violet only had eyes for him, watching as he limped his way back to her. Matt glanced briefly back over his shoulder to ensure that the drunk man was staying on the ground, and then crossed to her. The wide smile on her face was like a beacon, calling him to her.

"Are you all right?" he asked when he was close enough. "I'm so sorry that happened to you." He didn't think the man had been able to lay a hand on her, but he wanted to make sure. Matt's impulse was to clasp her hand, to pull her toward him, and to protect her in his embrace, but he restrained himself.

She nodded. "Thank you. I probably could have spent the whole night avoiding him, but this is better."

"If he couldn't find you, he might have bothered someone else."

"He probably would have." She nodded. "There's always something worse men like that could be doing. I haven't ever seen him before, but Elsa told me he had leered at her in town earlier today."

Matt shook his head, disgusted. "Men like that have no business in proper company."

"Do you think he'll really leave?"

"I do." Matt turned to look back at the man. He was still lying in the dirt. He didn't appear all that hurt, but his balance seemed to be off. After watching him attempt to get up another time, before collapsing back across the ground, Matt was satisfied.

"Let's hope he's the only one in there not able to hold his liquor. I thought this was a church function."

"It is, but Pastor Langdon likes to invite the whole town. Be welcoming and generous. Set a good example and all."

Matt chuckled. "Didn't appear to work with this one."

"No," Violet agreed. "But it's over now." She smiled brightly. Her dimple flashed when she smiled up again and Matt couldn't help but smile back, in spite of all his pain and frustrations.

"It is," he agreed. They were still in the doorway to the tent, and Matt looked over his shoulder at the crowd gathered inside. "I don't suppose you might— that is, if you haven't already been promised, would you like to dance?"

Violet stole a quick look down at Matt's bandaged leg. She had replaced the bandage for him herself just before they left home, so she knew precisely his limitations at this moment. But in spite of the fact that any other man in the place could perform better, she nodded quickly.

"I'd be honored."

He offered her his arm, and trying to limit his limp, led her back into the tent, onto the dance floor where a new song was just beginning.

"Oh, I love this song," she said wistfully as Matt wrapped his hand around her waist.

"Do you dance often?"

"Oh, no. No. The church only hosts one of these each year. This is probably the last time we'll have such entertainment until next spring. Elsa and I keep talking to Mrs. Langdon—the pastor's wife—about doing a Christmas dance, but we haven't talked her into it yet."

"And there's nowhere else in town?"

Violet shook her head. "Not in Juniper Falls. Maybe in Laramie, but that's too far to go just for entertainment."

"Would your father allow it?"

Violet bit her lip as she thought and gazed into distance behind him. With her attention elsewhere, Matt could take the opportunity to study the delicate features of her face unnoticed. Her narrow, slightly upturned nose and her full mouth and hazel eyes in her heart-shaped face. He memorized every detail.

She returned her gaze to him and smiled. "I think he might. He has always told stories of the gatherings his family used to host in Alexandria, where he grew up. Before the war. He's never been the type of Christian to frown on good clean fun."

"Then I'll take you sometime," Matt promised gladly. "We'll go to Laramie and go dancing."

Violet blushed. "Why— Matt, I'm not sure..."

"Not tomorrow. But someday. You deserve at least one dance with a man not limping from a bullet wound."

This made her laugh and hold back any concern she might have had about the practicality and propriety of the two traveling to Laramie. Matt knew it was just a suggestion, that it might never come to pass. But even having something hypothetical to look forward to was intoxicating. Though he didn't have any idea how he would make it happen, Matt knew he wouldn't give up.

"Other than dancing at a church social once a year, what do you like to do, Miss Conway?"

She smiled shyly. "I told you, call me Violet."

He grinned back. "Violet."

"I'm not sure what I like to do. Honestly, Mr. Hawke—"

"Matt."

"Matt." She smiled. "With keeping the house and occasionally helping with the animals, almost all my time is taken up on the ranch. But, you know... I don't mind at all. I get such a satisfaction from harvesting from our garden, or finishing sewing a new dress. In fact, just last fall, Mother and I took a whole week for canning and— please don't tell anyone this—I still go to the root cellar to admire the rows and rows of brightly colored jars. All those fruits and vegetables. All that food prepared to take care of my family. I did that. Or, helped at least. It's so satisfying."

"That sounds inspiring. I can understand why you would be proud of that."

"Thank you. But, I guess what I'm saying is... I do what I like to do. Mother helps direct how I should prioritize the tasks, but they're all things I'm glad to do. I suppose I might be happy as a storekeeper's wife helping wait on customers or a society matron back east somewhere with dozens of servants to keep the house. But really, here in Wyoming, on a ranch, taking care of people I love with my own two hands. This is what I like to do with my time."

Matt paused, considering slowly what to say next. Violet again was lost in her own thoughts and watching her light up like this made him want to give her everything she wanted.

"Then, I hope this is the life you get to have, Violet," he said gently.

"Thank you, Matt. I hope you get the life you want to have too."

The next ten minutes were the happiest of Matt's life thus far. Violet stayed in his arms for not just one dance, but three. She laughed at his jokes, she encouraged him in his own hopes, asking him questions and she floated gracefully alongside him as they slowly turned around the dance floor. Somehow in all of that, she also managed to get him to confide in her. Somehow, he trusted her enough to tell her about his struggles with his temper, his parents, and how he ended up in Wyoming.

After the third song, however, Matt could no longer ignore the pulsing pain in his leg. Violet had assured him it was healing, but that didn't mean he should stay on it very long.

"How about some refreshments?" he suggested. She had seen him wince, and he wanted to forestall any pity. "I could use something to cool down a bit."

Violet led the way, seeming to not notice his pronounced limp as he followed behind, weaving through the crowd. The table with cookies and punch was against the wall of the tent opposite the musicians, and when they reached it, Matt felt a hand clapped on his shoulder.

He turned to see Silas, beaming, with a young woman standing just at his side.

"Matt! You made it. I knew you would. I saw you two dancing already. That leg bothering you yet? Say, can I introduce you to my girl? This is Mary Ann Whitaker, like I told you about. Miss Whitaker, please allow me to introduce you to Mr. Matthew Hawke. And of course Miss Conway you know."

Further conversation was interrupted by shouting coming from outside the tent. Several male voices, confronting each other about something. The band valiantly played on, even after they could see that they had lost the attention of more than half of their audience. Most of the men, and some of the women, streamed out to the door of the tent, to watch the row happening in the field. Whoever had gone out there had likely been attempting to avoid notice, but raising their voices made that aim fail miserably.

Matt took Violet's hand and led her around the edge of the crowd. He thought maybe it was time for them to be getting home—he didn't want to be part of any more fights this night. But as more and more folks emptied out of the tent, he didn't see either of the Conways anywhere in the crowd.

"Stay close to me," he whispered.

She nodded, keeping her eyes fixed on him.

Still hand in hand, Matt followed the line of people going out to see what all the commotion was about. Men and women were spreading out in a half-circle around the shouting men, and Matt led Violet between couples in his quest to find her parents.

Matt looked up and over the crowd that was gathering, certain that he would recognize Mr. Conway any moment. The tall rancher had a full head of white hair and a stark white mustache. He was a man who stood out. And yet, even after several probing looks through the group, Matt didn't see him. Maybe he was still in the tent and they had missed him. Was he waiting by the wagon?

"Your father wouldn't have left without us, would he?"

"Of course not. Besides, I spotted Michael by the cookies. Pa must be here somewhere."

The shouting grew louder, and in that instant Matt thought he might recognize at least one of the voices. But in spite of his height, he couldn't see anything from where they were. There were far too many people gathered, tall hats and wide shoulders filling the space.

The words and voices of those fighting were too jumbled to make out.

"Did you hear that?" an older woman near him asked, looking shocked.

"Someone should stop them," another said.

"Two against one just ain't fair," a bearded man nearby mumbled, though made no move to take action.

"What is going on?" Violet whispered to him.

Matt shook his head, still trying to peer over the old man in front of them. He couldn't tell from where they were standing, but if the bearded man was right and there was a fight with two men against one, someone should do something. For not the first time, Matt cursed his luck at his injured leg.

"Violet, something is going on. I'll take a look, but I need you to stay here. Stay with these nice women. You'll be safe."

"You are not going wading into that fight, are you, Matthew Hawke?"

"Someone has got to. I'll be fine. It's not my fight, but maybe I can keep some poor sod from getting hurt too bad."

"If you get shot again, you're bandaging it yourself," she teased.

"That's fair." He squeezed her hand one last time before leaving her in the crowd. Pushing past the well-meaning folk trying to ascertain what was occurring, Matt drew closer to the arguing group. His suspicions were confirmed. The one man, facing off against two threatening bullies, sported a full head of white hair and a white mustache.

It was Mr. Conway, out here in the dark, in a neighbor's field, shouting angrily at ...

Matt wasn't even surprised; it was Sheriff Vance and Mr. Addison. Even from this distance, Matt could see the smugness on Addison's face. He walked closer, but none of the men saw him until he was standing nearly at Mr. Conway's elbow.

"Is there something I can help you with here, sir?" he asked.

Conway started, surprised to hear another voice but responded immediately. "You see here, Addison? You see what I am working with? Mr. Bullock confirmed the bank would honor the mortgage to the letter, which means that I still have a couple days to make that next payment—"

"That's three months that you owe, though. And then what will you do next month?" Addison interrupted smoothly.

"I— What?" Conway was flustered out of his train of thought.

"Next month. I have no doubt that you all will move heaven and earth to make this payment. But then you'll have to do it all again next month and the month after that, and so on. Why not just give up now and spare us all that?"

"I'm sure our friend the governor could recommend you for some commissioner's job or appoint you to some outpost or other," the sheriff said, smoothly. "After all, we're not heartless. We know a man needs to be able to support his family after his ranch is foreclosed on."

"That's enough," Matt said, stepping in for the first time and surprising even himself with his adamancy. But he could feel his temper rising again, incensed at the way Mr. Conway was being bullied. The older man was trying to be reasonable with these two, and was only being attacked. Conway was too kind to others, too generous to strangers to be able to stand up for himself when he needed to. Matt knew if he had to listen to much more that he might end up in a fight that he had promised Violet he wouldn't be in. "You can't do anything to any of the Conways tonight. They still have time to meet the terms of the contract. There's no point in discussing this any further. Come on, Mr. Conway. Let's just go."

"They threatened me, Matt," he said in a low voice. "They threatened my family. Violet and Michael, and even you. We can't let them get away with that."

"We won't. But remember what you told me just the other day when Bud Humphrey was coming after me?" he said gently. "He's not worth it. That was good advice then and it's good advice now. What would you tell Silas if he was in the same position?"

"Listen to the kid," Addison said.

Matt shot him a glare but managed to restrain himself just a little longer. Long enough, in fact to notice Mrs. Conway crossing the field toward her husband.

"That is quite enough for one day," Mrs. Conway said. "Let's go home, Richard."

He took a deep breath and looked around, finally registering the situation he had found himself in, with his neighbors and loved ones watching him scream at a couple of known bullies. Mr. Conway nodded.

"That's right," his wife said, taking his arm.

Mr. Conway began to lead her toward where the wagon stayed waiting for them. Violet broke away from the crowd, hand in hand with Michael, and met them partway back to the wagon. Suddenly, Mr. Conway stopped.

"I need... I can't..." He shook his head as though trying to shake something loose. "Mr. Hawke, would you please escort my family to the wagon. I need to get the horses. I need... I need just a few minutes to myself. I'll bring them over." He rubbed his eyes before looking at Matt.

"You sure you don't need help, Pa?" Michael asked. "I can do it. I know how."

"I know you do, son." He ruffled Michael's blond head. "But not this time. You take care of your mother."

"All right," the boy said glumly.

Matt watched the old rancher walk off into the darkness to where the horses were being watered. He knew the night had not gone to his expectations, but he prayed the older man wasn't losing hope.

For the first time in his life, Matthew Hawke felt as though he were part of something real, something bigger than him. Though he didn't know how they would do it, he vowed he would help the Conways keep their home.

CHAPTER EIGHT

The next day started quietly, as though the family wanted nothing more than to pretend everything was all right. Matt had not seen Silas again after he stepped into the disagreement between Conway and Addison. However late the ranch hand had stayed out with Mary Ann, Silas still arrived at dawn to begin his chores, dragging Matt along with him. He made jokes about all the men who had hovered around the refreshment table the night before and might be getting a late start this morning.

"I think that's probably why the pastor stopped holding these socials on Saturday nights. Too many men made excuses to miss church the next day." Silas chuckled to himself as he fed the chickens who had swarmed his feet.

"It was certainly an interesting night," Matt said, now that the two were alone. "Where were you when your uncle was getting threatened?"

Silas blushed, and didn't meet Matt's eye. "I told you,

Mary Ann was my priority all night. When you all started leaving the tent, we found chairs and a corner where we wouldn't be bothered."

Matt sighed. "Well, has Mr. Conway talked to you at all about the payment? Three missed payments to come up with in just a couple days. Do we know how he's going to manage that? I don't see how it's possible. Should we try to— I don't know. Hire ourselves to another rancher or sell one of the horses? I can't even think how he's going to get out from under this."

Silas shook his head. "He hasn't said anything for sure. I know he was thinking about selling part of the herd, but he'd have to do that at a loss and then we'd be even more trouble in a few months. I trust he has a plan, but other than that idea, I haven't seen any sign of one."

Matt nodded and continued his task. He was used to taking action. He was used to taking care of himself and having his full survival be dependent on his own steps. The only way he made as far as the Wyoming Territory was trusting in his own choices and making things happen. Waiting on another man was excruciating, but it was a lesson in patience Matt had a feeling he needed to learn.

Violet appeared in the doorway of the barn, two glasses in hand.

"I brought you some lemonade," she said, when the men noticed her.

"Lemonade!" Silas said, hurrying over to her. "There isn't anything we've done to deserve this."

Matt followed, limping slightly across the dirt. The look of surprise on Silas's face at the fact they had been brought a special drink was unmistakable. Matt had gotten accustomed to taking his refreshment from well water when he needed throughout the day. It was cool and satisfied, but was nothing compared to the sugary treat. The gift of lemonade, sweetened and cold, would be a bright spot of their whole week.

"If you two can see your way to taking a break, I wonder if Mr. Hawke might take a walk with me. I'd like to show you that tree I told you about."

Matt frowned, racking his brain for what seemed to be a lost memory. What tree? Had she told him and he had not been listening? That didn't seem likely. He thought he had hung on her every word. But from the way she was looking at him so intently, he knew he couldn't refuse the invitation. He would follow wherever she went.

"Of course." He took the second glass of lemonade from her. "Lead the way. Silas, I'll be right back."

She didn't glance behind her as she walked, but seemed to trust that he was there. The path she followed took them through the opening in the fence, around the perimeter of the pasture and to the grove on the far side. They were maybe half a mile from the farmhouse when they reached the wide, shallow creek that ran through the property on this side, providing the livestock with plenty of water at any season. The tall cottonwood trees overhead provided plenty of shade when they needed it in the middle of a summer afternoon. And the blanket of wildflowers—purple, yellow, orange—growing along the creek's edge provided a pop of beauty that, while not strictly necessary for survival, proved necessary for the soul.

It was into this grove of trees that Violet led him,

under the canopy, straight to the tallest, widest cotton-wood in the bunch. She turned to him, her back against the trunk.

"I'm so sorry, Violet," he stammered. "I don't recall what you told me about this tree."

"Oh, I didn't," she said, waving her hand dismissively. "I thought of it this morning and wanted to show you."

Matt looked at her quizzically. "I don't understand. Show me what?"

"Remember what I said about wanting to care for the people I love with my own hands? Well, I realized that this tree was the start of that. And I wanted you to see."

She turned back to face the trunk and placed her palm on the bark. Matt stayed quiet, watching, waiting. Whatever it was she wanted to tell him seemed impor-tant. Her shoulders rose and fell slowly as she took a few deep breaths. Finally, once Matt was almost sure she had forgotten about him, Violet turned back around and offered him a warm smile.

"We came out to Wyoming when I was only twelve," she began. "It had been weeks and weeks in a wagon all the way from Virginia. I don't even remember how long. Michael was an energetic handful, all legs and questions. With all Mother had to do to help Pa with the wagon and making camp, looking after my brother became mostly my job.

"I had, of course, helped with him since he was born, but never for so many hours in a row. Even though I'm sure we stopped places, and talked to folks, my abiding memory from the journey west is just weeks and weeks of the two of us riding in the wagon, cramped up and trying to make up games or tell stories to entertain him."

"Couldn't you get out and walk?"

"Of course," she answered with a shrug, "but he was only five, I think. His little legs couldn't do that the whole way. We would start out walking alongside the trail after breakfast, but he got tired within a few hours. I couldn't carry him. It wasn't all bad. When there wasn't too much dust from the road; we could pin up the sides of the canvas flaps and get some fresh air, and walk again in the afternoon. But most of what I remember from that trek was the tiny, hot, cloying space.

"When we finally arrived in Wyoming, I could not wait to just... rest. To have a place to stay put. But then —" She laughed at her thought. "When we finally came to this acreage and Pa told us this is where we would be living, I set off running. Mother called after me, but I needed to get out and get my muscles working again. I was so stiff, it felt like every step I might hurt myself, trip or pull a muscle, but I just kept running."

"I can understand that," Matt said with a laugh of his own. "That's part of why I wanted to come west at all. I never felt like I could run in Boston. There was always another brick wall or building standing in my way. Crowds at every turn."

Violet nodded. "The grass and the plains here are..." She trailed off, took another deep, contented breath and smiled again. "I am grateful every time I come out here."

She paused again, and looked up into the branches of the cottonwood.

"And that's the first time you saw this tree?" Matt prompted after a moment.

"Yes." She shook herself out of her daze. "Yes. This tree. It was the tallest then, just like it's the tallest now. It was like a beacon to me, calling to me as I ran across the grass. I had never been particularly connected to nature back in Virginia, but once we got here this ranch felt like home. Immediately. Before even the foundation of the house was built. And I think it was because of this tree.

"And, actually, that's why I wanted to show it to you. And to tell you this story. Keep in mind, of course, I was only twelve years old, but my immediate thought as soon as I arrived here breathless from running, was that I wanted to live in the tree. I would have hiked up my skirt and climbed all the way to the top if I wasn't afraid of tearing my dress and getting an earful from Mother. As it was, I pulled myself up to this first branch here."

As she reached up to touch the lowermost branch, she laughed self-consciously, glancing at him with a now-shy expression. She seemed worried about how he would react, maybe concerned he might find her silly or unfeminine.

But that couldn't be further from the truth.

It only made him admire her more. There was something brave and wild about such an admission. Only a strong woman would feel secure even imagining such a life for herself, no matter how unrealistic it really was.

"How long before your parents found you out here?"

"Oh, not long." She smiled at the memory. "But I was up in the tree before they got here." Violet laughed. "In fact, I climbed this tree every chance I got that first year. It wasn't many. We had a lot to do to get the house built and the garden planted, the well dug and the cattle settled. But every chance I got I came out to the tree. My tree. And every chance I got, I tried to convince them to build me a treehouse out here."

"Strange that they didn't support you living outside," he teased.

She didn't appear to hear him. She was miles away, back in a memory as she looked up into the branches of her favorite tree again.

"There's just a different feeling of belonging when I'm out here. I could climb to the top and see our entire ranch, all the acres in every direction. I think maybe that was when I realized this is what I want to do. When I tell you that I just want to take care of the people I love, I also mean this land. The Circle C Ranch is important to me, and every day I get to spend working on it is a day well spent."

"I'm sorry. This must be stressful for you, knowing that you might lose it."

Violet blinked back tears, and met his gaze bravely. "It is. But I trust my father. He's never let us down. I know it will work out. It has to. There's no other alternative for me. This ranch will stay in the family. Either with me or with Michael. Or both, for all I know. I've prayed about it, and I have peace. I know my father will take care of us."

Even with so much uncertainty, Matt felt a calm settle over him. Knowing Violet could be so attached to this land and still be at peace helped him stop worrying. She was right. They needed to rely on Mr. Conway. He had gotten to this point, knowing all along what the consequence was. The man wouldn't put his family and their home that they had sacrificed so much for at risk without cause.

And through it all, Matt wanted to be by her side.

"Violet," he began, reaching for her hand.

Whatever he was about to say would have to wait. His next word was interrupted. Across the expanse of pasture and Circle C Ranch, the crack of gunshot broke across the silence.

"What was that?" Violet asked in a petrified whisper.

But Matt didn't stay to answer; he had already started sprinting as fast as he could toward the house.

His leg wasn't healed, not even close, but he pushed through the pain, clenching his teeth to hold it together. With each step on the wounded leg, ache shot through all of him. But still he ran. Dodging cattle, dodging stumps, keeping one eye open for prairie dog dens or other holes in the earth, praying his strength would hold out.

Matt just wanted to get back to the house as fast as he possibly could.

Another gunshot pierced the air.

"No," he groaned to himself. He dug a little deeper to find the reserve of energy he didn't know he had. Blood was beginning to soak through his bandage, but he wouldn't stop.

A third, then fourth gunshot rang out as Matt finally stumbled his way to the yard in front of the Conways' home. An unfamiliar horse was ground tied near the well. Matt heard the sound of more horse hooves disappearing into the distance, but couldn't identify the riders. Instead, a tall man in a bright, orange-red flannel shirt standing in the middle of the dirt expanse seemed to be the only other creature in sight.

Where was everyone else? Who was—

But, then Matt recognized the figure.

He wasn't the only one there.

Bud Humphrey, gun gripped lightly in hand, stood over a prone body that lay in the dirt. The shock of white hair on the fallen man told Matt all he needed to know.

"No!" he shouted, still nearly thirty yards away.

Bud looked up at him. From this distance Matt couldn't read his expression, but his actions said plenty. As Matt picked up his speed again to try to detain the murderer, Bud scarpered. Leaving nothing but a body behind and taking nothing else with him, he ran to his horse, mounted and quickly galloped away down the road.

He was getting away, and Matt could not allow that. He looked around fruitlessly for something, another horse, anything he could use to make chase after him. Where was Silas? The entire area seemed deserted.

"No," Matt cried again. His voice cracked, as he recognized his impotence, frustrated at his total lack of options.

He turned his attention to Mr. Conway, lying motionless in the dirt. Maybe there was still time. He could staunch the blood and hold the wounds together long enough to get him to a doctor.

Matt rushed to the older man's side, falling to his knees next to him. He reached for Conway.

But he was too late. The bullets seemed to have pierced every vital organ. Even in his inexperience, Matt could see there was no chance Mr. Conway would survive it. His eyes were closed, his breath shallow and irregular. Matt kneeled in the dirt next to him, hardly noticing the tears running down his face as he took up the man's hand. The dust mixed with the blood pouring from the rancher and it soon turned to a coppery mud.

In mere moments, Mr. Conway passed without even noticing the young man by his side, the young man he had been beginning to think of as a son. Without any other member of his family able to reach him.

Matt gently lifted the older man's wrist, failing to find a pulse. He choked back a sob, as he shuffled back, away from the body. As the emotions overwhelmed him, Matt bent forward, over the prone form of Mr. Conway and allowed his tears to fall, dampening the man's already bloody shirt. Matt had never felt anger like this before. With as often as he may be inclined to lose his temper, always it had been mixed with frustration or futility. Never had he felt such a righteous rage searing through him.

This was not right. It wasn't fair; it wasn't just. He could not let this stand.

Matthew Hawke vowed—to himself and to the dead man in front of him—that he would have revenge. Bud Humphrey would pay for this murder.

CHAPTER NINE

Blinded by his anger, Matt couldn't decide what his first action should be. He knelt over the cooling body, paralyzed by indecision. He couldn't very well leave Mr. Conway's body out in the dirt, vulnerable as it was. Someone would have to contact the coroner. But neither could he allow Bud Humphrey to get a head start. The man was a murderer and Matt was determined to bring him to justice.

Where were the others? Where was the family?

Violet appeared at that moment, at the edge of the pasture, still dozens of yards away, but close enough to see everything.

"Pa!" she cried. Catching up her dress, she ran as fast as she could toward Matt and her father.

"Violet, wait!" Matt stood and stepped in front of the corpse. He held his arms wide, blocking her view of her father's broken body.

"Pa!" she cried again as she got closer.

She ran right to him, sobbing, brokenhearted and fragile, as he caught and held her.

"Pa," she wailed.

"Shh..." Matt tried to calm her, even though he knew it was futile. This was a young woman who loved her family. She had just told him the evening before that all she wanted in life was to take care of the people she loved. And now here she was faced with the reality that she couldn't always protect them. He couldn't imagine the pain in Violet's heart right now, losing her beloved father who meant so much to her.

"No," she sobbed out. "Pa! Why..."

She had thrown her full weight at Matt and as she went limp, he lowered her gently to the ground. Though he had thought to protect her, now that he saw the full depth of her agony, Matt knew he couldn't keep her from her father. With no thought to the state of her dress, Violet kneeled in the dirt and cast herself over the prone body of Richard Conway, sobbing and calling for him over and over.

Matt felt himself choke up. He had never witnessed such naked emotion. His own grandfather had died when Matt was still living at home, and though his mother was full of sorrow for nigh on a week, it didn't come close to this outpouring. His mother had shut herself in her room, yes. She had cried. But when Matt heard Violet's voice crack from the sheer torment, her throat raw, he recognized true grief.

He put his hand on her shoulder, with no thought to the propriety of the touch. Feeling her shoulders shaking under his fingers, Matt let the tears in his eyes spillover and down his cheeks. This would be a defining moment in Violet's life, as well as his own. He was a different man now.

At that thought, Matt wondered again where the rest of the family was. Surely Mrs. Conway and Michael had heard the shots, even if they hadn't been close to the house when Bud arrived.

He stood, and again looked around for any signs of activity on the ranch. He tried to listen for anything over Violet's tears. The ground all around Mr. Conway was disturbed. His blood, his falling, Matt's own footsteps. Most of the signs he could see in the immediate area were too confusing to tell him much.

He had been a city boy, and now on the western frontier he was in way over his head.

Matt backed up a few paces to look more at the scene as a whole. When he did, he realized the grass under the spruce tree, about forty feet away, was all torn up. He had overheard Mrs. Conway just the day before talking about how much she loved that patch of grass and shaded corner; her husband had suggested building a bench there. It had been a smooth lawn as recently as twenty-four hours ago.

But now ... Matt edged around Violet and her father's body to look more closely. There were ruts and grooves cut into it, and pieces of lawn were uprooted altogether. It only took a slightly closer examination for Matt to recognize the outlines of horse hooves within the damaged area.

This damage accounted for far more hooves than the single horse Matt had seen. Bud Humphrey might have been the last one there to pull the trigger, but he certainly had not arrived at Circle C Ranch on his own.

He couldn't read the tracks well, but their meaning was clear. Matt clenched his teeth. What a notorious bully. Bringing a whole gang to come intimidate a small family.

But where *was* the family? Matt realized in horror that they could be anywhere. If Bud had brought accomplices, they could have done anything with Silas, Mrs. Conway and Michael.

Though he didn't have the same trained eye that a bounty hunter or lawman might have, Matt could clearly see where the attackers' horses had been standing, pawing or ground tied, and where the men's bootprints led away from the tree toward the house and barn. It was a rough estimate, but Matt guessed four or five different pairs of boots marked the ground here. That would have been plenty to surprise and overpower the family. More than enough.

After one look back at Violet still sobbing on her father's chest, Matt followed the footprints to the house first. Though the door stood open and the interior held evidence of a tussle, the still silence convinced Matt immediately that no one was there. Mr. Conway had fallen close enough to the house that Matt would have heard someone, anyone, calling from within that building, even if they had been gagged.

He stepped across the threshold, holding his breath.

A terrifying thought hit Matt like lightning: What if they hadn't been gagged? What if there was another—darker—reason he could not hear anyone? What if the attackers had killed the family as well? Or taken them?

He didn't waste a moment, but turned and sprinted toward the barn, as best he could with his bandaged leg, hoping against hope to hear someone alive there.

"Hello!" he called as soon as it was in sight.

The faintest, muffled hollers sailed across the yard from the interior of the barn.

Matt almost started crying again in relief. Someone was still alive. Please let it be all three.

He reached the wide double doors and hauled open one side. As the sunlight cut through the dusty interior, the welcome sight of two missing family members alive and mostly uninjured met his eyes. But where was Silas? Matt didn't have time to dwell on that—he dashed forward, removed the gags from both Mrs. Conway and Michael and immediately moved to untie their bindings.

"What happened?" he asked.

"Let's go after them!" Michael shouted as he struggled against the rope holding his wrists together. "I can take 'em. Just give me a gun and a horse. We'll go after 'em!"

"Where is Richard? We heard gunshots..." Mrs. Conway asked, interrupting her son. "Michael, hush. Matt, please. Please..."

Just as he finished with the knot behind her back, Mrs. Conway lost all semblance of calm she had maintained over the previous half an hour. Though she had been able to hold her composure together for her son, now that the rush of fear and adrenaline had passed, she was just as emotional as her daughter.

Matt moved to untie Michael's hands, hesitant to look directly at the woman while he delivered the news.

"He's— Mrs. Conway, I'm so sorry. Your husband has been shot. He... He didn't make it. Violet is with him now."

"No..." she groaned, falling forward. "Where is he?"

She began to cry quietly, a less obvious grief than her daughter's but no less heartfelt.

"Did he really?" Michael asked quietly. He had stopped struggling.

He seemed unnaturally calm to Matt, as he worked at the boy's knot. "Michael, can you tell me what happened here? I was only gone with Violet for a few minutes."

Michael nodded. All evidence of the child that had been there just moments before was gone. In learning that one piece of news, he was now a man, handling the situation as an adult would.

"We were in the house. I don't know where Pa was. I was helping move one of the beds so Mother could sweep. Then we heard a bunch of horses and shouting outside. I didn't hear all they said, but by the time we got out to the porch, four different men met us. We tried to shut the door, and keep them out, but they were too strong."

"They broke my big porcelain mixing bowl," Mrs. Conway said. She had untied the rope from around her ankles and wiped the tears from her face. "My bowl that I got as a wedding gift and practically carried on my lap for the entire trip west. It shattered when they knocked into the shelf."

"I'm sorry, Mother," Michael said, putting his arm around her. "I'll fix it."

That sent his mother into another cascade of tears.

Michael cleared his throat, gently patting his mother's shoulder. "So, then, they had us, tied up and gagged and tossed onto the hay here. Silas was already bound in here when we got her. Then, two of the men came and grabbed him; we watched them drag him away. It took three men to subdue him, though," he said proudly. "My cousin ain't gonna go down without a fight, you can bet."

"Where did they take him?" Matt asked. "I didn't see any sign of him."

They looked at each other, each puzzled.

"I'm not sure," Mrs. Conway said. "I would have guessed they were taking him to the house, maybe just to keep us separated. But you didn't see him there?"

Matt shook his head. "I didn't go that far in. I can look again, but the house was silent."

"I bet they took him with them," Michael suggested. "That's the kind of thing they would do. Take a hostage."

"Michael," his mother scolded. "You shouldn't think like that. I'm sure Silas is safe."

"Why not? Someone's got to think like that if we're going to rescue Silas."

"He's right, Mrs. Conway. It makes sense. If they take one of ours, they have leverage if I go after them. They must know how important Silas is to the family."

"Oh, heavens, Matt. You're not thinking of going after them, are you? We should go straight to the sheriff." She looked at him with desperation in her eyes.

"Sheriff Vance? I don't know. Mrs. Conway..." Matt hesitated. Disagreeing with this kind and wonderful woman was the last thing she needed to hear at this horrible time. All the same, he couldn't let her think that Sheriff Vance would be their hope. "Sheriff Vance is the same lawman that supported Addison coming out here to threaten your husband. And the same one that Mr. Conway was arguing with last night. If we're lucky, he'll stay out of the way, but we can't assume he'll actually work with us."

"Does that mean you're going to go after them?" Michael asked hopefully. "Can I come? My aim's been getting real good lately."

"Absolutely not," his mother said before Matt could reply. He was grateful. He didn't want to have to be the one to turn the boy down.

"Let's get you two cleaned up," Matt said, as he stood. He offered his hands to Mrs. Conway, helping her to her feet. He hoped he could distract Michael from his question by assigning him responsibility here at the ranch.

As the trio exited the barn, Matt braced himself for the rest of the Conways to catch a glimpse of their fallen patriarch. After just a few more steps, they would turn the corner to the yard in front of their house. Matt clenched his fists, his insides twisting with worry.

His first impression after seeing the body again was that Violet hadn't moved. However, as they drew closer, he realized that though the body lay in the same place, Violet had taken the interval to fetch a bowl of water and a cloth. She now knelt again in the dirt and gently, lovingly was setting to work cleaning the blood and dirt off of her father's face.

"Richard," Mrs. Conway whispered to herself. She hurried her steps, catching up her skirt as she ran, in a near-perfect echo of her daughter only a few moments ago. As she reached her husband, Mrs. Conway kneeled on the other side of him, opposite of Violet and took up the man's cold hand.

Matt watched this tableau with renewed anger. How

dare Bud Humphrey take this family's pillar of strength, their protector and guardian against the hard world? Matt would avenge them, stepping in to protect as best he could. After everything the Conways had done for him, this would not make a dent in his debt.

Michael hung back with Matt, watching his mother and sister instead of joining in their mourning.

"That's your father," Matt said, nudging him. "It's best that you say good-bye now while you have the chance."

"I don't know."

"I didn't say good-bye to my father, you know."

Michael looked at him questioningly.

"And now I'm not sure I will ever get the chance," Matt continued. "Don't do the same as me. It's your job now to be there for your mother, and that starts with being by her side as she says good-bye to your father."

Their walk had brought them to the body, then to what was left of the family. After the slightest of nudges from Matt, Michael took the final steps and dropped to his knees next to his mother.

Matt turned his back. The Conways deserved this moment of privacy.

And he needed to get on the road after the murderer, Bud Humphrey.

He returned to the barn alone, to formulate a plan. First he would have to find the man, and then he would have to deal with him.

After a decent interval, Matt enlisted Michael to help him saddle one of the Conways' horses, Arrow, and Violet to pack him some jerky and a canteen of water. He was ready to be on his way. The family had plenty to take care of at home, and he could go after his target. Matt led Arrow on foot past the Conway home, past the family and to the entrance gates of Circle C Ranch.

He wouldn't rest until he had claimed justice for Richard Conway. Matthew Hawke would get his revenge.

CHAPTER TEN

Matt had never made the trip from Circle C Ranch to Juniper Falls by himself. When he first set out, for a brief moment, he was worried that his inexperience would needlessly delay him. But, fortunately, the road was straight, and the countryside familiar. Matt thanked God for his sense of direction, which got him to town with only a few moments of doubt. While he didn't travel as fast as he might have if he had been more familiar with the territory, Matt had far more pressing things to worry about.

Even though he had only just started to feel settled here in the Wyoming Territory, everything was different now. It seemed unnatural to him that life could continue without Richard Conway, and yet as he hurried Arrow down the road into town, he spotted signs of everyday life. Smoke curls rising above homesteads, horses being ridden casually, and neighbors stopping each other to chat. No one seemed to realize that his whole world had been turned upside down.

Though he wanted to be the reason Bud Humphrey never saw another sunrise, Matt had a responsibility to take care of Mr. Conway first and foremost. After a few harried inquiries once he reached Juniper Falls, he made his way to the coroner to inform Mr. Darrow of the rancher's death. The coroner assured Matt he would head out that way with his wagon directly and do what he could to ease the burden of the dead man's widow.

"Will you be headed back that way soon, Mr. Hawke?"

"I can't say, sir. I'm looking for Bud Humphrey. We've got to have words before I do anything else."

"Bud Humphrey is mixed up in this?"

"Have you seen him?"

Mr. Darrow scratched his chin thoughtfully. "Bud Humphrey? No, I can't say that I've seen him today."

"Oh." Matt could feel hope abandon him.

"But, of course, that's just because I haven't yet been to the Golden Eagle Saloon today," the coroner continued.

"What? What do you mean?"

"Why, Mr. Hawke. Surely you know. Bud Humphrey is almost never seen anywhere but the saloon. If he's not there now, he certainly will be soon."

"Is that so? Even if he's— well, that is, even if he knows someone might be looking for him?"

The coroner chuckled darkly. "It's possible in that case he might make an exception, but if I know that fool man he doesn't believe he will ever get caught or punished for a single thing. You might as well try to fly to the sun as try to convince Bud Humphrey to show any kind of propriety or caution."

Matt had already taken a step toward the door. "The saloon? You're sure? Please, sir, I can't afford any delay if I can help it."

Mr. Darrow shrugged. "That's the best I can offer you, young man. But I wish you luck in your quest."

"Much obliged, sir," Matt returned. "And thank you again for heading out to the ranch today. The rest of the family is all there and will be able to answer any questions you have."

The Golden Eagle Saloon was the last place of business Matt had visited when he was in Juniper Falls several days ago. It was the very place he had been trying to escape when Mr. Conway had found him. How life has a funny way of bringing things back around, Matt thought.

The coroner's office was close to the center of town, only a mere two blocks away from the saloon. With the prospect of finding Humphrey nigh, and the very real possibility of a battle of some kind looming, Matt found himself slowing Arrow's steps the closer he drew. Was he ready for this kind of showdown? Though his temper had been raging back at the ranch, now in the stark afternoon light the reality of what he was aiming to do had hit him hard.

He could be walking to his own death. He was heading toward irreversible choices.

He could obtain justice. Just a few short minutes from now, he could kill or capture the murderer of one of Matt's only friends. But that brought him to his next thought. Just a few short minutes from now, Matt could be about to kill a man. Was that something he could live with? Something after which he would be able to look himself in the eye?

Matt had a strong suspicion that his life would soon be split into the periods before Bud Humphrey, and after Bud Humphrey. If he was going to be realistic with himself, Matt had to acknowledge that there was no guarantee there would be a time after Bud Humphrey. He could bring about the end of Matthew Hawke altogether. The man had murdered Richard Conway and already shot Matt himself, after all.

At the thought of his own injury, Matt got a flash of memory—Violet cleaning and dressing his leg wound that first night he stayed at Circle C. Her thoughtfulness, her gentle touch, kind smile and amiable conversation had been a salve to Matt's wounded pride. It was for her he was fighting. For her future. For her family.

For Violet, Matt would take down Bud Humphrey.

He arrived at Golden Eagle Saloon, on the main street of Juniper Falls. It was still early in the day, but not so early that the place was empty. Tying Arrow to the post out front, Matt wiped his clammy palm on his shirt, drew the gun he had borrowed from the ranch, and entered the establishment. Matt had never been in a gunfight by any stretch of the imagination. He wanted to be ready without drawing fire unnecessarily. He held his gun by his side in what he hoped would be a nonchalant grip, and not draw undue attention to himself.

It took a moment for his eyes to adjust to the dim light inside. He glanced around the room and noticed a few faces he recognized, including Mr. Bullock. The banker nodded to him, acknowledging him before returning to his conversation.

As Matt inspected the saloon further, the sight that met his eyes after he crossed the threshold nearly deflated him. All other faces blurred into the crowd, and Matt locked eyes on Silas Denbow. The other ranch hand was seated at the bar, directly in front of and facing the door, flanked on either side by huge, filthy men laughing, drinking and spitting tobacco at—though not into—a nearby spittoon. Matt felt a flash of rage at the man's disloyalty before he noticed the expression on Silas's face.

The man seemed miserable. He was all but being tortured and, Matt realized when he finally looked closer, he was bound by a tight coil of rope, his hands pressed down between his thighs. Michael's original assessment that the men had taken Silas hostage seemed correct.

Before Matt could decide what his first step to free Silas should be, he noticed another familiar face in the crowd. Sheriff Vance sat at a table in the corner, a two-thirds-full bottle of whiskey in front of him. He was leaning forward at the table, staring down and seemed completely consumed by his glass. As Matt watched, the sheriff didn't make conversation or even eye contact with anyone sitting near him. He must have felt Matt's gaze on him, however, for he looked up, locked eyes and grinned at Matt.

He remained just inside the door, not yet having spotted Bud Humphrey and not yet having formulated a plan of any kind. But Matt knew he couldn't wait there indefinitely. He had to move.

He strode straight toward the sheriff.

"Evening, Mr. Hawke," Sheriff Vance greeted him,

tipping his hat slightly. "You have the night off from your duties at the ranch?"

"Do you know what happened at the ranch?" Matt asked hotly, trying to keep his voice down. He sat next to the sheriff and pulled his chair in close. "Did Addison tell you about the plan in advance so you'd stay away?"

Sheriff Vance scoffed, poured himself another dram of whiskey. "Stay away from what, boy?"

Matt couldn't say what it was that made him think twice. Maybe it was the sheriff sitting alone or maybe it was simply the bewildered chuckle. He would have to be the one to deliver the news.

"Richard Conway was just murdered," he said in a low voice.

Sheriff Vance seemed to sober up quickly. He sat up straight, put a strong hand on Matt's arm and peered into his face. "What did you say?"

"Bud Humphrey and a group of men came out to the ranch just an hour or so ago, and now Richard Conway is lying in the dirt, dead of four gunshots."

Sheriff Vance let his arm go, leaned back in his chair, and seemed to be thinking hard. Matt opened his mouth to say more, but was shushed by the sheriff. Finally, he turned his attention back to Matt and shrugged.

"So? It's your word against his, I'm afraid, if the only witness is dead."

"But I'm not the only witness," Matt said triumphantly. "Silas was there too. That's why those fellows have brought him here." He pointed, and noticed that Silas was watching him cautiously. "As insurance against ... well, I guess against me coming here to do this very thing."

"What thing? Tell me," the sheriff demanded. "Those boys are not nearly as dumb as you are."

Matt didn't take kindly to condescension, no matter if it was from a man of the law and his elder. He bit back a snappy retort and took a deep breath.

"Sheriff, I mean to get revenge for Mr. Conway's death. Something needs to be done. I'll figure out how to take Bud Humphrey into custody for you, but I need the law to work the way it's supposed to."

Sheriff Vance stared at him for a beat, and then laughed so heartily, the two men at the neighboring table turned to look at the commotion.

"You? You'll take Bud Humphrey in? That man has at least fifty pounds of muscle on you. And didn't he already shoot you once? No, Mr. Hawke. If Bud Humphrey needs to meet justice, it won't be by your hand."

"Then you do it, Sheriff!" he said, frustratedly. "Do your job. If you had been paying attention this never would have happened in the first place." He slammed a fist down on the sheriff's table, shaking the whiskey in his glass.

Anger flashed across the sheriff's face but before he could respond, the door to the saloon swung open again, and Matt heard the unfortunately familiar grating laugh of Bud Humphrey. Behind him through the open door, the orange and pink of sunset lit up the street. The day was closing. Wherever Bud had been earlier after he left the ranch, he was here now. All it would take was for Matt to take careful aim and compel Bud to give himself up. He hoped.

Matt swallowed down his fear that had quickly

snuffed out his frustration. For once in his life, he wished his anger and trigger temper were there to carry him through the next few moments. He needed that protection, even if it drove him to rash decisions. He hadn't expected to feel afraid when he finally got to it, but here he was, waiting in a shadowy corner of the room and watching his enemy saunter in.

"Speak of the devil," Sheriff Vance said with a small smile. "What was it you were wanting to say to Mr. Humphrey?"

"Aren't you going to arrest him, Sheriff?" Matt asked quietly. "Are you going to do your duty by the Conways and take that murderer into custody? How much more do you need? You have two witnesses."

"I might see my way to opening an investigation," he allowed. "Eventually."

Matt pursed his lips, furious. His heart hammered as the moment of truth drew near. "Eventually is not good enough."

He stood up, pushing the chair back across the dusty floor. Turning toward his foe, he called out loudly to be heard above the din. "Bud Humphrey. You need to answer for your actions."

The room slowly grew quiet, as one man and then another noticed Matt standing by the sheriff, erect to his full height, fury in his eyes and a gun pointed at Bud Humphrey. Slowly the final guffaw petered out as the laugher was elbowed by his neighbor, entreated to notice what was going on. No fewer than six men pushed past Bud, hustling themselves out of the saloon and away from the trouble they suspected was coming.

"Well. It's you," Bud Humphrey said lazily. He didn't acknowledge Matt with anything more than a passing glance as he crossed the room to the bar. He wedged his shoulders into the row of men, right next to Silas, and leaned forward on his elbows to talk to the bartender. "Whiskey."

The room remained silent, watching, waiting.

Matt didn't know what to do next. He felt almost silly, aiming his gun across a crowded room. The last thing he wanted was to hurt anyone else. If the man wasn't going to even take his threat seriously, what were his options?

He could back down, or he could follow through.

"Yes, it's me. I'm here to bring you to justice. You thought you'd get away with it, I know, but you didn't count on me still being at the ranch. I saw you shoot Richard Conway. I watched you do it and then run away like a coward."

A wave of murmuring coursed over the room. Three more men threw cash on the table and snuck out the door of the saloon before they could get caught in anything else.

"I saw it. Silas saw it." Matt pointed to the other ranch hand at Bud's left. "You are not going to escape the hand of justice, Bud Humphrey. Just come with me and no one else needs to get hurt."

Bud laughed and looked pointedly at Sheriff Vance, still seated near Matt and again fully consumed with staring at his whiskey.

"That so, Sheriff? Is this little boy arresting me?"

After a slow beat, the sheriff looked up at Bud. He

said nothing, but his expression implied more, eyebrows raised lazily. To Matt, it felt as though this were merely the continuation of an earlier conversation and Bud knew very well what the sheriff was thinking.

Bud laughed again and turned his attention back to Matt. "All right, then. Come and get me."

Matt raised his gun higher, to shoulder level, to aim directly at Bud Humphrey. The couple men still seated between them practically fell over themselves to get out of the way. He had never in his life truly aimed a gun at another human being. His hand threatened to quake, in his fear and uncertainty. Taking a deep, steadying breath, Matt drew upon his well of resolve, his determination to do what he could for the Conways. If anyone deserved this threat, it was Bud. A reminder of Violet wailing over the body of her father was all it took for Matt to be ready to do this. To follow through.

"Put your hands up, Humphrey," he commanded.

Bud ignored him, blatantly keeping his back to Matt, and sucked down his shot of whiskey.

"I'm taking you in," Matt repeated. "Surrender or be sorry."

Bud looked right in Matt's eye. "I'll be sorry? Prove it."

Matt glanced over his shoulder at the sheriff who remained seated. Taking another deep breath, Matt took a couple steps forward through the crowd, between the tables to where Bud still stood at the bar. He hadn't made it one yard before Bud abruptly discarded his shot glass and drew his own weapon.

Now both men stood staring each other down in a

crowded room, each with guns pointed at the other, neither willing to back down.

Matt swallowed hard. What should he do next? Should he threaten again? Should he shoot? Matt didn't want anyone else to get hurt.

Before Matt could make his choice, a shot from someone else's pistol cut through the air.

CHAPTER ELEVEN

When a gunshot rang out across the otherwise silent Golden Eagle Saloon, Matt ducked instinctively. He knocked over an empty chair as more shots were fired, then upended the closest table, barricading himself with the wall of the saloon behind him. The clatter of wood on wood was almost lost in the immediate mayhem that followed the gunshot. Somehow in the chaos, Sheriff Vance had disappeared. He was no longer at the table where Matt had last seen him. He was no longer even on Matt's side of the room.

As more men became enmeshed, more guns were drawn. Matt took a chance to look up over the edge of the table quickly and didn't notice Sheriff Vance anywhere in the room, in fact. Where had he gone?

More shots rang out. A bullet pierced the edge of the table Matt hid behind, not six inches from his face. He closed his eyes tightly against the wooden splinters flying through the air and ducked down again.

Time seemed to slow like molasses in winter. His

senses were heightened even as confusion reigned. Matt felt like he could hear every trigger pull, every flash of gunpowder, every curse and yell from the men all around him. The sounds of shattering glass filled the air as stray bullets pierced the shelves behind the bar. Heavy thuds shook the floorboards as tables were overturned and used as barriers.

And through it all, the mocking, carrying laugh of Bud Humphrey cut through the air, reminding Matt of where he was and what he had to do.

Before he could make another move, a large man ducked behind Matt's table against the wall and crouched next to him. Matt was surprised to recognize Mr. Bullock, the banker that Mr. Conway had introduced him to just the night before. Without saying a word, he nodded in acknowledgment and returned his focus to the firefight.

Matt couldn't quite understand what had happened. He had come into the saloon preparing to take Bud into custody, though at huge risk to himself, and now found himself with allies and not as completely alone as he had expected, though in the middle of a gunfight. A very cursory look around at his side of the room and he recognized several others, good, honest men who had been at the church social, who likely knew Mr. Conway or despised Humphrey. Or both.

Matt cheered internally. He might still get through this.

"You don't have to do this," he shouted to the other side of the room. There were at least half a dozen men surrounding and helping to protect Bud. "I only want

Humphrey! Hand him over and we all can go home, uninjured."

If they didn't agree, he didn't know how he could storm in there and seize the man. There was a brief moment of silence. Matt felt a surge of hope that the men could be considering his offer, before he heard a gruff voice return.

"Go to hell!"

This threat was punctuated by three more shots, all landing in the table and wall around Matt. He was being bombarded, under heavy attack, simply because he came after this murdering thug.

He hadn't yet fired a shot, but emboldened by the protestation, looked around the curved edge of the table and took aim. This would be the first time he ever fired at another man. His hand shook, but Matt reminded himself of what was at stake. If any man deserved this, it was this one. He couldn't see Humphrey; the man must be hiding behind or concealed by his allies. The muzzle of a gun poked around the edge of a table not twenty feet away, and as soon as Matt saw the pale flesh of the shooter's hand, he fired.

He missed.

Another man across the room chose that moment to stand, unprotected, to better take careful aim. Matt fired at him. He missed again, firing just over the man's shoulder and shattering the window behind him. Matt tried a third time; this time the bullet grazed the man's forearm. He cursed, stumbled back a few steps as the blood blossomed on the sleeve of his shirt.

But the wound must have been barely a scratch,

because he returned to his firing after only a moment's recovery.

Matt shook his head, frustrated and angry with himself. This was a matter of survival. These men were trying to kill him, and he had to protect himself.

"You give up? You don't seem too set on this whole justice thing."

Matt recognized that voice, carrying over the chaos. How dare Bud mock him? Without pause, without stopping to think, Matt popped up from behind his protective table. Bud was half standing, head, shoulders and torso unprotected above the edge of the table. Matt took aim and fired twice directly at him, sure that this blow would incapacitate the murderer.

One bullet lodged in the man's bicep, the other splintered the chair to the man's right.

Bud grunted in pain, and ducked back behind the table out of Matt's sight.

"Give up!" he yelled, frustrated. "I know you're hit. You can't get away now. Surrender, Humphrey!"

"I may be hit," he yelled back, "but one bullet isn't enough to take me down. You're going to have to do better than that, boy." Bud leaned out from behind his wooden shield and glared at Matt. The poison in the man's glance was unmistakable.

Matt took aim and fired again. Or, rather, he pulled the trigger to an empty chamber.

The gun clicked impotently.

"No!" he cried, falling to the ground again behind his protection. He frantically thought back, counting. Five. Five bullets. He remembered now. He had left the ranch without any extra ammunition and with only the five bullets loaded. He cursed his ineptitude. Why had he thought five would be enough? Why hadn't he considered all possibilities? He had, yet again, let his impulsive anger and his raging temper lead him to actions that came back to punish him.

And now here Matt was, in the middle of a saloon shootout, his life and his friend Silas's on the line, and he was out of bullets.

He had to think fast. Before Bud and his men figured out why he had stopped shooting.

Matt just had one chance. Quietly, to himself, he counted backwards.

Three. Two. *One.*

He bolted out from behind his hiding place and darted the several yards to the bar that lined the back wall of the saloon. With his running start, Matt launched himself over the bar, knocking over the few glasses that remained intact on the surface. They fell to the floor behind the bar, one cracking and rolling away, one shattering as Matt's feet landed directly on it, crushing the glass under his boots. Shots rang out all around him for the few seconds he was vulnerable and open to attack, but none landed.

He had been lucky thus far, but without a new weapon or ammunition to protect himself, he feared his luck would soon run out.

The bartender had long since fled. Crouched down behind the wide bar, Matt gave himself a brief moment to look around. The ground was covered in broken glass and spilled liquid. The stench of alcohol prickled his nose and made his eyes water. He had never been much of a drinker, and this much in such a closed space made him grateful for that.

It was darker behind the bar, but after a brief moment, Matt's eyes adjusted. He realized he wasn't the only one to have sought shelter back here.

"Matt," a hoarse voice whispered excitedly.

"Silas." Matt crawled forward as best he could around the broken glass. He brushed the larger pieces aside with his hands, resulting in a crisscross of cuts across his fingers and the back of his hand.

The ranch hand was still tied up, though not gagged. His hands were bound in front of him, and showed the unmistakable indication of Silas struggling to get himself free. Whoever had been in charge of his detainment had left him on his own when the fight broke out.

"Have you been back here the whole time? Are you hurt?" Matt fumbled for the knot holding Silas prisoner. In the dim light, he had only his now-injured fingers to see the way to untie it.

"I'm not hurt. Maybe bruised from falling, but I'm fine. How did you know to find me here?"

"I was looking for Bud. Silas, you have to help me. I'm out of ammo. Do you think there's any back here? Surely the bartender would be prepared, right?"

"Of course. In fact..." Silas looked around as Matt finished undoing the last loop of knot. "Over there, I think." He indicated with his head toward the end of the bar closest to where Bud Humphrey was fighting from.

"Here. You're free." Matt left Silas to shrug out of the loosened rope coils on his own. He made his way in a crouch to the far end of the bar that Silas had indicated, cringing every time the glass crunched underneath his boots. If anyone on the other side was listening over the roar of gun fight, they would know exactly where he was.

But the risk seemed to pay off. When Matt reached the corner of the bar, on a shelf deep underneath he found exactly what he was looking for: two rifles, a pistol and several boxes of ammunition. He marveled at what the bartender must have taken with him when he fled, if he saw fit to leave all of this.

Matt took a deep breath and made his choice.

"Which one is mine?"

Silas had freed himself and appeared at Matt's shoulder, looking at the same collection of firearms.

"No, Silas. Stay safely out of this. They already took you hostage once. You're the only living witness to what Humphrey did. You need to stay out of sight so you can testify against him. I can do this."

"Don't be a mushhead," he said as he reached for one of the rifles. "Uncle Richard is family and there's nothing you can do to stop me from trying to bring justice for him."

Matt smiled, sadly, and nodded. He took the other rifle, checked to make sure it was loaded, and let out a slow breath.

"Are you ready?"

Silas nodded. "Ready."

At that signal, Matt stood up from behind the bar, raised the rifle to his shoulder and took aim. He was closer to Humphrey now on this side of the room, and wanted to get this whole thing over with. The longer it went on, the higher the likelihood that someone innocent would get hurt. Matt didn't want to be responsible for any one of these men being injured, incapacitated, and somehow unable to take care of their families.

This needed to end. Now.

Bud's meaty shoulder was clearly visible around the edge of a table overturned on the floor. Matt would never forget that distinctive red and orange-colored shirt he had seen standing over Mr. Conway's body.

Holding the borrowed rifle steady, Matt took aim and fired. The kickback from the gun surprised him; he lowered the muzzle to shake it off before even seeing if the bullet had found his mark. But he couldn't waste any more time. He raised the rifle again, this time ready for it. Aiming again at Bud, Matt squeezed the trigger.

All around him he heard shouting, more shots fired, but he only had eyes for his enemy. He didn't see where any of the other players were. He had totally forgotten about Silas at his side mere moments ago. He was completely focused on ending the reign of Bud Humphrey.

One of Matt's shots had hit. Bud fell back to the floor, agonizing, groaning and holding both hands to his side where the blood swiftly soaked through his shirt.

Elated, Matt took aim again. "Surrender, Humphrey!"

Bud's gang was too fast for him, though, and dragged the injured man back behind another barricade. Surprised, Matt's gaze fell on the streak of dark blood across the dusty floor; it reminded him of the pool of dark blood that had spread into the dust around Mr. Conway.

"Get out here, Humphrey! Stand up! Fight like a man!"

Matt was livid. He began firing toward where Humphrey had disappeared, completely disregarding logic and any calm. He just wanted this to be over.

"Humphrey!"

He squeezed the trigger. Over and over. His fury gave him a tunnel vision that would have been useful if he could see his target.

He heard a thud nearby, but didn't look. Matt kept his eyes trained on where Humphrey had disappeared. He would get that devil if he had to wait all night, if he had to hunt him down.

He fired again trying to scare him out.

A movement caught his eye, surprising Matt, and he turned abruptly. In his haste, in his thoughtlessness, Matt's finger squeezed the trigger yet again. Though the rifle had not been aimed at anyone or anything, the bullet still fired, landing squarely in the middle of the movement Matt had seen.

In a haunting echo of Bud, Silas fell to the floor, crying out, writhing, and holding both hands to his thigh.

"No..." Matt froze, watching and unable to help for what felt like minutes. "Did I—Silas!"

"Bud's hit!" another voice cried out.

"I'm outta here," someone else said.

Whatever had happened, it seemed the end was drawing near.

"Matt..." Silas called to him weakly.

The sound of his name snapped Matt out of his fog. He had a choice to make. His friend Silas was injured, by Matt's own hand, and may not survive the wound. The amount of blood pouring out of Silas's wound seemed severe. He needed to be taken to safety and treated as soon as possible.

On the other hand, his enemy Bud was also injured, likely incapacitated and losing allies. He needed to be taken into custody, to be brought before the law and made to answer for his crimes.

Matt couldn't attend to both.

In that brief moment of indecision, two things happened.

Silas said his name once more and then appeared to pass out. The loss of blood must have been even more severe than Matt had suspected, and underscored the need to get Silas to safety.

In that same moment, the door to the saloon opened, Sheriff Vance walked in from wherever he had disappeared to. The lawman stood in the doorway and took in the sight of the destruction.

The eyes of the two men met across the room.

Matt couldn't read the sheriff's expression—a man of the law who seemed so unscrupulous was foreign to him. But the sheriff seemed to spot Bud, and immediately hurried across the room to where he lay thrashing with a couple of his henchmen.

That decided it.

He couldn't let his friend suffer. He would have to trust to the justice and honor of Sheriff Vance. Matt hoped that wouldn't prove to be a mistake.

Matt hurried to Silas. The door was clear, many of the men who had been involved in the fight had since abandoned it. They had seen the writing on the wall and got themselves to safety.

Matt wrapped his arm around Silas's waist and

heaved the man to his feet. With the injuries he had sustained, Matt couldn't rely on Silas to get himself out of the saloon. If Matt wanted the ranch hand to live, he'd have to take care of it himself.

Without waiting to see what the sheriff did, Matt dragged Silas out of the saloon and into the early evening streets of Juniper Falls.

CHAPTER TWELVE

With Silas's limp body weighing him down, Matt had trouble making it to his horse. He was strong, but he still had an injured leg himself. If only Silas was at least conscious. Just a little bit of assistance could make this so much easier, but as it was he had to carry the other man's full weight on his own. By the time he had limped his way to Arrow, Matt was out of breath and had sweat through his shirt.

The sounds of cursing and crashing continued from within the saloon, although the gunshots had stopped. Matt wished—not for the first time and probably not for the last—that he could have been the one to subdue Bud. He wanted to tie the man up with his own hands. He wanted to be dragging Bud to the jail, rather than dragging his friend to a doctor.

None of this had gone the way he had envisioned, but it was too late to stop now.

Matt took a deep breath, wrapped his arms around Silas's middle and heaved him up onto Arrow's saddle.

The body draped over the horse, hanging down on each side. Matt cringed to see the blood still dripping from Silas's leg. That sight ignited a fire under him; he was running out of time to help Silas.

Just as he was about to lead Arrow away, to find the doctor, he heard his name.

"Matthew Hawke! Stop right there!"

Matt turned to see a member of Bud's gang standing in the doorway of the saloon. It was a squat, round man Matt didn't recognize who swayed a little on his feet. Matt wondered how he could see to identify him if he was already that drunk. This man seemed to have been injured in the shootout, but that didn't stop him trying to threaten and come after Matt.

"You can't just walk away from this," he insisted, aiming his gun.

Matt's eyes widened in surprise, and he turned fervently back to his task.

"C'mon, boy," he said to the horse, pulling on the reins and guiding him down the street.

A shot fired. The dust cloud near his feet told Matt the man was serious in his threats.

"Faster," he told Arrow, breaking into a run, somewhat hampered by his limp.

"Come back here," he heard from behind him.

"Murderer!" someone else shouted.

Matt kept running. He had made his choice, and helping Silas was his priority. The next street was close, and he led Arrow around the corner. Faster and faster they ran, the horse almost galloping alongside Matt's limping sprint. The sun had already set, so they were able to stay in the shadows. Though he listened carefully,

Matt didn't hear anyone come after him. No more shouting, no heavy tread in the dirt. Maybe they were too caught up in the business of Bud's arrest.

After turning down two more streets at random, Matt paused to look around. This street looked familiar, though it took him a second to realize why. Matt had spent so little time in Juniper Falls, there were only a couple possibilities. There it was. Just at the end of the block was the coroner's office where he had just been earlier that day.

He started hurrying that way. Matt realized he had no idea where the doctor of Juniper Falls lived, or, indeed, if there even was one in a town this small. There must be one, but he didn't have time to be searching around. Mr. Darrow might be Silas's only hope. He slowed the horse to a walk so he could listen for any pursuers and led him down to the darkened building.

Matt tied Arrow to the post out front and knocked on the door.

There was no answer. He peered through the windows, but there was no light within either. Mr. Darrow must still be out at Circle C Ranch seeing to Mr. Conway's body. Matt cursed his luck.

Frantically, he tried the handle of the door, his good fortune returning. There was no lock on the door. He could at least get inside the office, away from pursuers, and provide Silas a place to rest. Matt would have to do his best to bandage up Silas himself. It certainly wasn't the ideal plan, but the coroner must have something he could use. He carefully, awkwardly, pulled the unconscious Silas off the horse, roughly gathered the man in his arms, and stumbled through the doorway into the dark office.

Silas's sticky blood dripped onto Matt's arms, and soaked through his sleeves. With no light anywhere, Matt merely found an open expanse of floor to lower his injured friend onto. He closed the door behind them—hopefully that would be enough to forestall any of their pursuers. Fumbling around in the dark, Matt knocked over an empty cup, and accidentally cast a pen to the floor before he managed to find a match and lamp to light.

Once the flame flickered into existence, Matt took a deep breath and began searching the office. This front room, where the coroner met with clients and families, seemed spare. A desk, drawers full of paperwork, a couple of armchairs and a spittoon. It wasn't built for comfort or welcoming, and unless Matt wanted to bandage up Silas with a stack of paid invoices, he would have to keep looking.

There was one closed door leading from the office into the back room. Matt knocked tentatively on the door, before pushing it open when there was no answer. As Matt carried his lamp into the back room, he realized this must be where the coroner did his examinations. There was a tray of scalpels, a bone-saw and other medical-looking tools. There were two an empty wooden buckets in the corner. And, finally, his eyes rested on a long, wide wooden table where Matt supposed a body would lay.

Matt closed his eyes, trying to block out the image of Silas lying dead on that table.

A step in the front office drew his attention.

"What the hell?" someone exclaimed.

Matt hurried back to find Mr. Darrow standing in the open door, gaping down at Silas on his office floor.

"Silas?" Darrow said in wonder. Once he looked up and realized who was holding the lamp, his next exclamation was even more surprised, less angry. "Matt?"

"Yes, sir, it's us. Could you close the door?"

"Well, I ... What is this all about, Matt? What mess have you dragged me into?"

"I don't know." He shook his head and hurried across the room. "But you've got to help me. To help *us*. Please, sir. Silas has been shot and I don't know where the doctor lives and I don't have time to take him there and I can't find anything to use to staunch the blood and I'm worried it's already too late."

Mr. Darrow smiled ruefully. "Sorry to say, my boy, but I'm not in the business of saving living people, you know. Those aren't the tools you'll find here. I don't know how much assistance I can be other than to point you in the right direction."

Matt stared at him, confused for a moment before realizing the reality of the situation. The mess he was in. Of course. Mr. Darrow only ever worked on the bodies of the already deceased. And Matt was trying to keep Silas from becoming one.

"But— I ... Mr. Darrow. What do I do?"

Darrow looked at Matt, then down at Silas, before letting out a long breath as though he had come to a decision.

"We can manage. It's not impossible. I'll do my best, but I am going to need your help. Come with me. Bring that lamp."

The two men entered the backroom, where the coroner led Matt straight to a tall wardrobe that stood against the back wall. He flung open the doors, and Matt beheld a stack of rough, though clean, folded pieces of fabric. Sheets of some kind, and something Mr. Darrow would need a lot of given how many were stored back here.

"Grab a couple of these," the coroner instructed before turning away again to rummage through another cupboard. "And grab that bucket."

Matt followed his instructions, and was right behind Darrow returning to the office carrying his load. The coroner's hands were full of blades and other equipment.

Mr. Darrow showed Matt how to fasten a tourniquet out of a ripped strip of sheet, tying it firmly around the injured man's leg.

"I did some medical work way back years ago, in the war, but I remember enough. He's lost a lot of blood," Mr. Darrow said, shaking his head. "I don't know about this, Matt."

"Just try. Please. Not even for his own sake. This is bigger than just Silas. He's the only witness who is able to testify that Humphrey shot Mr. Conway. We need him."

"I know," the coroner said, as he poured a small amount of alcohol on his scalpel. "I know. But ... Matt..." He looked the younger man straight in the eyes. "I don't want you to get your hopes up."

"I know." Matt lowered his eyes to Silas's face. His friend looked calm, peaceful. There was no hint of the pain he must have been in when he was shot. "Show me what to do."

Over the next ten minutes, Mr. Darrow spat out instructions and Matt carried them out as fast as he could. They had to clean the wound, retrieve the bullet, and bandage it back up all without the benefit of anything other than coroner's tools and a ripped sheet. At one point, when Mr. Darrow was trying to carefully probe the wound with a long set of tweezers, Silas's body seized.

"Careful!" Matt exclaimed.

"He's not awake," Mr. Darrow said, not taking his eyes from the wound. "His body is reacting the pain, but he's not going to be conscious for a bit, I'm thinking."

His prediction proved correct. Even after the wound had been taken care of and both Matt and Mr. Darrow had cleaned up the blood from their hands, the equipment and the floor, Silas still lay unmoving.

"Is he going to be all right?" Matt asked. He stood over his friend, drying his hands after scrubbing away the blood. There was still the hint of deep red under his fingernails.

"I think so, but ... Well, you know. You should have Dr. Gilpin take a look at him tomorrow. I can send word if you'd like."

"I think that's best. I don't want to take him back to the ranch tonight, and I'm not sure I trust his land-lady to look after him properly, even if I knew who she was."

"What will you do with him, then? You can't leave him here, you know."

"I know. I've been trying to think as we did all this. I might try to see if his ... well, that is to say, Silas has recently become very close friends with Miss Mary Ann

Whitaker. I wonder if she and her family would take him in."

Mr. Darrow smirked. "Miss Whitaker? Well, that seems perfect."

"Do you know where she lives?"

"I do. It's not far from here. I would caution you to be sure to use all deference with Mr. Frye, her brother-in-law. It is his home after all and if he in any way suspects that you will be bringing the law or trouble to his front door, he'll turn you away no questions asked."

Matt nodded. "I understand. I've met him, though I'm not sure he took to me. I'll do my best. Do you think Silas is all right to move yet?"

The coroner glanced at the younger man still lying prone on the wooden floor. "I don't know. I'm sorry, Matt. This is not my area of expertise. I'd say if not now then never, though. After being shot and jostled and then my clumsy hands on him, I'd say things can only get better for our friend Mr. Denbow. He may not be conscious, but he's alive. And where there's life there's hope, as they say."

"I understand. Then, Mr. Darrow, if there's nothing else I think I'd like to get a move on. The sooner I can get Silas settled and safe, the sooner I can finish what I started and make sure Bud Humphrey gets what the law has for him. I can't thank you enough for your help. And your understanding that I just let myself in."

"Tell you what, Matt. I'll help you carry Silas out to your horse, if you help me carry Mr. Conway into my workroom."

For the brief time when he was handling the emergency of Silas's wound, Matt had forgotten where the coroner had been that afternoon. Matt felt himself pale at the thought of seeing the corpse again, but agreed. It was his duty to see this all the way through, and if that meant helping to deal with the body, so be it.

"Show me what you need from me," he said.

CHAPTER THIRTEEN

Reciting Mr. Darrow's directions to the Frye family home in his mind, Matt quietly led Arrow down the dark streets of Juniper Falls with Silas's still unconscious body firmly draped over the saddle. Though Matt still feared their pursuers, at least now Silas's leg was securely bandaged and he wasn't dripping any blood into the street to reveal their track or whereabouts. Once he found the right place, Matt would be able to turn Silas over into the care of those who loved him best.

Then Matt could turn back to his original plan: ensuring Bud Humphrey had been brought to justice.

He still wasn't sure how the gun battle in the saloon had concluded. He had left as soon as it was clear Silas needed immediate medical attention. With the fat, drunk man shouting after them as they left, he couldn't be too careful. The dark shadows and side streets could keep them hidden until Matt was ready to make his presence known.

Miss Whitaker lived with her sister and brother-in-law about half a mile off of the main road. As the school-teacher, Mrs. Frye would need to be close to the school-house. As Matt led the horse down the street, past a couple homes, he wondered how many of these neighboring families knew Silas. Maybe they had seen him come calling on Mary Ann, or watched the young couple stroll down the street arm in arm. Matt pictured Silas offering to help one neighbor shovel snow or another build a shed. He wondered if the neighbors would be able to help care for the unconscious Silas. He wondered sadly if they would have all been invited to an inevitable wedding and what they might have to give up if Silas didn't make it.

According to Mr. Darrow's instructions, the Frye house should be just up the street a little farther on the right. It should be just past this next—

Matt paused. The lights from the house he stood in front of cast a glow into the street through the narrow window, but it wasn't enough to see anything too clearly. Shadows moved and obscured what was real. The broad outline of the building barely showed against the night sky. Matt realized he could be walking into anything hidden there in the darkness.

Without the visual warning, Matt would have to rely on his other senses. And his ears were telling him there were people up ahead. He couldn't hear conversation, but some mixture of heavy breathing, occasional grunting, shuffling steps and what he suspected were whispers reached his ears.

Though he had no way of knowing who waited for him ahead in the dark, Matt had plenty of suspicions. There were only so many people who might think to go to Mary Ann's house at this time of night and hide, ready to ambush him.

He looked around quickly for somewhere to hide, but he had to deal with his cargo first. Matt had a horse and an unconscious man to keep safe, and the only places nearby were small homes of innocent townspeople. He needed to get farther away.

Matt backtracked, as quietly as he could. At the end of the street, he led Arrow around the corner to where a wide tree stood in front of another home. This was far enough off of the Fryes' street that Matt hoped no one passing would notice it. He couldn't explain to Arrow to be quiet and he couldn't very well leave a note for Silas in case he woke up. Securing the horse to this tree was the best he could do.

Once Matt was sure that Arrow would stay put, and had quietly promised to return as soon as he could, he darted back through the shadows behind the row of homes that neighbored where Mary Ann lived. The residents inside these homes were oblivious to the danger that lurked in their street. They all ate their suppers, cleaned their faces, and read their Bibles for their nightly devotions, even as Matthew Hawke was risking his life.

Crouching below windows to avoid being seen, Matt made his way back to his original target. The Fryes' next-door neighbor had a couple of outbuildings in the yard behind the home that Matt used to his advantage. Where the shadows grew deeper, he hid. He removed his lightly colored hat, poked his face around the corner of the shed and peered into the gloom. Now that he had reached this close to Mary

Ann's house, he could finally visually confirm what he had suspected.

In the dark, leaning against the side of the house and dimly lit by the orange ember of their cigarettes, three men stood silently, about five feet apart and covering the entire length of the house. The longer Matt watched, the more it seemed clear they were waiting for something, watching for someone. Each man held a gun loosely in his hand. Matt recognized the one in the middle as the man that had chased them out of the saloon, and suspected the other two were of the same alliance.

This suspicion was confirmed when Sheriff Vance walked by one of the lit windows inside the Fryes' home and peered out. Matt ducked down behind the corner of the structure he had hidden behind, though he didn't think he had been spotted.

His mind raced at possibilities. Why was the sheriff there? Was he looking for Silas? Was he reporting Mr. Conway's death? Was there something else totally unrelated he had to do with the Frye family? Matt hadn't stuck around the saloon long enough to notice what anyone else there was doing. He could only speculate now. Even as he worried about Silas left alone down the street, Matt was grateful he had not just walked into whatever was happening here.

When Matt dared to look around the corner again, he was surprised to see Mary Ann visible in the window talking to Sheriff Vance. Matt couldn't read lips; he couldn't hear what they were saying. All he could do is make his best guess based on their body language and interactions. And whatever the man had said to her, she looked upset.

As they stood inside the room, just inside the window, Sheriff Vance held her hand gently, patting her in what he probably intended to be a soothing way. The expression on the sheriff's face—condescending and wheedling—made Matt shudder. Mary Ann, fortunately, didn't seem to be paying that close attention. Whatever the sheriff had already said to her was enough to keep her occupied.

The man leaned close to her, murmuring something else. Mary Ann brushed a tear away, only seeming to partially be listening. Another woman, older with her dark hair pulled back in a neat bun, walked into the window frame and handed her a glass of water. Matt guessed it could be her sister, Mrs. Frye. She put her arm around Mary Ann, and squeezed her tightly.

Matt needed to know what was being said. Maybe once the sheriff and his men had delivered their news and left the family alone, Matt could sneak Silas in and find out everything.

When he had lived in Boston, after he had run away from his father's house and was making his way on his own, Matt often had to stay hidden from his pursuers. Though it seemed counterintuitive, it had always seemed to Matt to be easier to evade someone if you knew what their plan was and what precisely they were looking for. This often meant him staying closer and more vulnerable than would otherwise feel safe, but had so far worked out.

Once, he had just stolen a potato from a crate behind the shop itself, when the back door opened and the shopkeeper walked out. In the split second that Matt had, he managed to squeeze himself behind the open door, squished against the building. It was when he was hiding there that he heard the man say he was going to walk around to the front. If Matt had followed his initial instinct and run down the alley instead, in all likelihood he would have been seen. And subsequently caught.

And Matt couldn't get caught.

Especially now. He had a task ahead of him.

Mr. Conway had taken him in, fed him, protected him, and promised him a new life here in Wyoming. Matt wouldn't rest until he had his revenge, which meant that he needed to use all the skills at his disposal to stay out of the sheriff's clutches.

The Frye family and Sheriff Vance had left the space by the window and Matt was again left without any clue what was occurring.

He decided to make his move. If he was fast enough and quiet enough, he could dart through the farthest part of property, farthest away from the light of the houses, and travel in a wide arc around the men on guard. He looked down at himself. His clothes weren't as dark as he would like them to be in order to stay hidden, but they would have to do. Matt peered again around the corner of his shed, judging the distance and trying his best to guess the timing.

He watched the men, looking for patterns or tells. Hoping one of them would get fed up and leave, or for the sheriff to come out and distract them. One of the men looked like his cigarette had almost been smoked all the way down. Maybe when he went to light a new one that could be enough of a distraction to give Matt a window to run.

He was aiming for the back door of the Frye's house. After the sheriff left out the front, Matt could knock on the back door. He could slip in without the lawman seeing him, he hoped. Mary Ann would remember him, surely; they had only met a couple nights before. He could get Mr. Frye to help carry Silas in. And then Matt could move on to the next step of his quest.

The man closest to the back of the house, leaning against the wall, tossed the butt of his cigarette into the dirt at his feet. This was it. Matt held his breath, watching raptly for the exact moment the man began to pat his pockets for the next smoke. Here it came. Any second— There!

The second the man looked down, Matt set off in a sprint. He made it all of three strides before he skidded to an abrupt stop, almost losing his footing in the dirt. The back door of the house was opening. Sheriff Vance stood in the doorway, making one last comment to someone standing behind him, before he finished opening the door.

Matt had to move. Now.

In his haste to turn around, he lost his balance, and stumbled heavily to recover. He was sure he was making enough noise as to draw the attention of everyone on the street. Spinning completely around, Matt all but leapt the few steps back to his hiding place. His heart pounded. His leg wound ached. His breathing was shallow, but he didn't dare try to take anything like a deep breath for fear of being heard.

And yet, even in his blind panic Matt knew he needed to focus.

Standing as close to the edge of the building as he could, without risking looking around the corner, Matt listened intently.

"Yes, right here will be just fine," Sheriff Vance was saying. "Again, I'm sorry I can't say for sure where your friend Mr. Denbow is. Matthew Hawke could have taken the body anywhere. Once we find him, we find Denbow and we can lay him to rest as a good Christian man like him deserves."

Matt blinked in surprise. They thought Silas was dead? That must have been why Mary Ann was crying. His heart broke for her; she should never have been put through such torment unnecessarily.

"I'll leave some of my men here, staking out the place. They'll be on hand to guard and watch out in case Hawke tries to contact you," the sheriff continued. "Rest assured, Miss Whitaker. Mrs. Frye. We'll apprehend this criminal and restore order to Juniper Falls as soon as possible."

"How will you do that?" Mary Ann asked, so softly Matt almost didn't hear her.

"Just leave it to me."

Matt didn't hear any more of what the sheriff was telling the family. He had already begun to back up farther into the dark corners of the neighbor's yard. How was it possible that he the criminal Sheriff Vance had mentioned? Especially after all Matt had told the sheriff directly. Humphrey was the murderer; Humphrey was the one that should be brought in front of a judge.

Matt needed to figure out more of what was going

on. He needed more information. He needed to get back to the Conways and the ranch. If the sheriff was setting up guards around the Fryes' home to it was only a matter of time before he did the same around the Conway home.

He had no time to lose. Matt needed to get to the Circle C ranch. He still didn't know how he would be able to get justice for the family, but he certainly couldn't do it on his own with all these men looking for him.

CHAPTER FOURTEEN

As silently as he could, Matt backtracked away from the hidden corner where he had been watching and listening. He crept back through the dark yards, hiding behind outhouses and darting from shadow to shadow until he reached the end of the street where the Fryes lived. A quick left turn, and his horse Arrow should be around here …

Any minute he should see the animal, with Silas's body draped over the saddle …

Any minute.

They should be right around here. He was sure of it.

Matt walked slowly past the large tree where he had tied up the horse to wait for him. Though it was getting late at night, there was still enough ambient illumination for Matt to see the horseshoe imprints in the ground. This was where he had left Arrow.

Matt began to panic.

He didn't have time for this.

How had he lost a horse *and* a person?

He spun in a circle, slowly, trying to calm his heart rate and think about this step by step. Though it was technically possible that a horse could have wandered away, Matt had been reasonably sure the rope and reins had been tied tightly. Had Arrow somehow miraculously learned how to undo a knot?

"Arrow!" he called in a hoarse whisper, though he had no way of knowing if the animal came when it was called.

This was yet one more reason he wished he had had more time with Mr. Conway. With the whole family. Matthew Hawke was a man from Boston. The skills he had learned growing up in a bustling city were nowhere near what he needed for a small ranching town out west. Experience with firearms and animals and even building outbuildings was so far from him. Who would teach him everything he needed to know about horses with both Mr. Conway and Silas gone?

"Matt?"

Matt froze, certain he was hearing things after stumbling around in the dark like he had. That was his name. Someone was calling his name. Someone who sounded an awful lot like Silas Denbow, who Matt had left unconscious and then somehow misplaced.

"Matt!" the familiar voice called again in a carrying whisper.

"Silas?" Matt hissed into the darkness. "Are you—Where are you?"

He heard the gentle steps of a horse being led in his direction. Matt spun around to see man and beast walking toward him from the dark mouth of another side street a farther forty feet up the road. Even in shadow, Matt could recognize Silas's bouncing walk, surprising given the ranch hand was so severely injured.

"Where'd you go?" Silas asked as he got closer. His tone seemed relaxed, matter-of-fact, as though he had not just been unconscious for nearly an hour.

"Where did *you* go?" Matt demanded. "Actually, don't answer that. We don't have time; we can't stay here. Give me the reins, and you go home."

"What?" Silas stood stock still, not handing over anything.

"I don't even know how you're able to walk right now." Matt shook his head. "I saw the bullet wound. You're in no shape to do anything but rest."

"You think I should go home?" Silas frowned. He seemed too confused to even understand the basics of what Matt was suggesting.

"I had planned on taking you to Mary Ann's, so she could nurse you. I didn't want to leave you with the coroner—"

"Why would I be with the coroner?"

"—but that was when you were unconscious. And before I knew the sheriff and his men were waiting there to ambush us. Now that I see you can walk, it's best if you just go home and rest up. We've got to make sure that leg heals properly. You can be at the ranch to protect the Conways. The rest of them."

Silas shook his head, as though trying to shake something loose.

"Make sure *my* leg heals? What about your leg? You think you're just going to drop me off at someone's door and be on your way, leaving me behind to just sit?"

Matt was too surprised to answer right away. "Well... But ..." he sputtered inarticulately. "Yes?"

"You don't get to decide that."

"I don't?" Now Matt was the one too confused to grasp what the other man was getting at.

"No. You don't. First you shoot me, then you leave me unconscious and alone in the dark. And now you're telling me you're just going to desert me? I don't think so."

"Wait," Matt said, suddenly aware of where they were. "Just wait. We can't be seen out here. Lower your voice."

Even with so little light, Matt could see the glare that Silas shot him.

"You don't get to decide that," Silas repeated deliberately, though more quietly.

Matt took a deep breath to try to calm himself; the more Silas disagreed with him, the more he felt his temper rising. "Look, Silas... Let's just— Let's find somewhere off the road." He looked over his shoulder toward the street he had just left, certain that any moment the sheriff or one of his men were going to come around the corner. "I can explain it all better."

For a moment, Matt was sure the other man would reject his suggestion. But finally, Silas nodded brusquely and turned away.

"Over here," he muttered, still leading Arrow.

Matt followed him silently to the same dark alley that Silas had emerged from. As he looked around, Matt realized they were walking around the corner of Mr. Frye's hardware store, a business that would still be closed for another several hours and behind which, hopefully, they could stay undetected.

Once they were far enough around the corner, Silas spun around again, pointing a finger harshly into Matt's face.

"Now, I'll say it again. You don't get to just leave me behind. I know what you're up to, and I'm not going to be left out of it."

"But, Silas. Hear me out. Mary Ann thinks you're dead."

Silas paled, paused, and swallowed. "She does?"

"Yes. I'm sorry. You're hurt, and she's hurting. I saw her crying over the news. The best thing you can do right now is rest up and then go see the sheriff in the morning to tell him what you saw Humphrey do to Mr. Conway. You're the only witness other than me."

"And while I'm doing all that and keeping my head down, what will you be doing?"

Matt let out a long breath and shook his head. "I don't know. I just ... I don't know yet. I think I over-heard the sheriff calling me a murderer, so I have to ..."

Matt trailed off, his throat seizing up. He swallowed hard. It had been a long time since he had been so frus-trated he was brought to tears, but this current situation he had found himself in could be his undoing.

"The sheriff is looking for me. I'm not even sure if Humphrey has been arrested. I need to figure out how to make sure your uncle is avenged. And then, on top of all that, I still only have a couple days to come up with the payment on the Circle C mortgage."

"We," Silas said.

"What?"

"*We* need to do all that. You kept saying I, but there's no way you're going to do all that on your own. I'm going with you."

"But, Silas—"

"I heard all the reasons you think I should go home, but I'm just not going to do it. You can't stop me, so stop trying."

"You've been shot!" Matt finally shouted.

"So have *you*," Silas shouted back.

That silenced Matt. He was right. He and Silas were in almost the exact same position, with the exception being that Silas was actually kin to the Conways. How could Matt deny him that family connection, in spite of everything else."

"Besides," Silas continued, his tone lighter. "What do you know about this horse, huh? I bet you didn't even saddle Arrow yourself, did you? You need me, Matt."

"I..." He paused, trying to think what his next step would be and came up with nothing. Without Silas, he would be floundering in the wilderness, maybe even literally. He didn't know his way around the countryside outside of Juniper Falls. He could barely find his way back to the ranch. "All right," he said finally. "But, Silas, we need to make sure you stay safe. I know I've already said this, but we can't forget that you are the only person who can attest to Bud Humphrey's murdering Mr. Conway."

"I know. Believe me. I want to stay alive as much as you want me to." He grinned.

Matt shook his head. "I still can't believe he left you alive."

Silas shuddered. "I know. I got lucky, or maybe he didn't realize what all I had seen, or ... I don't know."

"He knew enough to think to kidnap you. Maybe he had something worse for you planned, if we hadn't gotten you out of the saloon."

"That's true. But, you know, Matt. That's one more reason maybe I should stay on the road with you, hiding from the sheriff. What if they realize what I know and try to silence me like they did to Uncle Richard?"

Matt nodded, finally warming up to the idea. "Okay. Yes. Okay." He nodded more vigorously. "Okay, good."

"So...?"

"So?"

"What's next?"

It was now nearing midnight and though the path to Circle C Ranch wasn't long, the men decided they should try to stay off the road as much as they could. That, combined with the fact that they only had one horse between the two of them and a leg wound each meant that they needed to get moving if they wanted to return to the Conways' ranch before sunrise.

In spite of the ranch hand's injury, Matt let Silas lead the way. He had lived in Juniper Falls for years, and could pick their way through the darkness. He led the way through the shadowy alleys, past the now-dark homes on the edge of town to the flat plains that stretched into the darkness.

"Keep your pistol handy," Silas warned. "Any animals will probably hear us coming first, but just in case."

"I'm out of bullets," Matt reminded him.

"Oh. Well, then ... Any animals will probably hear us

coming first," he repeated with a confident nod. "Just follow my lead."

With Silas's leg injury being far more severe, he rode Arrow slowly while Matt walked alongside. The black night swallowed them. The men made their way over grass and hills, toward the home waiting for them.

CHAPTER FIFTEEN

It was nearly dawn when Matt and Silas finally crept over the low hill across the road from the Circle C Ranch. It had been slow progress, trying to stay quiet and out of sight. Cutting across country, in the dark, through the property of neighbors while they slept had the dual result of both allowing Matt to feel safer and more hidden from the sheriff, but also anxious about disturbing the men and women whose homes they were walking right past. If anyone were to see them, the two men could very well look like the outlaws the sheriff seemed to consider them.

Along the way he had held his breath every time they came within a hundred yards of a home, certain that a dog would smell them and start barking or that some ranch hand had been set to guard against cattle rustlers and shoot them.

All in all, when Matt finally saw the Conways' ranch across the road, he breathed a sigh of relief.

The very faintest light, the warm orange glow of just

before sunrise, illuminated the countryside around them as the two men crested the hill. Down the other side of the hill, only fifty yards away, was the road that Matt had been familiar with leading to the ranch. And just on the other side of that was the gate to Circle C, now closed against visitors for the first time since Matt had been here.

The men paused at the top of the hill to confer.

"Do you see anything?" Silas asked, squinting. "I can't tell if we're walking into an ambush or not."

From where they stood, a wide grove of spruce trees stood between them and the Conways' farmhouse. It was a sparse enough grove that Matt suspected they should be able to see lights of the home if any were lit, but he wouldn't swear by it. There was too much at stake for him to be certain of anything. With the rising sun, the shadows and darkness were lessening, though nothing became clear.

"I don't see anything but the trees," Matt said.

"I wish there was a way to send a message ahead. Just in case."

"Like a telegram, just across the road?" Matt chuckled at that idea. "Yeah, that'd be nice."

"Instead, we just have to walk into whatever it is and hope we can deal with it," Silas said sullenly.

"Not necessarily," Matt assured him. "There are still plenty of ways to sneak back onto the property if we have to."

Silas nodded and squinted again at the ranch stretching into the distance ahead of them.

"Regardless, though," Matt continued. "We should make tracks. We can't risk the sheriff getting here before us. With the new day dawning, we have to assume anyone could show up at any minute. If news of Mr. Conway's death spreads we could have all the neighbors coming by, even if it's just to bring food and offer condolences."

"Right. Let's be quick."

Matt led Arrow, with Silas riding on top, down the hill quickly and quietly hurrying across the road to the gate. He was relieved to find that though it was closed, it had not been locked. Almost as though the Conways knew the men might be coming back. As Matt lifted the latch to swing the gate open, Silas dismounted. He grunted in pain as he landed on the ground, but waved off Matt's look of concern. Without exchanging a word, both men knew what the other was thinking, both deciding what sacrifices they were willing to make to stay quiet, stay safe and get onto the ranch.

Though Matt didn't have experience in tracking or hunting, he still knew enough to recognize if the scene looked off. Gratefully, even though he had been gone twelve hours, everything about the ranch seemed to be in order, and just like he had left it. No unfamiliar footprints or cigarette butts. No destruction or new bullet holes. He noticed some wagon wheel tracks cut into the dirt and hoped that was from the coroner's visit the previous evening. The farther they got toward the Conway home, the more confident he could be that Sheriff Vance or any of his men hadn't been here. Not yet, at least.

Silas elbowed Matt, breaking him out of his focused searching of the ground. He gestured toward the left, pointing farther into the grove of spruce trees. Matt looked where he was indicating and nodded. They would make an arc around the main yard and house, watching for any other sign of intruder. This direction would take them toward the barn, shed and other outbuildings, which would be perfect for hiding behind if necessary.

The sun was now over the horizon, and the country-side was illuminated with the warm light of dawn. Matt took a deep, soothing breath as he and Silas trekked quietly through the trees. Though he hadn't slept all night, this fresh morning did wonders for him. He needed some food, maybe some coffee, and then he'd be ready to revisit his plan to get justice for Mr. Conway.

Seeing Violet again would only make this day even better.

Silas paused behind one of the wider trunks in the grove of trees.

"What is it?" Matt asked in a whisper.

Silas shot one final glance through the trees, before turning his full attention to Matt. "I don't see anything or anyone, but that doesn't mean they're not there."

"Right."

"Are you prepared to risk it? Are we ready?"

"Are *you* ready?" Matt said, pointedly looking at the wide bandage around Silas's thigh. Though it had kept securely overnight, the final few steps and jostling had caused the wound to start to bleed again. A dark red patch was just beginning to show through the torn sheet.

Silas glared. "I'll let you know if I'm not ready. Don't worry about me."

"All right, then. I'm ready."

Silas nodded. "Follow me."

He looped Arrow's reins around a low branch, patted

the horse on the neck and whispered something reassuring to him that Matt didn't hear. He then turned his attention again to the structures, watching for one more long moment. Silas beckoned Matt, and the two darted half-crouched toward the barn.

As they reached the side of the building, a shot rang out, cracking against the otherwise silent and calm morning.

"Shoot!" Matt exclaimed. "They've seen us!"

The bullet didn't hit either man, but shattered the branch of a tree several yards behind them. In just a couple more quick steps, they were protected behind the side of the barn.

"Did you see where that came from?" Silas asked frantically.

"From the house, I think. Just one. Did they only send one man?"

"Probably. Or they would have come out in more force. More than one shot."

"Come out from behind there with your hands up," a familiar voice yelled at them.

Matt and Silas exchanged a puzzled look. Was that who they thought it was? Matt couldn't help a grin spread across his face.

"Wait—" Silas began, but it was too late.

Matt gladly threw his hands high above his head and walked around the corner of the barn, hoping that the shooter could see clearly who it was he had captured.

"It's me, Michael," Matt called out. "Matthew Hawke. You know me."

A moment of tense silence followed, long enough that Matt began to doubt himself and what he had heard. After another long moment, he heard another familiar voice.

"Matt?"

"Mrs. Conway? Are you folks all right?" he called.

Matt didn't dare lower his hands yet; the family didn't sound sure of his identity and he didn't want to risk spooking them. The sun dappled yard cast long shadows over him. But he took another several tentative steps toward the house. The closer he got, the better they could see his face and the safer he would feel.

"It's me, Mrs. Conway. I'm back. I brought Silas. I need to talk to you all."

The door to the house opened slowly. Though it was still early morning light, and though she was still almost seventy feet away, Matt would have recognized Violet anywhere. She wore the same pale green calico dress as the day before, and Matt's heart broke a little wondering if she had rested at all in the intervening hours. Such a strong, brave woman. She held a shotgun cautiously, pointing it down, and walked the few steps down to the dirt.

"Matt?" she called to him.

He heard the hope in her voice. He walked another several steps, keeping his hands up.

"Matt," Violet said again as she recognized him. She set the gun down carefully before running for him.

"Violet!" Mrs. Conway called from the house.

But Violet was heedless, disregarding any warning or caution as she ran to Matt and threw herself into his arms.

"Violet," he whispered into her hair as he wrapped his arms around her. "Violet Violet Violet. You're okay."

"Oh, Matt, it's been awful. I'm so glad you're home."

"Tell me everything."

"Well," she drew back to look into his face. "I didn't see you leave. I didn't know when you went. I— You were just gone and I didn't know what to do."

"Wait, Violet. There's someone else that came back with me." He took her hand in his, wanting her to feel safe and secure, and turned back toward the barn. "Silas! Come out! It's all right."

The ranch hand peeked his face around the corner, a suspicious scowl on his face. "You're sure?" he asked in a hoarse whisper.

"It's just us," Violet said. "It's safe. I promise."

He stepped around the corner and took in the sight of Matt holding her hand. Silas nodded. "Let me go back and get Arrow."

He disappeared again briefly and Violet led Matt back toward the house. She seemed remarkably calm for someone who had undergone such trauma in the previous twenty-four hours. What a remarkable woman she was.

"I'm sorry I had to leave you," Matt said. "All of you. I've been so worried since I left. But you understand I only had a small window of time to follow Humphrey. I couldn't risk him leaving town and getting away with your father's murder."

"I understand." She squeezed his hand. "And I'm so grateful. I was just disappointed you weren't here, but you're right. You did exactly what you needed to do."

"And Mr. Darrow came out, right?"

"Oh, yes! And, oh, Matt ... Thank you for taking care of that. I'm not sure any of us would have been able to go into town for another several days. You thought of everything."

"Not everything."

But he was interrupted in his explanation by Michael bounding down off the porch excitedly to meet them in the yard. He almost crashed into Matt in his exuberance.

"I almost shot you!" he cried. "Did you see that? Did you see how I almost got you?"

"Yes." Matt tried to hide his smile. "That was great work, Michael. You were defending your home."

"I know!" He nodded vigorously. "Now that I'm the man of the house I gotta start taking care of stuff like this."

"Michael Conway," his mother scolded. "I will not have you shooting at everyone that comes through that gate."

"But Mother—"

"Matt and Silas are here now, so I want you to put down that gun."

Violet and Matt exchanged amused smiles. Matt was so grateful to be back here again, among this family, in the place that felt like home.

Before he could make any remark to this effect, however, he was interrupted.

"Hide!" Silas shouted as he ran forward. "They're coming!"

CHAPTER SIXTEEN

As the sun continued to rise in the morning sky, Matt faintly heard the sound of horses coming closer. The day had arrived, and with it visitors to Circle C Ranch. He had only gotten there just before the enemy, and hadn't yet had a chance to establish a defense. While he and Violet had been connecting again, Silas had spotted the new arrivals, and alerted the rest of the Conways.

"Hide!" Silas said again. "It's Sheriff Vance. I recognized his laugh. They can't know we're here."

Matt froze for a split second before turning to the Conways and issuing instructions.

"Do not let them know we are here. Do not let them know you saw us or heard from us or even know we're alive. Please." Violet nodded, while Michael looked stunned. "Silas, you're going to take care of Arrow?"

The ranch hand nodded, swung up into the saddle and galloped toward the pasture and the far side of the ranch.

"What can I do?" Violet asked.

In the face of danger, she was calm, which Matt couldn't help but admire.

"Pepper him with questions. Find out everything you can. Cautiously; don't give away our hand. Be polite, though. We don't want any more trouble if we can help it. I only have a small idea of what the sheriff is after and what happened after I went after Bud. If you can get out of him if they're looking for me, why, what they think is going to happen. Anything. I can fix this, but I need to know."

She nodded.

Mrs. Conway put her hand on Matt's shoulder and squeezed. "You can trust us, dear. We want you boys safe."

"Michael," Matt directed, "do not shoot them."

"I *know*," he said petulantly.

Matt wanted to believe the kid, but was worried about what he would do in his eagerness to be helpful. But they were out of time. Matt could now hear the horse hooves from where he stood at the foot of the steps to the house. He only had maybe seconds before the sheriff and his men opened the gate and rode into sight.

"Be careful," he entreated the Conways before running for his hiding place.

The ranch boasted several wells throughout the property, including one that lay close to the house for the family's use. As Matt sprinted to it, he wished he had gloves, or something else to help protect his hands. He was going to have to hold on to that rope for who-knew-how-long. He threw his leg over the stone wall, grasped the rope that led down to the bucket, and lowered himself as quickly as possible.

Fortunately for Matt and his haste, going down would be easier than climbing back up. Within moments, he was perched awkwardly on the bucket, arms wrapped around the rope, and praying it would hold his weight as long as he needed it to.

The sound of horses grew closer. He had only just made it out of sight. Matt tried to breathe as quietly as possible so he could listen, though the sound barely reached over the stone and down to where he hung.

"Good morning, ma'am," Sheriff Vance's unctuous voice called out.

"Good morning, Sheriff. Awful early for you to be calling."

Matt could hear the warning in Mrs. Conway's voice, but wasn't sure if the sheriff would pick it up. He silently praised her for her coolness. Another woman may have started wailing and attacking, but not Mrs. Conway. She was smart. She remained composed, as though she had no cares at all.

"What can we do for you?" she continued cheerfully.

"We've come to offer you our condolences." Matt could imagine the man removing his hat, and putting on a mournful expression in an attempt to exhibit a sorrow he didn't actually feel. "Mr. Darrow told us about the sad tragedy of you losing your husband."

"Did he now?" There was a brief pause. "What did he say?"

The cool metallic scent of the well water reached his nose from where he perched on the bucket. Matt suddenly remembered how long it had been since he had eaten or drunk anything. As soon as he had that thought, his muscles began to twitch. He was young and he was strong, but no one could keep going forever. He just needed to hold on long enough until the sheriff had said what he came to say.

"Well." Sheriff Vance cleared his throat. Matt wondered if he was stalling. "As I understand it, your husband suffered a bullet wound."

"A bullet wound," she repeated. Matt silently willed her to keep calm. "Well, as I understand it, he suffered ... several."

"How dreadful. That surely is a tragedy. As I say, we came to offer sympathy and see if there's anything you need from us. A widow left all on her own with two children must need help. Or is your ranch hand still around to do what needs doing?"

Matt held his breath. There was no reason for the sheriff to ask specifically if Silas was around. She was being baited. He knew it, and he hoped she knew it.

"Thank you so kindly, Sheriff," Mrs. Conway said after a brief pause. "There is only one thing I can ask of you at this time, and that is that you apprehend my husband's killer. We can manage everything here, but appropriate justice is beyond my capabilities."

That was it. That was the weight dropped to upend the delicate balance of the entire conversation. Matt reflected that it could have been worse, but pointing out to the sheriff that she knew her husband had been murdered was revealing.

"Killer?" he said, with feigned surprise.

Matt was furious, gripping the rope more tightly to

remind himself to stay put. His temper had always gotten him in trouble, and he was half glad he was so far down this well so as to not reveal himself out of spite. How could the sheriff wriggle out of this corner? As a man of the law, he should want to investigate every crime or claim of crime, which in this case rightly should include interviewing Mrs. Conway at the very least about what she knows about her husband's death. On the other hand, if the sheriff was trying to protect Bud Humphrey, and maybe even Mr. Addison by extension, he couldn't dig too deeply into it.

"Why, yes, Mr. Vance. My husband didn't take his own life. He didn't accidentally fall into several, well-placed bullet wounds. He has been murdered. That same ranchhand witnessed it. And, forgive me, but I thought that unraveling these mysteries was the duty of the sheriff, is it not?"

"I see."

There was a long, quiet moment, during which Matt agonized over the fact that he couldn't do anything. Or, more specifically, that he *shouldn't* do anything. He hoped that Silas was staying away as well. They would have to trust the women of the Conway family to handle this careful maneuver.

Thank God for these Conway women.

"I'll certainly look into it," the sheriff said smoothly. "In fact, I've also come here to look into something else."

"Oh?"

"Yes."

Matt's heart hammered, anxious and wondering about what the sheriff was about to say.

"Your husband is not the only man who has been killed in Juniper Falls in the last day."

"Oh?" Matt heard Mrs. Conway's voice crack, as though her throat was closing up.

"You haven't heard from Silas Denbow lately, have you?"

"Silas?" a new voice asked, alarmed.

Matt recognized Violet's voice. Just that single word revealed in her tone a combination of wondering and panic. He had not had time to explain to her what he suspected about what the sheriff knew about Silas.

"Mr. Denbow was here yesterday," her mother said calmly. "I didn't see him leave in the afternoon, but I'm certain he was working yesterday morning."

"Well, ma'am, no one has seen him since yesterday afternoon. After ... well, there was an incident at the Golden Eagle Saloon. Denbow was shot in the fracas and we have reason to believe he died of his wounds and his body disposed of."

Matt frowned to himself. This tale the sheriff spun was frustrating. Why would the first thing they assume be that Silas had died? Wasn't it equally likely that he recovered and that's why they haven't found him? He couldn't understand how the sheriff kept thinking he would get away with this story.

"Oh, no!" Violet exclaimed. "Silas dead? What happened? Who would shoot him? Everyone loves Silas."

Matt gritted his teeth, wishing she hadn't asked that specific question. He could almost hear the smarmy grin on the sheriff's face.

"I'm so glad you asked that, Miss Conway. It so happens that there is a man who is new to Juniper Falls who somehow in the last week has ingratiated himself to multiple people, getting involved in others' business and, in fact, starting a shoot-out in the saloon late yesterday."

"What—"

"We suspect this man to be responsible for shooting Silas Denbow. Multiple witnesses have testified to the fact, actually."

"There isn't any—"

"Further," Sheriff Vance continued over her, "we are certain this man fired the shot that killed Bud Humphrey."

"Who are you talking about?"

Matt could hear the worry in Violet's voice.

"And now that you have enlightened me as to the circumstances behind your husband's death, Mrs. Conway, I will be looking into the likelihood that this same man is responsible for his death as well."

"Oh, well, I'm not sure that's—"

Violet interrupted her mother with a more pointed question. "Sheriff Vance, why would this suspect have killed Silas, though?"

"Perhaps he was getting rid of the one witness to his murder of your father, as your mother mentioned earlier. Cleaning up his mess, so to speak. This newcomer, after all, would have nothing to lose by skipping town, as he had nothing keeping him here. No hearts to break."

Violet let out a choked half-laugh that Matt couldn't interpret. If he knew who the sheriff was referring to, he had to assume Violet did as well.

In a terrible way, it all made sense. With Humphrey gone, and without Silas around to testify, of course they could pin the death of Richard Conway on Matt. With a groan, he realized he should have seen this coming. He was an easy target. Sheriff Vance was telling the truth in that bit at least. Matt was new to town. He had ingratiated himself to the family awfully quickly. From an outsider's view it seemed remarkably easy to conclude that he was a blood-thirsty murderer, flying through town to wreak havoc.

Matt was almost tempted to climb up out of the well then and there and turn himself in, if only to save the Conways any more hassle. If Silas was around, he might even do it, but he was too afraid of being shot on sight, especially since he was clearly hiding from the law at this moment. For the first time he cursed his telling Silas to flee to the far side of the ranch. His existence—his simple presence—would be the key thing that exonerated Matt.

Well, from Silas's murder, at least. They may have more trouble clearing him of the other two deaths. Especially as Matt was out of bullets. Especially as the sheriff likely spoke the truth about the witnesses that could attest to Matt's shooting Humphrey. He hadn't seen the man die, but he knew at least a couple of his shots had landed, and that building was full of men who didn't care for Matt.

If only the sheriff had done his job in the first place, not only in keeping the Conways safe from Addison and his gang, but also in pursuing the real murderer when Matt had told him so plainly.

Above him, the conversation continued.

"Well, we certainly hope you apprehend the *guilty* party, don't we, Violet?" Mrs. Conway said. "And, as I say,

Sheriff. I'm happy to cooperate in any way I can as you look into the death of my husband."

"Thank you, ma'am."

"Now, if there's nothing else, sir, we all have some chores to be getting on with. Best get started on our day."

"Actually, there was one other thing. I'm so sorry to be bringing this up on a day like today when you're certain to be grieving, but needs must."

"All right."

Matt heard the suspicion in her voice.

"I'm not sure if you're aware, Mrs. Conway, but over the last week your husband has been in talks with Mr. Bullock at the bank over the missed payments for a second mortgage on this ranch."

Now it was Mrs. Conway clearing her throat to give herself more time.

"Well, perhaps as you say I don't know all of it, but I had thought that we still had a couple days before the payment was due."

"Well, yes, of course, the contract does say that, but you know ... if you don't have the money or any prospect of getting it, it may be best to start thinking about your next steps after that day passes."

"I see," Mrs. Conway said coldly.

"There are plenty of options, and these boys here with me would be happy to help you move any of your furniture or—"

"Sheriff Vance," she interrupted, "while I can assure you I appreciate the offer of assistance, I must insist that it is misplaced. You have just said yourself the payment won't be late until the third. My husband might be gone, but neither my pride nor my faculties are. I must implore you to not count your chickens before they hatch."

Matt stifled a laugh. It was as though she were an elderly aunt scolding him for bad manners.

"Just as you say, ma'am," the sheriff said stiffly. He cleared his throat.

"Now, again, if you'll excuse us, Sheriff. My family has plenty to be getting on with, and I believe you have a murder investigation to begin."

"Hm. Yes. Well ... Good day, then. I'll be in touch, I'm sure."

"I'm sure."

Matt listened to the sheriff call to his men, giving instructions and leading the group off of the ranch. The horse hooves died away, but he didn't dare show his face until one of the Conways came to tell him it was safe.

A slight shadow passed over the dim light of the interior of the well. Matt looked up to see the silhouette of a small head peering down at him.

"They're gone," Michael called down.

CHAPTER SEVENTEEN

Fifteen minutes later, Matt had climbed out of the Conways' well, Michael had run to the far side of the pasture to fetch Silas, and both men were now settled in the kitchen of the ranch home, hands wrapped around mugs of fresh coffee. Both Violet and her mother had donned aprons and were hurrying around, making sure the men were fed and safe. They had been promised hot baths, clean bandages, and all the food they could eat.

The morning was passing quickly and they had plenty to do.

"And then, once you're all recovered, Silas needs to go see the sheriff," Mrs. Conway concluded.

The two men looked at each other.

Matt shook his head.

"I don't think he can," he said hesitatingly. "I'd be worried about Silas's safety."

Violet paused in her stirring of the oatmeal and turned to look directly at Matt. "You don't think Silas should go to the sheriff? What do you propose then?"

"Well, I'm not sure."

"Then he should go," Mrs. Conway said decisively. "Silas will tell the truth."

"Thank you, ma'am," Silas said. "But sometimes the truth isn't enough."

"What do you mean?"

"Well, see... You said that Sheriff Vance accused Matt here of killing me to get rid of a witness, right? What's to say he won't do the same thing when he sees me alive?"

"That's true," Matt piped in. "They were waiting outside Mary Ann's home for him, after all. Just looking for a reason. Sure didn't look like a welcoming committee."

"But..." Violet looked lost.

As a faithful member of the church, Violet had been raised to believe that if she was good and honest and did her best, she would be rewarded. Matt reflected it must be a hard realization the first time you learn that the truth isn't always enough. Instead, they had to be sure to get the truth into the hands of the right man.

"Is there a U.S. Marshal nearby?" he asked.

Mrs. Conway and Violet exchanged a look. The younger woman shrugged. "Maybe," she said, returning her focus to her cooking.

Matt felt a heaviness in his chest. He had hurt her. Whatever needed to happen, whatever options he and Silas had, none of that mattered if he hurt Violet Conway. She had been trying to help and he had refuted her. He watched the back of her head for a few moments in silence, worried about how he could fix this.

"I think what Silas and I need to do is seek out the

marshal, if we can. Someone who doesn't have a hand in the local politics, who should be able to look at all our facts objectively, instead of whatever Sheriff Vance might be inclined to do. This is getting too big for all of us."

Mrs. Conway and Violet exchanged another look that Matt couldn't decipher.

"I hate this," Violet said quietly, still staring down into the pot she was stirring. "You didn't do anything wrong, but you have to hide."

There was a moment of silence as each person considered what she had said. She was right, of course, but as Matt had learned in his break with his own family back in Boston, it didn't always matter whether you did anything wrong or not. He couldn't change the past, he couldn't change the circumstances that got him to this point. All he could do was choose how to react to those same circumstances. And in this case, that meant finding the next lawman up the chain and convince him to help mete out the necessary justice.

Mrs. Conway sighed. "You should be able to find a marshal in Cheyenne. I think his name is Hollis. You could just send a telegram, of course."

Matt shook his head. "Too risky. We'd have to go into Juniper Falls and be seen. Can we trust the telegraph operator? I don't know. No, it'd be better if we go to Cheyenne on our own. See him in person."

"Besides," Silas said with a wry grin. "Maybe Sheriff already sent his own telegram and told him I'm dead. We can take him the genuine article, this way."

Mrs. Conway sighed and shook her head indulgently. "You boys are going to send me to an early grave with worrying, you know that."

Silas got up and wrapped one arm around her shoulders, squeezed her tight and kissed her cheek. "We know, Aunt Susan. We'll make it up to you."

"Yes, well. See that you do." She smiled up at him. "But I suppose in the meantime we should put together a pack for you. Something to keep you alive a little longer."

"That would be... Thank you. We would be so grateful," Matt said.

The next several hours were a mixture of delay and anxiety. Matt wanted to be getting on the road to Cheyenne, the better to hide from Sheriff Vance and get the trip underway. But at the same time he couldn't bear to leave Violet and the rest of her family. Not again. He hated to think about how they would be left unprotected after he and Silas left. He could imagine all sorts of reasons the men would come back here. Bud Humphrey was out of the way, but Addison had any number of additional men at his beck and call.

There were still almost two full days left before the mortgage payment was due and Matt didn't put it past them to leave well enough alone until the deadline. The murder of Mr. Conway must have been a delaying tactic to ensure Addison got his hands on the ranch. Though they still didn't know how they were going to make the payment, there was still time. But in that time, Addison could sabotage.

That couldn't be helped. Matt and Silas had to get to the marshal in Cheyenne.

While Silas was tending to the two horses they would take, and Mrs. Conway was rustling up all the dried fruit she could find, Matt finally got a moment alone with Violet. She was out on the front porch folding clean laundry, including an extra shirt that Mrs. Conway was insisting Matt take, even though he kept telling her they'd be back that night.

They stood on the porch of the house. He had found her looking out over the ranch, out toward her favorite cottonwood tree by the creek where just the day before they had shared an intimate moment. He wondered if she wished she was up in that tree at this moment.

"I'm sorry," he said quietly. Her back was still toward him, but he saw her shoulders relax at the sound of his voice. "I wish things could be different, but this is the only way I can see making this all work."

"I understand." She turned toward him. Her smile seemed genuine, though a bit sad. "I do. Really. I hate that there's not another way, but I trust you. This is the only real solution forward."

"Thank you, Violet. And, while Silas and I do this, there's something I wonder if you can do, too." He took one of her hands in both of his. It was warm and soft, small in his big ones.

"Of course," she said, looking up into his face with trust and adoration.

He almost couldn't make himself leave this beautiful, vulnerable creature. But she was strong, he reminded himself. She had already withstood the death of her father and was unflinching enough to carry on despite the trouble bearing down on them. She was trusting him to take care of the safety of her family; he could trust her to do her part while he was gone.

"We need to come up with that mortgage payment still. Even if we can find the marshal in Cheyenne and make all this right, none of that fixes the fact that your home is at risk."

She nodded solemnly. "I know. You're right. I've been thinking about that."

"Silas and I talked about the idea of selling some of the stock, but I don't know how easy that could be at this last minute."

"That's true. I bet the only one around here with the money to even do that would be Mr. Addison."

"So..." He shrugged helplessly. "If I had the money, I'd pay it immediately."

"I know."

"But I don't. I'm sorry. If there's anything else of value on the ranch we can sell... Jewelry or ... if there's any family members you can telegraph for a favor ... I'm sorry, I'm just at a loss for how we are going to be able to fix this, even if we find a way to get the law from pursuing me."

She nodded again and looked down to where he held her hand. They stood in silence a moment, both thinking, both worrying, both grateful the other one was there and they didn't have to do this alone.

She gasped. "I have an idea," she said, suddenly excitedly. "It's possible ... I overheard Pa talking about it months ago, so maybe I'm misremembering or maybe something has changed."

"What is it?"

"Well." She hesitated, as though embarrassed. "Maybe I should talk to Mother about it first. I don't want to get your hopes up."

"It's not my hopes you need to worry about," Matt said with a smile. "What can I do to help?"

She shook her head, but her smile grew even wider. "Nothing. Not yet. Let's go now to talk to her. Maybe this will fix everything."

The idea of fixing everything seemed a bit unrealistic. Matt didn't have the heart to tell her there was far too much that needed fixing. But Violet had an idea, she might even have solution, and he wasn't going to be the one to take it from her.

"Let's finish up here first," he suggested. "Whatever your idea is has waited this long; it can wait another few minutes. We told your mother we would fold up these clean shirts to take."

She giggled a little, now heartened by whatever plan she had come up with. "You're right. I'd rather spend time with you as long as I can, anyway."

As Matt grabbed for the last piece of fabric, Violet watched, impatiently hovering over his shoulder. The second he set down the shirt, she grabbed his hand.

"Let's go talk to Mother," she said excitedly.

"You're not going to fill me in on what this is all about?" Matt asked as they all but ran back into the house.

Violet didn't answer him, but instead called for her mother. The older woman called back when she heard her name; she was in the root cellar below the house when they found her. The trap door had been cast open, and she had climbed down into the dark space looking for more food she could send with the young men on their journey.

Matt trailed along behind, still questioning what it was they were doing.

"Mother!" Violet called down to her. "I know what to do!"

"What, dear?"

Her voice sounded far away, but within moments she was climbing up the ladder with one hand, while her other hand held the edge of her apron, which she was using to carry a pile of dried apples. Matt hurried forward to help her climb out through the trapdoor and back into the kitchen.

"Violet and I have been trying to think of what we can do to help you pay the next mortgage payment," Matt explained. "She thinks she's found us a way out."

Violet's eyes shone with pride as she laid out her plan to her mother. "I think— that is, you probably know better, but didn't Pa have a life insurance policy? Wouldn't... um..."

Her voice choked up. She blinked back tears and trailed off as she tried to speak more. Matt took up the thread of thought, as Mrs. Conway emptied the contents of her apron onto the kitchen table.

"Would that policy pay out now that he's gone, you mean? Goodness, Violet, that's a wonderful idea. Would that work, Mrs. Conway?"

The older woman looked surprised, with one hand to her bosom and staring off into the space past the other two. Matt could see she was thinking, she was trying to remember something, and he held his tongue for fear of breaking her concentration.

"I... Violet, you might be right. I can't remember the details right off, but I seem to remember him saying that very thing. But I don't know— Wait, let me check."

Matt watched her dart from one corner of the house

to another, turning it over to seek out any paperwork they might have. Looking between the pages of the Bible, in the trunk at the foot of their bed, even under the mattress. He couldn't help search and dig into her personal items, but he questioned her further as she looked.

"You're sure there's a life insurance policy?"

"Well, no, I'm not certain," she said over her shoulder as she dug through the pockets of Mr. Conway's coat that had been hanging on a hook inside the front door. "I'm sure he told me he was going to do it. But I never saw any paperwork or heard if he had. Oh, no." Mrs. Conway looked deflated, sitting back on the floor with debris spread over her skirt in front of her. "Maybe he never did it."

"Don't say that, Mother," Violet said, from where she stood in the kitchen. "He wanted to take care of us. He must have. Just have faith. We'll find it."

"You'll find it," Matt repeated hopefully.

"What are you looking for?" Michael asked. He had just entered from outside where he was collecting water. Walking awkwardly to the kitchen, he stepped over his mother's legs where she remained on the floor.

"Oh, just some papers," his mother said, reaching the end of the stack in front of her. "Never mind that now. Did you finish helping Silas?"

As her mother got up, Violet continued to search. She glanced up at Matt, who gave her an encouraging smile. This was a good idea—a great idea, in fact. The question was, would it be enough.

CHAPTER EIGHTEEN

The family all focused their efforts, all working toward one goal, and Matt and Silas were on the road before noon that day. Mrs. Conway had fed them as much as they could hold, further packing a saddlebag full of dried fruit, bread, jerky and two canteens of water each. With the sun high overhead, Matt was grateful for the periodic shade of the spruce trees they passed under. It shouldn't take them very long to get to Cheyenne, but all the preparations the Conways had done on their behalf made him feel more confident about their mission.

Though he had traveled west from Boston only the previous few weeks, Matt had not yet allowed himself the opportunity to really notice where he was. The countryside around him was remarkable and yet he had barely experienced it. He had been so focused on getting out of the city on the water, and then on getting to the first town west of there, and then westward on and on until he got where he was going. The problem, of course, was that Matt had had no idea where he was going. He had been restless. He kept moving west, looking for the next thing instead of stopping to see what he already had.

In doing so, Matt had traveled through countless counties, states and territories without noticing any of them.

But now ... Juniper Falls was different. Wyoming was different.

Matt didn't know if he had started to notice this part of Wyoming before Mr. Conway found him, or if the Conway family had been the reason he had paused to pay attention for the first time. Either way, Juniper Falls had made him halt in his tracks and had changed the way he felt about his future. He had made friends here. He was learning what was required to run a ranch, and to be a man of the west. He had finally started to notice the beauty of the open frontier.

To the right of the road, almost parallel to it, but crossing back and forth periodically, ran a narrow creek. Along the creek bank were spruce trees, towering over the road and the water, and offering shade and protection. Wild animals appeared periodically—elk, foxes, bobcats—watching the humans curiously from yards away. Matt took a deep, slow breath, smelling the scent of prairie grass and wildflowers in full bloom.

It was springtime in Wyoming, and a whole host of plants and scents accosted Matt. Flowers he had never seen before. Fauna he would need to learn about if he was to stay here. The wild countryside of the Wyoming Territory was a whole new world to Matt, fathoms away from the congested city life back east.

In Boston, he had regular coughing fits from all the

smoke that hung in the air. Here—Matt took a deep, cleansing breath—the scent of a campfire was soothing. The streets of Boston had been dirty and crowded. In contrast, this dirt road to the next town over had been empty for their entire trip since leaving the ranch. Even the people in Wyoming were different. Sure, he was running for his life at the moment, but everyone else had been accommodating, welcoming, and generous.

Just like, for example, Mr. Bullock at the social the other night. The banker had offered help if he could. Even Matt's own father hadn't been that supportive.

There was something about the cities back east that changed people. Or maybe it was that something about the countryside here freed them. Matt didn't know what it was. All he knew was that he was glad he had decided to come west, no matter the impetus. He could feel his whole life opening up.

The expansive frontier was good for him.

Or, would be, as soon as he solved this crisis, cleared his name, and saved the ranch for the Conway family.

Though this trek was one of desperation, Matt couldn't help but be grateful for the opportunity to be outdoors, on the road, with a sturdy horse under him. Circumstances were less than ideal, and yet God was blessing them with a beautiful day.

Ahead of him, Silas took off his hat and fanned himself with it. The two men had ridden in silence for miles, Silas in the lead, Matt following behind, both armed and alert. They had a deadline to make with unknown obstacles between now and then. There was no telling who had seen them leave or what they might run into on their journey.

Matt suspected all kinds of possibilities. He couldn't tell if he was imagining it or not, but he kept thinking he heard someone or something behind him. At one time he thought maybe it was just a wild horse neighing; at another point he could have sworn he heard a man's cough. But each time he stopped Arrow to listen more intently, there was no further clue. He had to conclude that his imagination was conjuring up threats.

The narrow dirt road from Circle C Ranch headed southeast, away from Juniper Falls and toward the U.S. Marshal's office in Cheyenne. After only a couple hours, the two men stopped to water the horses.

"What's between here and there?" Matt asked, as he led Arrow through the grass to the nearby creek.

"A couple small towns, I think. Maybe three. As far as I know this countryside is filling up with cattle ranches, with beef prices the way they are."

"Should we go around? Stay off the road? What if Sheriff has sent out word about us to the other towns?"

Silas looked thoughtful. "That might be a good idea..."

"I mean, me, I guess," Matt said, correcting himself. "They claim to think you're dead, so I would be the dangerous outlaw to look out for."

Silas guffawed loudly. "Yeah, so dangerous."

"Hey, now. You don't know," Matt said with a grin. "I could have been a bank robber in Boston. Or a kidnapper."

"Sure, Matt. I bet."

It felt good to be relaxed with Silas, even for a short moment. The threat of capture still hung over them, and their window of opportunity to get the funds to save the ranch was slowly closing, but for this brief pause, with the scent of wildflowers and the sound of a babbling creek around them, Matt felt at peace.

"I think I need to take a break for a minute, Matt."

When he looked over at Silas, the other man had dismounted his horse, and was bent over double, examining the bandage around his thigh.

"Are you okay?"

Silas glanced at him briefly, before turning his attention to his leg again. "Yeah, I think so. But this is starting to ache and bleed through. Mrs. Conway gave me fresh bandages before we left, and I think I want to change it."

"Already? Seems awfully soon, doesn't it? Maybe you should turn back."

"Yeah. I know. But..." He trailed off as he slowly lowered himself to the ground, next to the creek bank. "I'll be quick."

Matt looked around, making sure they had not been spotted as Silas got to work. They needed to keep moving, but Silas knew that. Matt didn't need to remind him. Silas wouldn't be delaying them if he didn't absolutely have to.

Since he had the time, Matt ground tied Arrow and wandered downstream a little ways. The water was both deep enough and clear enough for Matt to see foot-long mountain whitefish under the surface. He glanced back and saw that Silas was still deep in the middle of his project, so Matt took off his boots and waded in.

He gasped slightly; the water was freezing cold. He was probably walking into snow that had melted and made its way down from the Laramie Mountains overhead with the warmer weather. Matt entertained a short moment of wishing he had a fishing pole or net. Maybe after this was all over he could finally take the time to settle in, to learn to fish.

"Hey! Matt!"

Silas called for his attention, and Matt turned back upstream to where Silas was now standing.

"Don't go too far," he called. "Nature calls. I'll be right back and then we'll go." He slung his thumb over his shoulder, indicating his path through the copse of trees farther upstream.

Matt nodded and turned his attention back to the water and wilderness around him.

His feet grew numb in the cold water, but still Matt waded farther downstream. Under him the rounded river rocks threatened to shift and tumble with each step, but he kept his balance, staying within a couple feet of the riverbank. Up ahead, a toad rested on a larger stone jutting out of the current. Matt paused quietly to watch it.

It wasn't very big yet, maybe only two inches across, and sat in a cool, dark, damp corner where the bank curved around the stone. Matt stood, frozen, watching as the toad's eyes seemed to be scanning constantly, watching the air all around him. Though Matt couldn't see what the toad saw, he could imagine.

In a flash, with a tiny movement, the toad lunged forward and snapped something out of the air. A bug. A whole meal for him.

And then, another half second after the toad had swallowed its prey, it hopped off the stone, into the water, and swam away into the dark.

Matt smiled to himself. Nature was fascinating, in the most beautiful way. He never would have been able to watch anything like this in Boston. But, like the toad, he too needed to get going, get on the road and move on toward his goal.

He turned back toward his friend.

"Silas," he called.

Matt treated himself to another several minutes in the cool water, walking back upstream with the water just above his ankles instead of climbing out to the grass on the bank. As the afternoon got hotter, the time would come that he wished he was still relaxing in the creek instead of riding under the hot sun. But they needed to get to Cheyenne by that evening and couldn't stall any longer.

Matt was carefully watching where he stepped, intent on not stumbling on a rock and falling in, so he had to pause his progress to look up for Silas. The ranch hand's hat was still sitting in the grass by his used bandage and canteen. How long had he been gone?

"Silas?" Matt called again.

He hurried his steps upstream, taking long steps to cover more ground. Had his wound gotten worse? Was Silas incapacitated somewhere, unable to walk, unable to call out to him.

"Silas!" Matt called for a third time, as loudly as he could.

When there was still no answer, he stepped up out of the water, dried his feet as best he could on the long grass and put his boots back on. Once so attired, Matt headed toward the stand of trees he had seen the other man disappear into.

Before he got more than a step, though, two figures appeared out of the darkness. Their silhouettes loomed, blocking Matt's way; one held a gun to the side of the other.

"Looking for him?" the voice said.

CHAPTER NINETEEN

Matt froze. He held his empty hands out from his sides, instinctively showing he had no weapon.

He was out of the creek now, though the bottom hems of his trousers were still wet. He had only just put his boots back on, only just stood up again to go searching for his friend. He had spent the last twenty minutes relaxed, letting his guard down, enjoying the countryside. And now he had been blindsided and was completely unprepared to deal with the strong, squat man standing in front of him at this moment with a gun pointed at Silas's side.

"I... uh..." he sputtered.

"Matthew Hawke?" the man asked. He took a step forward, the dappling of sunlight illuminating his face. "You're Matthew Hawke, ain't ya?"

Matt glanced at Silas. His eyes widened at Matt and he shook his head almost imperceptibly. The squat man was grinning as though he had discovered some rich treasure. His gloating was unmistakable.

He didn't wait for Matt to answer. "Come on. Move." He poked Silas in the ribs with the muzzle of his gun and nudged him forward, out of the trees, closer to where Matt stood still frozen.

The other man seemed distracted for a split second. Moving as slowly as he could, Matt gradually, inch by inch, reached for his own gun. Having the weapon pointed at Silas was a risk, but maybe—just maybe—Matt could get off a shot quickly enough. But before he could even release the loop, the squat man was yelling.

"Hands off, Hawke," he commanded. "In the air, or your friend here is going to have a hole in his gut to go with the hole in his leg."

Matt pursed his lips and reluctantly raised his hands above his head, farther away from his weapon and his one chance of escape.

"Now," the man continued, continuing to mosey toward him. "You're Matthew Hawke, right? You match the description. That looks like the right horse. I just didn't know you'd have an accomplice." He eyed Silas up and down as though disgusted.

Matt's mind whirred. Who was this stranger who had been looking for him? His graying hair and beard were unkempt and his face tanned and worn from thousands of hours in the sun. Though Matt had only been in Wyoming for less than a week, he didn't think this stranger looked familiar; he certainly wasn't any of the same men Sheriff Vance had kept around him for protection or muscle.

Matt weighed his options. Was it better to cooperate with this ruffian, in hopes of finding answers and opportunity? Or would it be better to keep his mouth shut, not reveal anything in hopes of staying safer longer?

"Who's asking?" he responded.

The squat man grinned, and Matt noticed he was missing one of his canines. The man was several inches shorter than Silas, but easily a hundred pounds heavier and mostly muscle. This was a man who knew the value of throwing his weight around, both literally and figuratively. Matt quickly scanned his clothing, looking for signs or signals of who he was and where he was from, and maybe, if he was lucky, how to overpower him.

The muscles of the man's immense arms twitched under the thin woolen shirt he wore. If he had worn a coat, he had discarded it in the afternoon heat. His sleeves were rolled up to reveal equally powerful forearms. Matt counted one more revolver visible in the holster, and who knew how many knives or smaller guns the man had hidden on his person.

In a final glance, Matt noted the man seemed surprisingly ... clean. Worn attire, yes, but tidy and dust-free. Wherever he had come from hadn't been very far; he couldn't have been on the road very long. Maybe not any longer than Matt himself.

Who was this stranger?

"Here's what we're going to do," the squat man said, ignoring Matt's question. "You, Mr. Hawke," he gestured with the gun, "are going to pick up that rope hanging off the side of that saddle there."

Matt remained where he was, hands still in the air, but reluctant to follow any other instruction. His eyes darted over the man, checking for some weakness. He hoped if he stalled long enough some miraculous plan would occur to him that would get him and Silas out of this mess. The ranch hand was injured, presumed dead by most of the people in Juniper Falls, and now captured by this stranger. No one was coming.

It was up to Matt.

How had they ended up like this? His one moment of relaxing his guard and this brute had snuck up on them.

In the split second it took him to assess the situation, Matt had a revelation. Like a bolt of lightning, he gained clarity about his life instantly. Matt was newly resolved to somehow get free of this mess and build himself a life here in Wyoming where he could dip his feet in a creek for a few minutes without finding himself captured by an armed villain. An image of Violet and him walking through a field of wildflowers flitted into his brain.

That's what he was working toward. That's who he was doing all this for.

Matt was jolted out of his reverie by the man yelling at him again.

"You hear me, Hawke? I said grab the rope. I know you ain't deaf or dumb. Get to it, now."

Matt moved his gaze to Silas who still looked petrified.

"What do you want?" he said evenly.

The squat man chuckled. "I'm taking what I want, or didn't you pick up on that part? I didn't realize you could be even stupider than you look."

"Just ... I'll do it. Fine. But, you gotta at least tell me why."

The stranger chuckled menacingly. "Grab the rope, Hawke."

Matt felt his temper rising. His heart beat faster. The fact that he was unarmed seemed a mere inconvenience when paired with his righteous fury. He glared at the stranger. Matt kept his hands in the air, but moved forward a couple steps.

"Other way, Hawke," the man said, moving his gun to point at him instead of Silas. "I know you probably think you're tough, but I'm here to disabuse you of that notion."

Matt took another step forward, glaring at the man, furious that he had found himself in this situation.

The squat man tilted his head looking at Matt as though he were merely a curiosity instead of threat. Calmly and deliberately, he sighed, lowered the muzzle of the gun and shot. A wedge of grass flew into the air from a spot on the ground not six inches from Matt's right foot.

"Gah!" Matt yelped, jumping back.

The shot had surprised him more than scared him, and his heart raced even faster. For a full five seconds, Matt weighed the possibility of running at the man, of putting his shoulder to the man's ribs, of knocking him down, tackling him to the ground. Could he physically overpower him?

But Matt's self-preservation won out. He had promised Violet he would return safely. He had promised himself no harm would come to Silas. He couldn't go around throwing himself at armed, brawny strangers.

"You going to follow directions now, boy?" the man said with a cruel grin.

Silas stayed silent, but Matt could read his expression. His eyes pleaded with him not to give the man any more reason to fire his weapon.

Matt backed away from the man, whose name he still didn't know. He kept his attention on the gun, feeling back with his feet the several steps to where Arrow was tied up and waiting patiently for the journey to continue. He didn't dare make a sudden move once he was close to the horse; he couldn't risk the innocent creature getting accidentally shot because the squat man had fired at him.

With a final awkward step, Matt backed into Arrow's side. The rope he had been directed to grab was looped around the pommel of the saddle, behind Matt's right shoulder. He groped over his shoulder, but couldn't manage to bend his arm to the correct angle while he still faced their captor.

"I, uh ... I need to turn to get it."

The squat man narrowed his eyes at Matt, then nodded brusquely. "I'm watching you."

Matt nodded, turned and lifted the coil of rope to loop around his arm, keeping his left hand raised the whole time. When he turned back to the man he tried again. "Who are you?"

The squat man grinned again, wider this time. Matt's eyes were drawn to the gap in his teeth, a dark, menacing hole that threatened any number of things, including the fact that this man had somehow withstood an injury of that degree.

"Name's Frank Cutter," he said. "Now bring that over here. No more questions."

Matt nodded. "Okay. But—"

"I said no questions. Do I need to show you again that I'm serious?"

Matt bit back his retort. In spite of the heat of the moment, he reflected he was getting better at keeping his temper. Violet would be proud.

He held the rope out in front of him, again with his other hand high in the air, and walked back over toward Cutter. Matt took his eyes off the stranger for a moment to steal a glance at his friend. Silas looked petrified. His eyes were wide and unfocused, and even from this distance Matt could see that his breathing was rapid. All that blood coursing through his veins, his adrenaline up, couldn't help his leg wound to heal.

Matt needed to try to calm him.

"Here's the rope. Is there— Can I ... I mean, what is it you need?"

Cutter snorted a laugh. "You offering to help me? Why the hell do you think I'd want help from a murderer?"

"I'm not—" But Matt stopped himself. Arguing with the armed man wasn't going to do him any favors. "How do you know my name?"

"Wrap that rope around your friend here," Cutter commanded, once again ignoring Matt's question completely.

Matt locked eyes with Silas and tried to get close enough to whisper to him without Cutter overhearing. He inched around the side farthest away from Cutter but the other man was too intent on keeping the muzzle of his gun right up against Silas's side.

"Around him. All the way. I want them arms pinned to his sides."

Matt sighed and obeyed, thankful at least that he wasn't having to tie himself up.

Once the coil of rope was wound around Silas several times, Cutter stopped him.

"That's enough. That's right. Now, give me the end there." He held out his free hand, moving the gun to be trained on Matt now. "We're gonna make sure this here one is set and then we're going to take care of you."

"All right, fine," Matt said.

No brilliant escape plan had occurred to him, but the longer they took to follow Cutter's instructions, the more time he bought them.

"Walk ahead of me. That way, now."

Cutter gestured into the far cluster of trees, away from the horses, away from the creek. Toward where he had emerged with Silas already under guard.

"You know, if you tell me all of what you're trying to do, it's more likely that I'll be able to do it quickly for you."

"Give me a break, kid. There ain't no way in—"

But the rest of his retort was cut off abruptly by the sound of a branch crashing to the ground. The crack of wood, the rustle of leaves. All three men turned to peer into the trees ahead of them.

"What was that?" Silas asked, speaking for the first time.

Matt opened his mouth to answer, before realizing he had no idea. It sounded like something heavy had been perched in a tree and misjudged the strength of the branch.

"Who's there?" Cutter shouted.

No answer. Nothing stirring.

"Maybe it was just an animal."

"That weren't no animal," Cutter muttered, not taking his eyes off the woods.

Matt's breath caught in his throat. With their captor so distracted, was this the opportunity he needed to take advantage? Could he be fast enough?

He held off, letting Cutter get a few steps ahead of him in his haste to investigate the noise. Matt eyed him carefully. He had to disarm the stronger man first, without the help of Silas and without allowing him to get off a shot. Two steps. Three. Cutter wasn't paying any attention to Matt.

This was his chance.

He crept up behind Cutter as quietly as he could, slowly, steadily moving his hand to his holster. He undid the hammer loop, wrapping his fingers around the gun.

Matt was within half a second of drawing his weapon when Cutter whirled around again.

"Move an inch and you die," he said coldly.

Matt froze. The gun was aimed directly between his eyes. At this distance there was no way that Cutter could miss. His heart pounded as he splayed his fingers, eager to show the other man that he was unarmed. Arms raised high above his head again.

"Now then. What shall I do with you?" Cutter said. The calm in his voice was unnerving.

CHAPTER TWENTY

Matt cleared his throat before speaking again. The scare Cutter had given him when he almost got caught drawing his weapon was enough to stop his heart, but once given a moment to breathe, he reassessed his situation. Silas was tied up, bound completely around the torso. His feet were free to run or walk, but he would be useless for shooting, or even for untying his own knot.

Matt had almost succeeded in getting the jump on Frank Cutter, when a distraction had miraculously manifested from the trees ahead of him. He hadn't been quick enough in his taking advantage of it.

Cutter approached Matt and relieved him of his weapon. "See, now? I was trusting you and you blew it. You won't be needing this."

Back to his first plan: cooperate as best he could, stall, figure out what to do later.

"All right, you're walking in front of me now. March."

Cutter gestured wildly with his gun, holding the

length of Silas's rope in one hand and jabbing at Matt with the gun in his other.

"I'm going," he said, sullenly. "I still don't understand what's going on. We're just two ranch hands on our way to the next town. We can't possibly have anything you want."

"That's all you know, Matthew Hawke."

"How do you know my name?" Matt asked over his shoulder.

Maybe he shouldn't have confirmed his identity, but he was running out of ideas. He walked as slowly as he could get away with, closing the several-yard gap between them and the stand of spruce trees that grew near the creek bank. He didn't like his odds of escape once Cutter got them in those trees, penned in with limited visibility.

"For Christ's sake," Cutter said, exasperated. "Ain't you never even heard of me? Frank Cutter? *The* Cutter?"

"What?" Matt stopped and turned around, confusion written all over his face. "Heard of you? For what?"

"Goddamn it," Cutter swore under his breath. He spit angrily into the grass near Matt's feet. He looked up at Matt again and shook his head. "You're a goddamned idiot, you know that? Some outlaw."

"I'm not an outlaw," he said, exasperated. "I'm not a murderer. Is this ... Are you—"

"Yeah, that's right, Hawke," Cutter said, interrupting. "You're an outlaw. You are wanted for the murder of Richard Conway and Bud Humphrey, and the suspected murder of Silas ... someone or other. I didn't memorize it."

"Silas Denbow is right here." Matt gestured. "The

man you have tied up. This guy. Right here. This is Silas, demonstrably alive."

If Matt thought that would prod Silas into speaking, he was mistaken. The ranch hand still looked pale and petrified, barely shuffling along fast enough to keep pace with them.

Cutter laughed, eyeing his captive up and down. "Well, how about that? Tell you what. I'll bring him back too. That should knock your murder charge down to a kidnapping, maybe. And then there could be a reward for his safe return."

"Why are you doing this? Are you a bounty hunter?"

"Very good. You finally figured it out," he said mockingly. He slowed down his speech to make sure Matt heard every word. "I am a bounty hunter and there is a bounty on your head. I am going to claim that reward and you are going to meet justice."

"But I didn't murder anyone!"

"That's not for me to decide. If you're good, I'll take you back alive and the law can hear your case."

"*If?*"

"The bounty also applies to your corpse so ..." He shrugged. "Me? I don't like to have to kill a man if I don't have to. So don't you go and make me have to."

"But— I can't— I mean, I didn't—"

"Hush up, Hawke. Let's just get this over with. Keep stepping. My horse is on the other side of these trees."

Matt stopped and looked back at the bounty hunter. "How much?"

"What?"

"How much am I worth?"

Cutter grinned. "Two hundred dollars."

Matt shook his head in wonder. Two hundred dollars. Who would be providing that fee? Addison? Even though there was no actual proof he had done this terrible thing? Sheriff Vance must be praying that some bounty hunter decided to take in his corpse instead of capturing him alive, so he didn't have to deal with actual justice. Matt needed to cooperate now more than ever. He couldn't risk Cutter changing his mind.

"Keep moving."

Matt kept his hands in the air and took the final few steps until he was within the shade of the trees.

"What're you planning on doing with that two hundred dollars?"

"That's none of your damned business, boy."

"All right, all right. Just making conversation."

"Well, quit it. There ain't nothing you have to say that I care to hear. You're gonna— Wait. Hush. Did you hear that?"

Matt had heard that. He had heard the small, stifled sound that had made Cutter interrupt his own ranting. He could be wrong, but to Matt's ears it had sounded like a cough. A man's cough, coming from somewhere ahead and to the right of them. His visually scanned the canopy overhead. Not much sunlight made it through the spruce branches; the trees were growing so close together that the dappled shadows played tricks on his eyes. But somewhere out there was a man. He was sure that's what he had heard.

In fact, Matt realized, the sound had probably come from roughly the same place that the branch had crashed to the ground just moments earlier.

Who could it be? Most likely, if there was another

man out there somewhere, it was another bounty hunter come to claim him. Matt sighed, preparing to be the center of some misguided fight between two strangers. If Matt got caught between two hard, greedy men, who knew what would happen? A shootout with him and Silas in the middle.

He turned to look back at Cutter and Silas and saw that the ranch hand somehow managed to look even more afraid than he had before. Even in this shaded area, he was sweating.

Matt thought fast.

He coughed.

"It was me. Sorry. This all..." He gestured around vaguely. "I'm not used to Wyoming yet, I guess."

Cutter narrowed his eyes at him. "You?" He paused long, stared hard.

Matt coughed again.

Cutter cleared his throat and looked around furtively. "I'm pretty sure you're lying, Hawke."

Matt shrugged. "All right, then. You want me to go looking for whoever made that noise, then?"

The confusion was evident on Cutter's face. "Shut your mouth, I said. Keep walking. All the way through the trees."

Matt turned back around to continue his trek, but this time kept as quiet as he could to better hear whoever might be out there. If he could manage to get to Cutter's horse and out of the area before the new hunter came down on them, maybe he and Silas would have a better chance.

If only Silas would ... *do* something. Help in some way. Matt could understand that the other man was frightened, but he seemed almost like a dead weight. Matt would need to snap him out of this stupor if he wasn't going to be a burden and they were going to be able to escape.

Matt continued his trek through the woods. The canopy let sunlight down to the ground, though the shadows remained harsh. He marveled that a few minutes ago, he was wading through the creek, taking a short moment in the middle of all this chaos to admire nature. And now? Now he once again was under attack and having to scramble to save his own life.

His arms began to tire with as much as he was holding them over his head in surrender. He walked about three paces ahead of Cutter and Silas, knowing that the bounty hunter's gun was pointed at him the whole time. With as thick as the trees grew together, he couldn't lead the group in a straight line. Each time he had to make an adjustment, Matt chose toward the left, closer to the water and farther away from where he thought he had heard a stranger cough.

So far, Cutter hadn't noticed.

And, so far, Matt hadn't heard any other sign of a stranger in the woods near them.

"How much farther?" he asked over his shoulder.

"Hush your mouth! Don't make me tell you again."

Matt walked on several more yards in silence. Only the sounds of grass rustling and twigs breaking under their boots indicated the men were there at all. Even Cutter had somehow muffled his breathing. Matt forced himself to tune out the sounds of the creek babbling to his left, or the birds chirping in the trees all around him.

"Stop there, Hawke," Cutter commanded.

Matt halted, confused. This part of the trees looked exactly like every other part of the trees. He couldn't see any reason why they should be pausing in this spot. He didn't have much time to consider, though, before Cutter pushed forward toward him.

Careful to keep his gun aimed at Matt, Cutter looked around, peering between the tree trunks ahead of them. He walked around both Matt and Silas in a wide arc, keeping the gun trained on them, though more and more carelessly. If Matt were more sure of himself he might risk trying to overpower Cutter in this moment, but he couldn't be sure whoever he had heard out in the forest wasn't watching them, and wasn't waiting for his own moment to nab them from their current captor.

The more Cutter looked, the more he seemed to be getting frustrated.

"Is something wrong?" Matt asked.

He happened to meet Silas's eyes in that moment. The ranch hand must have heard or seen something Matt had not. He widened his eyes and barely nodded his head to the right.

Matt sent him a questioning expression back, but the two weren't able to communicate any further before Cutter had wedged himself between them again.

"What did you do?" he demanded, more fiercely than Matt had seen him yet.

"Do?" He was bewildered. "I just— I'm just standing here, arms in the air like you told me to do. I didn't do anything."

"Don't give me that bullshit. Who else are you traveling with?"

"What—"

"Where is my horse?"

"Your *horse?*"

With each question, Cutter grew more frantic and more livid. Matt was flabbergasted, trying to keep up with his train of thought. Did Cutter think whatever they had been hearing elsewhere in the trees was someone they knew? Matt almost laughed. He wished that were true. He wished they had more men on their side, that they had not been completely alone. Trying to fight against the entire town of Juniper Falls, or at least the law, had nearly gotten them killed. It had required him to literally cling to a rope in a well, as well as fight his way out of a shootout in the saloon.

If whoever was following them now wanted to help Matt and Silas rather than capture them for the bounty, he'd gratefully shake their hand.

"The hell did you do?" Cutter demanded, spittle flying from his lips as he got up in Matt's face.

"Nothing." He met Cutter's glare with one of his own.

As the two were staring each other down, another unfamiliar sound emanated from the trees just out of their range of vision.

"Who the hell is that?" Cutter screamed, whirling around.

He still had a hold on Silas's rope, but it was weak, barely a grip. With the bounty hunter's attention elsewhere, this was Matt's best chance to get him and Silas out of this mess. He needed to go for it, to take the leap, to make the brave choice. For him, and for Silas, and for their futures.

Only pausing to take a deep breath, Matt sprung at

Cutter's broad back, wrapping his arms around the other man in an iron grip. Cutter was so wide, Matt could barely make his hands meet in front but he stretched; he held on tight. He would take this man down.

"Get OFF!" Cutter yelled, firing his gun wildly into the trees in his attempt to shake Matt from him.

Although the bounty hunter was far wider than Matt, the younger man was more determined. He was desperate. And he knew he could do this.

CHAPTER TWENTY-ONE

"Silas, run!" Matt shouted at his friend.

He clung to the back of the squat, strong bounty hunter that had tracked them down on the road to Cheyenne. With his arms were wrapped around the other man's shoulders, Matt was doing his best to pin his arms to his sides. If he could keep Frank Cutter from raising his gun, maybe he could get out of this. If Silas could get away while Matt had the man at a disadvantage, maybe they could both escape. Matt squeezed more tightly, trying to cut off circulation in Cutter's arms, trying to induce him to let go of the rope that still bound Silas.

He couldn't even see Silas at times, since Cutter was jerking and twisting around so much to try to disengage Matt from his back.

For his part, once Matt had made his move Silas had finally woken up from the frightened stupor he had been in for the last half an hour. Ever since the moment that he had been cornered by Cutter, Silas had been silent and pliant, not even meeting Matt's eye, seemingly unable to do anything in in his own interest. But now that Matt had disturbed the delicate balance, Silas was moving. Finally.

His arms were bound to his sides by the rope that was still wound around his torso, but his legs and feet were free. Silas ran, pulling the bit of rope still held in Cutter's hands taut until the bounty hunter could barely hang on to his grip.

Matt tried to pull harder on his end, to lift his feet so Cutter was forced to bear his full weight, to wrap one leg around the other man's to trip him up. While Silas pulled in the other direction, Matt used every trick he could think of to bring the bounty hunter to the ground. The rope slipped further; Cutter cringed as it cut into his palm. Matt noticed a slight shade of pink staining the hemp where the bounty hunter's blood began to run.

Cutter held tightly, but Matt thought they were wearing him down. He tried again to wrap his legs around the bounty hunter's; maybe he could trip him or knock him off balance somehow. And the whole time he needed to keep an eye on the gun. Cutter still held it wildly and erratically to the left, nowhere near Silas.

"Go, Silas!" Matt shouted again at his friend.

"No, you damn well don't!"

Cutter jerked his right arm toward him, trying to strengthen his grasp on the rope, but with Matt pulling on him from the other direction and doing his best to knock him over, Silas managed to stay on his feet.

With one arm still around Cutter's shoulders, and now holding him tightly across the chest, Matt scrambled to reach his own gun. Cutter had disarmed him earlier, but the gun still sat loosely in Cutter's own holster. This might be the very moment of chaos that Matt needed to reclaim his weapon. The bounty hunter's broad back required all of Matt's length and strength to hold him tightly. His fingers fumbled, barely able to reach the butt of his gun.

"No!" Cutter shouted again, this time spinning around to knock Matt off balance.

He lost the minuscule hold he had had on the gun and had to focus on not falling to the ground and getting utterly crushed.

But he miscalculated. In his attempt to knock Cutter off his feet, Matt had tangled himself up in the other man. When Cutter spun, trying to shake Matt off, both men lost their balance and collapsed. Matt hit the ground hard, his back flat in the dirt, the wind getting knocked out of him from the force of the fall. Not half a second later the bigger man fell on top of his legs, which had already been twisted at odd angles to try to take down Cutter.

"Gah!" Matt cried out. He hadn't felt anything break, but the strain, and weight of a two-hundred-plus-pound man crushing his knees would leave him in pain for a while.

In his fall, Cutter had almost let go of the rope. Silas stumbled backward as the slack was released from his binding. Matt didn't see it exactly, but Silas must have tripped on a root or rock; he staggered backward a couple steps as he tried to get his feet back under him, but soon fell to the ground, landing on his rear end in the dirt.

With Silas temporarily immobilized, Cutter redoubled his grip on the rope, wrapping it around his palm, even as he still lay crushing Matt's legs.

"Get off!" Matt cried, pushing him.

No sooner had the bounty hunter rolled off of him than Matt realized he had missed his chance to grab for his gun again. Now all three men were on the forest floor, but still nothing had changed. Matt was slow to get to his feet, slow to be able to bend his knees again, to catch his breath, to put his weight on his legs. Silas was still bound from waist to neck, and held captive by Cutter. The bounty hunter still held the rope, both weapons and all the strength.

Matt had to think fast.

Cutter was climbing to his feet, awkwardly since his hands were both occupied. Though Matt was moving slowly himself, he wouldn't again have a chance like this.

"You little—" Cutter began.

His cursing was cut short by Matt ploughing into him, ramming his shoulder into the man's ribs. It was clumsy. It was ugly. Some men might even think it wasn't fighting fair, but what choice did Matt have. Even as Cutter was climbing to his feet, Matt swung his leg in a wide arc, cutting the other man's legs at the knee and smashing the delicate joint as hard as he could.

"Argh!" Cutter screamed as his leg was bent the wrong way and he again lost his balance and fell into the dirt.

Matt scrambled forward on his hands and knees.

But Cutter was no idiot. Even as he collapsed to the ground, he rolled farther away from Matt's grasping hands. In doing so, he pulled Silas along the forest ground with him.

"No!" Matt had been so close to being able to take this man down and now it eluded him.

Frank laughed as he rolled onto his knees and then quickly climbed to his feet. Matt put his hands in the air, as the bounty hunter aimed his gun at him again.

Shaking his head in frustration, Matt did not take his eyes off the gun pointed in his direction.

Silas still lay on the ground where Cutter's dragging had left him. Matt cursed his luck. He would never be able to get out of this now. The best he could hope for was that Cutter would keep him alive to claim the bounty, instead of bringing in his corpse.

"What the hell did you think would happen, boy?" Cutter said condescendingly. "Some outlaw you are. I'll not leave you for a second now. My horse should be right around here, but seeing as it is not, I'm not going to waste any time looking. We're going to return to your horses and get moving back to Juniper Falls."

"But—"

"You shut your mouth. Walk, now." With the gun, Cutter gestured back toward where they had come.

Matt took a deep breath and walked slowly back. He had missed his chance. Whatever or whoever had distracted Frank in the first place was gone now. Whatever had happened to Frank's horse wasn't worth waiting for, apparently. Despite what the horse meant to the man, the bounty hunter would have Arrow now, after all. As well as a couple-hundred-dollar reward. As much as he hated to do it, Matt turned his back to the armed man and started walking.

"Hold up," Frank commanded.

Matt stopped and turned to look. Silas was struggling

to get to his feet. Matt watched as he repeatedly lost his balance, without being able to use his hands or arms at all, and with a bad leg injury to boot. His friend seemed to be catching his eye more frequently than he needed to, but Matt couldn't tell whatever he was trying to communicate. He frowned. What did Silas expect Matt to do?

He didn't have time to figure it out before several things happened in rapid succession.

First, the same cracking noise they had heard earlier echoed around the trees, this time much louder. Much closer. Matt looked around frantically.

Second, the source of the noise made itself known. Even as Matt was visually searching the wooded area, a glimpse of movement caught his eye. He turned to face it and watched a man—young, a little scrawny, clean-shaven—barreling between the tree trunks at them.

Matt didn't know where to turn. He kept his hands in the air but backed up several big steps, trying to get out of the line of this stranger running at them.

What mess had he gotten into now?

Silas still hadn't managed to get to his feet, hampered as he was by the rope binding him. In the chaos, he scooted through the dirt back out of the way. Moving farther away from Frank pulled the rope taut, but the bounty hunter still didn't let it go.

While Silas scrambled away, Cutter turned to face their new attacker, firing off two shots that embedded deep in tree trunks around the man.

Though the new person could only weigh maybe half of what Cutter did, he had the strength and power of surprise behind him. He rushed the bounty hunter and without preamble or warning, hit him as hard as he could with his fists.

With three rapid blows to the head, the new stranger knocked Frank Cutter to the forest floor. He wasn't quite unconscious, but certainly dazed. The power of the punches was enough to finally get Cutter to let go of the end of the rope he had been holding the entire time. Matt backed up a step as Cutter writhed on the ground, blood pouring from cuts on his lip, eyebrow and the bridge of his nose.

The strange man stepped toward Matt, who immediately put his hands up. He wasn't quick enough to grab either of the guns that lay in the dirt around Cutter.

"We don't want any trouble, mister," Matt said. "See? I'm not even armed."

Before the newcomer could respond, they heard a heaving groan come from the bounty hunter on the ground. Cutter must have had some kind of reserve of energy, still going after taking such a beating. He rolled over once, got to his feet and darted off into the trees before any of the others could react.

Matt considered for a moment running after him, but without knowing who this new person was, his intentions, or even having his hand on any gun, it was too risky.

The bounty hunter disappeared. Maybe he found his horse; maybe he kept running. Being knocked to the ground had apparently made him lose interest in the bounty he had been after, which Matt could be grateful for, at least.

As they lost sight of Cutter, the strange man caught up the end of the rope that still held Silas captive, wrapping it several times around his bicep in order to keep the ranch hand in place while still having both of his hands free for shooting.

"Now, then. Matthew Hawke. And Silas Denbow. Yes, I know exactly who you are. You're both coming with me."

Matt heaved a deep sigh. Out of the frying pan and into the fire. He had spent the last near-hour in the control of bounty hunter Frank Cutter. He had done his best to cooperate so the man would take him back to Juniper Falls alive, rather than dead. And in spite of all that effort, he still now found himself under the gun of yet another strange man.

This one, at least, looked familiar, though Matt couldn't place him.

"Curtis?" Silas asked in amazement.

"Oh, *now* you say something?" Matt asked, frustratedly. "You know this guy?"

Silas nodded. "This is Curtis Bullock."

"Bullock? Wait. Are you related to Mr. Bullock, the banker?"

"That's right," Curtis said, though he seemed a little embarrassed by it. "He's my father."

CHAPTER TWENTY-TWO

Curtis Bullock grinned at Matt and Silas. "Glad I finally caught up with you boys. Looks like you really needed my help."

Matt eyed him cautiously. He couldn't read that grin. He didn't know this other man. He had met his father, yes, but as Matt himself knew you couldn't always judge a son by his father. Matt's own father was a cold, uncharitable man. If anyone had asked his neighbors as he was growing up, Matt would have guessed those good, Christian men and women would have written off Matt entirely. His own father's selfishness reflected poorly on him.

And now he stood here with a gun trained on him. His friend Silas still being bound up with a rope that was in the control of Curtis Bullock, the banker's son.

"Curtis?" the ranch hand asked. "Do you think you could help a little?" Silas's arms were bound to his sides, so he couldn't even gesture to what he was referring, but instead looked pointedly down at the rope imprisoning him.

There was a slight pause when Matt was sure that Curtis was going to refuse, but instead the other man relaxed slightly and laughed nervously.

"Of course. I'm sorry, Silas. I guess I just ain't used to this."

"It's all right."

Matt stayed silent, still watching the gun trained on him. Either Curtis didn't trust him or had forgotten that he had the weapon out. Though he lowered it slightly, he didn't return it to his holster. Instead, he tried to help free Silas using just the one hand and Matt had to stand to the side helplessly, hoping he didn't squeeze the trigger accidentally.

He didn't dare draw attention to himself. For all Matt knew, this man was here to collect the bounty on him same as Frank Cutter had been.

Curtis was clumsy, his fat fingers soft and unused to whatever knot Cutter had tied. Silas tried to crane his neck around to see what his friend was doing.

"Maybe if you..." He trailed off. From that angle, he couldn't see well enough to offer any suggestions. "Matt, could you?"

Matt held his breath, waiting for Curtis to give him the go ahead, but the banker's son seemed oblivious to the situation and continued to focus on the mess in front of him.

"Matt?" Silas asked again.

"There's a, uh..." He cleared his throat. "There's still a gun pointed at me."

Matt tried to sound casual and unconcerned, but no

matter how often it happened he couldn't relax when there was a weapon pointed at him. It was taking such situations for granted that got other men killed. Matt didn't want to make that mistake.

"Curtis?" Silas said. "You planning on shooting Mr. Hawke?"

Curtis looked up at Silas, noticed where the other man was indicating, and then looked between Matt and the gun in his own hand. As before, he paused briefly before reacting and in that breath, Matt was sure his worst suspicions would come true.

"Oh. Right." Curtis seemed to shake himself out of his stupor, as though he hadn't realized where he was or what he was doing. "Sorry, friend. I'm just... Well, as I said this is new to me."

"What part is new to you?" Matt asked. He wanted to keep the other man talking, the better to keep his mind from the weapon that remained between them.

Curtis holstered his gun, then flexed his hands, making a fist and then relaxing it again, as though his hands weren't used to holding such a thing.

"I guess I'm just ..." He trailed off and looked more closely at the knot in the rope behind Silas.

As Curtis looked down, his hat fell down farther over his eyes and Matt caught his breath. That hat was familiar. That looking down, that shirt and vest under the chin. That was all familiar. Where had he seen this man before?

"You're just ... what?" Matt asked.

He walked in a slow, cautious arc around to the back of Silas. He needed to stand close to Curtis if he was going to be able to remove his friend from his imprisonment. At the same time, this new person in their company was an unknown factor. In spite of his apparent intention to help, in spite of the gun being holstered, Matt still wasn't sure.

He tried to feel his way through undoing the knot without taking his eyes off of Curtis. The other man still seemed to be avoiding his gaze.

"I'm just not used to ... being safe? No, that's not it."

Matt hid his surprise; he had never heard another man talk that way. He wished he could confer with Silas out of the hearing of their new friend, but that was impossible.

"What do you mean?" he asked gently. But before Curtis could answer, Matt suddenly realized why he looked familiar. He backed away a couple steps. "Wait. I know you. You've been running around with Sheriff Vance and Bud Humphrey. You were there at the ranch when they came and threatened the Conways."

Curtis grimaced. "Yeah, I was. Sorry."

Matt stepped back abruptly, putting space between them. "What are you doing here? What do you want?"

Silas looked from one man to the other, helplessly still tied up. "Aw, come on, boys. Can we just— ? Free me and then let's figure it out."

"What are you doing here?" Matt repeated.

Curtis raised his hands in surrender. "I'm not really one of those guys. I'm on your side. I came to tell you that the rest of the Conway family is still in danger, like your uncle."

Matt was suspicious. "Well... they already are under Addison's thumb because of the mortgage, and now they're having to deal with it all without Mr. Conway or either of us. What else could Addison or the sheriff possibly take from them?"

Curtis looked grim.

Silas asked quietly, "Curtis, what will happen to the ranch if all the Conways are gone? Is that something your father told you?"

Curtis swallowed hard. "Mind you, no one told me anything directly. This is just... I heard them talking."

"Talking about what?" Matt asked more urgently. "What *exactly* do you mean when you say they are in danger like Mr. Conway?"

"Well, the mortgage past due, right? But they still have a few days. If, uh..." He looked down, avoiding their eyes as he scratched the back of his head. "If during that time all the Conways were to, somehow, die, well, then I guess the bank would just be able to sell it off sooner. I think ... that is, I'm pretty sure I heard Addison talking about staging an attack on the ranch to look like an Indian raid."

"How?" Silas asked, flabbergasted. "We're so close to the fort. We haven't seen a raid or massacre in years."

Curtis shrugged. "I know, but... it only needs to *look* like a raid, doesn't it?"

"Why are you telling us this?" Matt asked quietly. "Surely your father didn't send you."

"I just got tired of not being able to sleep at night." He sighed heavily. "I'm not a bad guy. My mama raised me better than this. I don't know what I was thinking, getting mixed up with Sheriff Vance. I knew he was doing some shady dealings, but I thought maybe this would be a way for me to get out from under my daddy's shadow."

"So, you joined up to be one of the sheriff's heavies?"

"Yep. Thought I could catch bad guys or something, but instead he's just had me doing some intimidating for his wealthy and powerful friends. I'm done with it. Mr. Conway's death was the last straw for me. I'd known that man ever since the family landed here years ago. I was only ten, but my daddy and me helped them put up the house they're living in now. I couldn't just stand by and let Addison take everything away from that family."

"That, and you're sweet on Violet Conway," Silas said with a teasing wink.

Curtis grinned. "Yeah, maybe. But I'd a done this either way. I know I'm not the one for her, but the whole family deserves a better chance than Sheriff is giving them."

Matt rubbed his face hard, thinking. If the man cared that much about the Conway family, he was probably all right. Curtis had the chance to take both of them in for the two-hundred-dollar bounty, and instead had put his weapon away and explained himself. Apologized, even. Matt couldn't ask for much more than that.

"You satisfied, Matt?" Silas asked.

He nodded. "For now. I have more questions, of course. And we'll have to figure out a plan for when we go back. But for now, this explanation'll do."

"Good," Silas said with a firm nod. "Now can you *please* see your way to untying me."

Matt laughed. "Sorry 'bout that."

He and Curtis both moved back to work side by side behind Silas, fiddling with the knotted rope. Cutter had tied it firmly, and a bit messily, so both men had to dig at it with their fingers.

"Should we just cut it?" Curtis asked. "One of you got a knife?"

"No, we might need this," Matt said, furrowing his brow as he concentrated harder on the problem. He felt the burn from rubbing his skin hard against the hemp, but he kept at it. They couldn't do much else until Silas was free.

While they worked at the knot, Curtis filled them in a little bit more on what had been happening in Juniper Falls outside of their experience. About what he knew about the bounty on Matt and the plans to take the Conways' ranch. About how Bud Humphrey had died writhing in pain from the multiple gunshots he had suffered in the shootout in the saloon.

"I thought I only hit him twice," Matt said.

"Yep, which means you're not the only one to get him. Dr. Gilpin can't say if one wound in particular did him in."

"So then maybe they can't get you for that murder," Silas said excitedly.

"Maybe." Matt sighed. He had known what he was risking by going after Bud, but all the same ... it was a shame another man had to die, even if it was that bully. He hoped he could end this cycle of revenge soon.

"There," he said, pulling the last loop of knot free. Once this last piece was straightened out, the coils around Silas loosened immediately and fell to the ground, leaving Matt and Curtis both just holding loose pieces of rope. "How do you feel, Silas?"

"Sore." He shook out his arms and rolled his shoulders. "I'll probably find some bruises tomorrow, but it wasn't all that bad."

"Great. Now that's settled, let's go. Finally. Please." Matt started coiling up the rope to take with them.

"Wait a minute, now," Silas protested. "Where are we going? We already had one plan in motion."

"Back to the ranch. We gotta make sure Violet and the rest of the family stays safe."

"But, what about the marshal in Cheyenne? Don't you remember? The whole point of us leaving them in the first place was to make sure that we could get this all legally sorted the right way. We still need a higher up to help us."

"Shoot," Matt said under his breath. After the chaos of being captured by the bounty hunter, he had forgotten the full breadth of catastrophe they had found themselves in. "You're right."

"If I may," Curtis said cautiously interrupting. "The solution seems pretty clear to me."

Matt and Silas exchanged a glance. Matt still wasn't sure whether or not they could trust this guy completely, but if Silas was on board he was willing to try. He had known Curtis for years, at least.

"What's that?" he asked.

"Well, there's three of us, aren't there? We can split up and accomplish more than one thing."

"We couldn't ask that of you—"

"You're not asking. I'm offering."

"Curtis," Silas began, "we don't want you putting yourself any more at risk than you already are. The Conways are my blood. Matt has his own reasons for being involved, but you don't have to."

"I want to. Really. Please. Now, look, you say you were on your way to Cheyenne? Why not just stop at

Harrisville and send a telegram to the marshal from there? That next town is probably only thirty minutes' ride from here."

"Well, Matt's a wanted man," Silas said with a gesture. "There's that enormous bounty on him. And they all think I'm dead. We couldn't risk walking in somewhere that they'd be on the lookout for us and being captured before we could send the telegram."

"That's smart. I forgot about that," Curtis said, nodding. "But no one's looking for me, are they? I made reasonable excuses to the sheriff to account for my disappearance. I can be seen in Harrisville without worry."

"Are you sure?" Matt asked. "You need to be absolutely certain you want to take this on."

"Sure I'm sure. I'll hurry to town, send a telegram to Cheyenne, and then head back to Circle C to see how I can be of help."

"Do not put yourself at any more risk than you have to," Matt admonished. "Do not make me responsible for you getting injured or killed."

Curtis grinned. "Not to worry, Matt. I know my way around. Don't forget I spent the last few months at the sheriff's side."

"Well, if he's going to take care of that," Silas said, "we best be getting back, then, don't you think?"

Matt nodded. "As fast as possible. We don't know when Addison and his men are going after the Conways, but if we can set up some kind of defense all the better."

"I'll go see to the horses."

"Curtis," Matt said, turning to the other man and

offering his hand. "Thank you. Sincerely. I don't know how we can repay you. This is more than generous."

Curtis ducked his head, looking embarrassed but still shook Matt's hand. "Don't mention it. Just see to that family. That's all you have to worry about now."

Matt and Silas both nodded somberly and mounted their horses to head back to Juniper Falls.

CHAPTER TWENTY-THREE

Matt and Silas galloped swiftly back up the road. They had to get back to Circle C Ranch before the sheriff did. Before the Conways found themselves cornered with no way out. Though Curtis had given them an idea of what they were walking in to, the truth was there were more questions than answers. What they needed more than anything was more time. Matt prodded Arrow on, urging him to greater speed.

He wished he hadn't loaded the poor animal down for what they had thought would be a longer journey, but that couldn't be helped now. Instead, he was thankful that they hadn't made it very far away from Juniper Falls before they were stopped and captured by a bounty hunter. Matt supposed he could thank Frank Cutter for that. It could have been far worse.

Arrow seemed to sense his rider's urgency, keeping his head up, his steps sure. Every mile brought them closer to the Conways and closer to providing the family the protection and support that Curtis and said they needed.

Matt didn't know what they would do once they arrived at Circle C Ranch. The bare minimum he could hope for was that all three members of the family were present and accounted for, that they were safe and healthy ... and that they had plenty of ammunition. He didn't know what Silas usually carried with him, but Matt himself only had a handful of extra bullets. He could hardly believe that only twenty-four hours earlier, he had been emptying his pistol in the shootout at the saloon.

But maybe the Conways had what they needed. Situated as they were so far outside of town, with wolves and other predators to contend with, Matt was hopeful that they could make do. They must have more weapons, more ammunition, more ideas for how to defend their home.

And, really, make do was as much as he could ask for with all the chaos raining down him.

Who knew where Cutter had disappeared to, but Matt had to assume he ran back to Sheriff Vance as soon as he could, maybe hoping to leverage his knowledge of Matt's whereabouts to a share of the reward. Who knew what Vance and Addison actually had planned; Curtis had only sketched out the barest of suggestions to them.

All-in-all, Matt reflected, they were riding as fast as they could, headlong into trouble.

But they made record time doing so. They had gone and come back in just an afternoon. As the two men rode through the gate onto Circle C Ranch, the sun was nearly set behind the hills in the distance. The soft purple light cast over the homestead gave the place a calm, welcoming appearance, though Matt knew better.

The silence that greeted them was ominous.

Instinctively, Matt stayed quiet, reining in Arrow to a slow walk and was gratified to see Silas doing the same. The two of them didn't want to draw any more attention to themselves than necessary, not until they figured out what was going on.

This entire situation felt very much like when they had returned to Circle C just earlier that morning. It was amazing what all could happen in a day. Matt expected to hear Michael shouting at them any second. The interior of the house remained dark. Maybe Matt had guessed wrong and the family had left.

Keeping his eyes open for clues, Matt slowly grew more and more relieved to not find any. It seemed as though no one new had visited the Conways since they had left. Maybe they could still yet pull out of this situation with everyone still healthy, uninjured and keeping their home.

It wasn't much, but even a sliver of hope helped.

By the time the two men reached the yard in front of the house, they were more or less certain that they had made it here before anything worse happened. Silas sent Matt a questioning look. He nodded.

"Hello?" Silas called.

"Mrs. Conway?" Matt shouted.

"Matt?" a faint voice answered.

"Violet?"

The door to the house opened. The interior remained dark, but in the faint sunset light, Matt could make out the figure.

"Violet. Are you all right? How is everyone here?"

"Matt, thank goodness." She ran down the steps of the porch to him; Matt dismounted and held his arms open to catch her.

"What happened?" He pushed her hair out of her face, looking at Violet intently.

"Did Curtis find you?"

"Curtis? Curtis Bullock came here?"

Mrs. Conway came out onto the porch at that moment, holding a small candle flickering with just the tiniest amount of light. Michael stood behind her, not yet up to her shoulder, but hefting a rifle longer than his arm.

Violet nodded. "Right after you left, he came knocking, looking for you and full of stories about what the sheriff and Addison had planned."

"You trust him?"

"I do," Mrs. Conway said. "I know his parents. I know he's a good boy, or tries to be. He may have made some poor choices of late, but I think his coming clean with us is a good first step in a new direction for him."

Matt nodded. "I met Mr. Bullock at the social the other night. He seemed like an honorable man, but I wasn't sure about Curtis."

"Mr. Bullock does his best. He's the one that got Richard the mortgage on this place after all. With as favorable terms as he could get away with. I know if it wasn't for him, we may have had to pull up stakes and go back east long ago. Mr. Bullock is the reason that we have this home and life that we do. And I'm happy to extend my gratitude to his son."

"So, then, Curtis was here?"

Violet picked up the story from her mother. "He came looking for you all. Once he finally believed us that we weren't hiding you in the hay loft or down the well —" Matt grinned "—he told us all about the sheriff's plans."

"We've been hiding ever since," piped in Michael. "I told them they should let me go, too. I'd find y'all right quick."

"I told you not this time, Michael."

"I know," he said sullenly.

"Has there been any sign at all of anyone since Curtis left?"

"Not a hair," Mrs. Conway said. "We've been keeping quiet and watching."

Matt turned away briefly to take another look around and think. He ran a hand through his hair, racking his brain for some answer, some solution. They could wait here, hiding, or they could go and leave the whole ranch up for grabs.

"What should we do, Matt?" Violet asked quietly.

He met Violet's gaze. The fierce light in her eyes reminded him of how she had looked under her favorite cottonwood tree, telling him all about how much she loved this land. She was committed to her roots here, and stability for her family.

With just that look, Matt knew there was really no option. The Conways would never leave their home— even if he asked them to and he never would. Instead, they would have to make their plan around staying on site.

"Matt," Violet said cautiously. "Did you all get to Cheyenne?"

He smiled, hoping that he was able to keep his expression neutral and calm.

"No, we didn't. But, Curtis Bullock said he'd go on and take care of notifying the marshal for us."

"Oh, good. How did he find you? You had gone on ahead so much earlier."

"We, uh ..." Matt realized he was embarrassed. This might make her think less of him. "We were waylaid by a bounty hunter."

"What? Oh no! How did that happen?"

"It seems that there is a bounty on my head. A lot of money. For the murder of your father and Bud Humphrey."

"But," Violet frowned, "you didn't do that. Either of those things."

"True, but if the sheriff wants people to believe I did, all he has to do is declare that there's a bounty out for me. Let the court sort it out later, if then."

"Oh, no. Matt ... What do we do?"

"We have to prove my innocence, I suppose. Or..." He smiled wryly. "You could always turn me in for the bounty. That amount could pay for the mortgage, at least."

Violet smiled and pushed him lightly. "Don't you tease about that, Matt. What would we do without you? If Curtis can reach the marshal, I won't worry about it. There are too many other things pressing on us right now."

And if Curtis couldn't reach the marshal, Matt didn't know what they would do. Worrying certainly wouldn't help.

Taking another tack, Matt asked, "Were you able to

find your life insurance paperwork? If we can use that to secure or promise the mortgage payment, maybe we can fend off any attempts by the sheriff to get you off the property."

Mrs. Conway shook her head sadly. "I looked through everything. We even looked in places it didn't make any sense to keep an important document. I'm not even sure Richard took out the policy, but if he did I don't know where he put the paperwork."

"Maybe it was in his pocket when he died? Maybe the coroner has it?" Violet suggested.

"Maybe," Matt said doubtfully. "I don't know why he would have been carrying such papers around with him. Even if the coroner does have something, though, can any of us really risk going into town to check?"

Violet sighed. She walked a few steps away from the rest of the family and gestured Matt to follow her. Once they seemed to be out of her mother's hearing, Violet turned back around to him. In the darkness, he couldn't make out her expression, but the way she was standing so close to him Matt knew she was about to say something just for him.

All he wanted to do was take her hand in his and promise her the world. If he could have made this all go away, if he could have taken care of her, paid the mortgage, unseated the sheriff, he would have. He would have done anything he could to keep her safe and to keep her family secure.

But at this moment, all he could do was listen.

"Matt," she said quietly. "I don't like this." She squeezed his fingers. "You were going to be safely out of the way if you went to Cheyenne, but now you're back.

The sheriff could show up any minute with an excuse. If there's a bounty on your head, you're not safe here or anywhere near here. If anyone sees you, they could shoot you immediately with no questions asked. I don't know..." Her voice caught as she fought back tears. "I don't know how our family can manage this without you, but I also don't know what I would do if anything happened to you."

All the promises he wanted to make bubbled to his lips, but he withheld them. The prospect of breaking a promise to her was more dire than soothing her anxiety right now. If this was the beginning of a life lived together, he wanted to start it on a foundation of honesty and integrity.

"I'll do my best," he said. "But, you know I won't be happy if I ride off and save my own skin and leave you and your mother and brother here to deal with it all without me."

There was a slight pause, and in the dim light, Matt could see that she had lifted her chin to look directly at him.

"I know. That's one of the things I like best about you, Matthew Hawke."

Matt smiled, and wanted nothing more than to take this beautiful young woman in his arms and kiss her, but that moment of delay could be their lives.

He needed to focus on their plan of defense and get the family ready for what lay ahead.

"Let's go see about Circle C," he said.

She nodded and led the way back to where the others waited. Silas had joined them by this time, after having brushed down and stabled the horses, hopefully getting them safely out of the way of whatever happened next. Matt wanted to ask the other man about how the barn looked, what resources they had, what his ideas were, but first things first.

"So, we're agreed, then?" he asked the group. "We all stay here and defend the ranch?"

Before anyone could answer in the affirmative, something else caught Matt's attention.

Maybe it was because Matt had so noticed and admired the light cast over the ranch as the sun set, but his attention was promptly drawn to another shift in the light. He looked around, curious about what it could be, praying that it was maybe just a fluke, or that Silas had lit a lantern.

As he turned, Matt realized where the new light was coming from.

The light was moving. It was scattered and shapeless, creeping ever nearer. It wasn't close yet, and he had to peer through the trees between the house and the road to get a handle on it. Once Matt focused, however, it was unmistakable. Coming up the road, toward the ranch, just outside the gate, were at least a dozen lit torches carried by a gang following Sheriff Vance.

CHAPTER TWENTY-FOUR

"Get in the house!" Matt shouted. "Now! We don't have much time. They're coming."

He ran to help Silas who was carrying their saddle-bags and supplies back into the house, even with his leg injury. Matt glanced over his shoulder periodically to keep an eye on the progress of the gang that was now making its way onto Circle C Ranch. There were at least a dozen men, maybe more, on horseback riding toward the house. Many of them carried torches to light their way as the crossed over the border and invaded the Conway family's property. In the dim light, Matt could not make out expressions, but the gang's quiet determination spoke volumes.

They were here to destroy any chance, to remove all hope that the family could keep their land and their home that they had worked hard to improve. If what Curtis Bullock had said was true, this could be a fight to the death. This group of thugs was intent on slaughtering every member of the family that Matt had come to love, and making it look like Indians had attacked.

They were here. He had run out of time, and they would not leave any survivors. There was so much Matt had meant to do to prepare the family and the property against this attack, and now he never could.

Sheriff Vance led the group, riding slowly, deliberately, as though they had all the time in the world. Maybe they did. Maybe they would take all the time they needed to get this job done. There only remained one more full day until the mortgage payment was due, and all they had to do was keep the Conways from finding or making the necessary money until that moment. And then once that time ran out, Addison could buy or seize the property for his own.

Even if the group of men didn't kill the family, they could still ruin their lives.

All the men had to do was wait out the bank's time limit.

And with a dozen flunkies at their beck and call to help stall, or help intimidate the family, the results seemed assured. The light grew brighter as a dozen torches, flames burning high, drew closer to the house.

Matt closed the door behind him, doing a quick head count to make sure everyone had made it inside. Women, a child, and two injured men. That's all that he had to work with to defend the entire ranch against these insurmountable odds.

"Help me," he said, gesturing to the furniture in front of him.

He had assumed Silas would jump to assist, but was

surprised and impressed to see Violet immediately at his side as well.

"We should move the table?" she asked.

Matt nodded. "The table, the chairs. Any furniture that would be heavy enough."

"That's my favorite chair," Mrs. Conway said weakly, watching Matt wedge the sturdy wood back between the wall and the table.

"Silas," he said, pointing. "The window."

The ranch hand nodded and hurried to the far side of the room where the one large window lay looking out over the pasture and toward the barn. It was one of the loveliest parts of the large family room, but also the most vulnerable. Immediately next to it was a tall sideboard with shelves full of dishes.

"I'm so sorry, Aunt Susan," he said quickly.

He leaned his shoulder into it and shoved the heavy piece of furniture to block most of the window. Matt winced at the sound. The legs of the sideboard gouged and scratched the wooden floor underneath. In the movement, Silas also tipped the shelves slightly, enough that most of the dishes went crashing to the floor.

Matt winced.

If they survived this, they could worry about the damage wrought then. The most important thing was getting through the night alive.

"Show me the other windows," he said.

"There's just one other. Come this way."

Quickly Violet led him to the larger bedroom, where her parents'—or, rather, her mother's—room looked out onto the other side of the ranch.

Matt stood in the doorway, struck for a short moment by what had happened just a couple days earlier when he stood in this same spot. His hand stole to his pocket where he ran his fingers over the delicate etching in the silver of the pocket watch. Mr. Conway had been so kind to him. So generous. So welcoming. Protecting his family and his property was the best way Matt knew to repay him.

"Matt?" Violet asked.

He blinked a couple times and remembered where he was.

"This is the other window. What do you think we should do?"

Looking around the room, there didn't seem to be any tall furniture he could move to guard in front of the window. It wasn't quite as large as the window in the main room, but it was plenty vulnerable. Anyone could easily break that glass, shoot through it, and get at the family inside. He needed to protect it at all costs. Feeling helpless for a moment, Matt briefly felt his temper rising. But he quelled it. He forced himself to take a deep breath. He closed his eyes and took a short moment to think.

When he opened them again, his gaze fell on the wide bed that had held both Conways only a couple nights earlier.

That was it.

"Silas!" he called to the other room. The bed would be far too heavy for him to lift on his own. "Michael!"

He moved to the side of the bed, lifting a corner of the thin mattress and dragging it to the ground. Violet again anticipated his intentions and ran to help. She caught up the pillows and quilt in her arms, carrying them out of the room and out of the way. When Silas and Michael appeared in the doorway, Matt had already half-drug the mattress to lean against the wall. Though it sagged a bit, it was still large enough to protect them.

"We'll lean this up, against the wall to block the window. It's the best we can do," he explained as he lifted. The legs of the bed stuck out toward the center of the room and at one point Michael had to duck to keep from getting hit. Next, they dragged the mattress to lean against the bed frame; the weight should help keep it in place, blocking the window from any breach.

As they frantically worked, the firelight from outside grew even stronger. Matt chanced a peek out the window as they maneuvered the heavy wooden pallet into place and thought he counted a handful of torches. If he could see the flames from this window, that meant they were already getting to surround the house.

With Michael offering additional support, Matt and Silas got the bed and mattress into place and stepped back to check the work. Would it hold? Would it be enough?

"Is there any other way into the house?" Matt asked the boy.

Michael frowned as he thought. "I don't think so. There's a crawl space under the house, but you'd have to go through a floorboard to get in."

Matt shook his head. There wasn't any way they could guard against anyone coming in throughout the entire floor of the house. They just had to hope that the sheriff and his men wouldn't think of that.

The crack of a gunshot interrupted his thoughts. Matt ducked instinctively, but after listening for a moment, he wasn't sure the bullet pierced the house. He looked around, trying to identify where it had gone.

"Y'all come on out, now," Sheriff Vance said, loudly but with complete calm, as though he were discussing the price of a chicken. "Matthew Hawke. We know you're in there. You're a wanted man. In the name of the law of the Territory of Wyoming, I am placing you under arrest. You are making these fine folk into criminals, aiding and abetting you as they are, and I know you don't want to be doing that."

"How does he know you're here?" Silas asked in a loud whisper.

"Frank Cutter ran off, remember? He must've run straight to the sheriff," Matt answered grimly.

He hurried to the window in the main room. The sideboard blocked some but not all of the window, and Matt could crouch down, out of sight, and watch what was going on outside. Sheriff Vance held his gun in the air above his head—he must have just shot a warning, rather than deliberately at anything. His men were spreading out in a circle around the house, but the sheriff was casually directing his horse back and forth, from one side to the other.

The Conway farmhouse was surrounded.

"What's happening?" Michael asked in a fierce whisper. He was crouched behind Matt, trying to see out of the same tiny sliver of dark glass.

"Shhh," Matt scolded.

"Matthew Hawke," Sheriff Vance said again. "Surrender and no one has to get hurt. Wouldn't want to drag that fine family in too."

"Don't you dare," Violet said in a hushed voice.

Matt moved away from the window and looked at the family surrounding him, supporting him, putting themselves in danger for him.

"Now, you all heard what the sheriff said, didn't you? You're committing a crime by letting me stay in here with you."

"I don't want to hear another word, Matthew Hawke," Mrs. Conway said. "We know what we're doing. We know which side is the right one."

Matt smiled, gratified. "All right, then. I won't argue with you. Let's get these fellows taken care of. Do you have any other weapons in the house?"

Violet nodded, indicated to her brother about something in the drawers by the stove and then left the room herself. Silas had already drawn his own weapon, but as they were barricaded within the house, he seemed to be nervously shifting it from hand to hand.

Matt sat heavily in the middle of the floor where the family's kitchen table had rested not two minutes earlier, overwhelmed and at a loss.

Where had he gone wrong?

This had all started when this man had come to the ranch to threaten the kindhearted Conway family, and somehow now they were essentially imprisoned in the ranch house. Was this his fault? Had Matt been the one who made a mess of it?

He rubbed his face vigorously, thinking, considering.

He felt stuck. Cornered. After inadvertently provoking Bud Humphrey's ire, he had dragged Silas and the Conway family down with him, and they refused to be let out of it.

When he looked up again, Violet was watching him.

Her expression when he met her eyes wrenched his heart. She was trusting him. Trusting him to take care of them, and to do the right thing. She was trusting him to come back safely to her after all this was over.

But all this came back to Matt's desire to get revenge for Richard Conway. Violet's father. Mrs. Conway's husband. The man of this house and Matt's first and only example of what a good father could look like.

He would not back down now.

Matt stood, wiped his sweaty palms on the front of his shirt and took control.

"I've got this. We'll get through this. You all can count on me."

Before anyone else in the family could respond, they once again heard Sheriff Vance making threats from outside the house.

"One way or another, Matthew Hawke, you're going to have to account for what you've done. We can wait here all night."

Matt began making plans for how they would spend the night trapped in the house.

CHAPTER TWENTY-FIVE

After the sheriff brought his gang to surround the house and intimidate the Conway family into giving up, they settled in for a what amounted to a siege. The night dragged on inside the Conway family ranch house. For the first several hours that the family and Matt were barricaded inside, they had plenty to keep them busy. There was the matter of reinforcing the windows and door, of uncovering all the weapons, and of changing Silas's bandage again so he could be as nimble and useful as possible. But once all that was completed, all they had left to do was wait.

They lit only one lamp, keeping it hidden behind their bodies and what furniture remained as much as they could. The hope was that if the sheriff did not know where in the house they were huddled, he would hesitate before trying to enter. They stayed quiet, thoughtful, not yet giving up.

Mrs. Conway was the first to think through the practicalities of being trapped within the house and after a few minutes of her son asking for a drink, she had made the decision they needed to ration their water. Matt wished he had thought of that before he corralled all of them within the house, but there had been no time to gather any additional supplies as the sheriff rode up. All told, if they were careful, they probably had enough water for everyone through the end of the following day.

Matt prayed this stand-off would be over long before that.

Fortunately, at least, their food supply could last longer. The Conways also had a narrow, beginning of a root cellar dug under the house. Though it was nearly empty now that they had just gone through the Wyoming winter, it was still stocked enough to keep the family fed for a few more days.

It had gotten late. Matt pulled out the pocket watch that Mr. Conway had gifted him just a couple days ago. This was a symbol of how he had been adopted by this family, and now he was using it to check how much longer he could help them survive.

It was now past eleven o'clock and Michael was curled up, asleep in the corner of the big room with a quilt draped over him. He had stayed awake as long as he could with promises of sharp-shooting and getting revenge of his own, but even a twelve-year-old boy runs out of energy eventually. Mrs. Conway and Silas were in the large bedroom, near the other window, the ranch hand keeping a lookout in that direction.

Matt tucked the watch back in his pocket, and glanced through the dim moonlight at Violet. The two of them sat up by the one window in the main room of the ranch house, both sitting on the floor, leaning against the wall where the sideboard used to stand. This was the closest they had come to being alone in days, and every time Matt looked in her eyes he had a difficult time remembering that they were in the middle of a dangerous siege.

The peace he felt with her was welcome. She had a calming influence on him. His temper, which had always been a point of personal struggle for him, had abated lately. He had been more and more successful at bringing himself back from that edge, from that point of no return where he could do or say something he would later regret. Even now, as their whole world was upside down and their very lives were in danger, Matt could manage to focus on the little he could control and think rationally about his next steps.

Their next steps. Together. Because he could not have done any of this without her support.

It was almost midnight, almost the morning of the day when the Conways' mortgage payment was due. Whether the would run out of food or water or time first, Matt didn't know. All that mattered was that this stand-off couldn't last forever.

Violet's head lolled a little on her shoulders. She leaned it against the wall and closed her eyes. Matt held his breath. He didn't want to disturb her; she should sleep when she could. But the rest didn't last long. She jolted awake after only a moment.

"You should sleep," he said softly. "You've had a long day."

She smiled sleepily at him. "So have you. And you didn't sleep last night, either."

"I can't sleep," he said. He rose up on his knees just

enough to glance out the window. There were still plenty of torches burning, although it seemed as though the men the sheriff had brought were also resting for the night. "My body feels like it's thrumming. I've got too much to think about. But I'll stay on guard so you can sleep."

She closed her eyes again. "Maybe just a little."

Matt watched her body relax and settle as sleep overtook her, in spite of her protests.

And all he wanted to do was protect her and give her every chance. Even if it was only staying awake so she could sleep.

As soon as he was sure she wouldn't wake, Matt stood carefully and walked on tiptoes to the other side of the house where Silas was keeping guard by the other window.

"Anything?" he asked in a whisper.

Silas shook his head without looking at Matt.

Matt stood in the doorway a moment longer before leaving Silas to his vigil. They had all night. All night to think over their options. All night to worry about the attack that would undoubtedly come. If not the next day, then soon after.

Matt walked back into the main room and lowered himself to sit next to Violet again.

He couldn't wait for an attack. They didn't have more than just the following day. There was the mortgage payment to make. Waiting in the house for safety would only result in them losing the house.

He had to do something.

Hours passed as the Conway family dozed around him. Michael woke up with nightmares several times, the third time waking Violet as well. But Matt never slept. He never once dropped his guard.

"Is he okay?" he asked Violet when she returned from comforting her brother.

"I think so. He will be. Once this is all over, we'll just have to make sure he has some time to be a carefree twelve-year-old again. When I was his age, everything seemed huge and monumental in my life, but even in crossing the states in a wagon, I don't think I ever experienced such a rough time like this."

"That poor kid."

She nodded.

They sat in silence another moment before Matt found the courage to tell her what he had been planning.

"I've come to a decision, Violet. And I'd like your opinion."

"All right," she answered solemnly.

"We can't stay in here forever. You know that. We can't even stay in here another day if we want to be sure to have the mortgage paid for."

"That's true."

"So, I think our only option is … I might … Well …" He cleared his throat, stalling.

"It's okay, Matt. You can tell me." She rested her fingers on his arm.

He took a deep breath. "I'm going to try to talk to the sheriff. And I might turn myself in if it means you all can be free."

"Oh, no, but—"

"I'm the one that brought all of this on us. And maybe the law will be fair. Either way, it's not right for your whole family to suffer because I happened to have been in the wrong place at the wrong time."

"I can't let you turn yourself in."

"Violet, I know." He wanted to cup her face in his hand and pull her close, but he couldn't allow himself to be distracted. "I know. But, what other choice do we have? Your mother and your brother need their home. This is the only way."

"I ... I know you're right," she said finally. "I don't like it, but I trust you."

"Thank you. But, I need you to not try to help."

"What do you mean?"

"You're strong, Violet. You are always the first one to volunteer when something needs doing. But when I go out there, I need you to stay inside. I need you to stay away from the gang and stay as safe as possible while I take care of it."

She didn't answer right away. She looked him over, studying his expression as though weighing the value of something very precious.

Finally, she nodded.

"But, Matt? Can I ask one thing?"

He looked into her clear, hazel eyes.

"Wait until dawn, at least?"

Her teasing smile told him all he needed to know. He had her support in spite of the dangerous circumstances. Dawn would be here soon and he would take action.

In answer, he placed his pistol on the floor for the first time since they entered the building. In its place he reached over and took Violet's hand, as he moved to sit closer to her. She squeezed his hand back and rested her head on his shoulder.

That's how they sat for the next few hours. She might have fallen back asleep. She might have stayed awake with him. All Matt knew is he would treasure the memory of these hours sitting with Violet as long as he lived.

He hoped that would be past dawn of the coming day.

Finally, when he thought he could hear stirring in the yard outside the house, Matt pulled out Mr. Conway's pocket watch again, and ran his thumb over the etching slowly, thinking, admiring. He opened the face and checked the time. Dawn should be here any moment. He could no longer let this family wait at his expense.

It was time to move.

CHAPTER TWENTY-SIX

It was time. Dawn was just arriving over the mountains in the distance and the warm orange light peeked through the tiny gaps around the covered windows. The new day had arrived—the day that the Conway mortgage payment was due and the last day that Matt had to solve all of these problems and avoid being jailed himself.

The crowing rooster to mark the day was Matt's cue. All this would take was a moment of deliberate action and he could end the whole thing. With Violet searching through her father's things and Silas on guard, Matt enlisted the help of Michael to move the furniture out from behind the front door. They had done such a great job of barricading themselves inside, and now it was time to undo that. After chipping some wood, scratching the floor and breaking the dishes, Matt felt terrible that he was now reversing the whole thing, but he trusted Mrs. Conway's understanding.

Silas came to stand in the doorway, holding his revolver and watching.

"You'll stay here, right?" Matt said to him over his shoulder, as he and Michael worked. "I need to be sure that I'm covered in case it all goes wrong."

"Of course," the other man said solemnly. "You can count on me."

Michael picked up the other end of the solid wooden table that had been providing the bulk of their reinforcement, and he and Matt moved it a couple of feet to one side. Just enough so that Matt would be able to squeeze through the open door.

"Here it is," Violet said as she emerged from her parents' bedroom. In her hand, offered to Matt, was a plain white cotton handkerchief.

"This is perfect," Matt said as he took it from her. He held it carefully, forcing himself to pay attention and not just wad it up in his clammy fist as was his wont. "Remember what we agreed. You all stay in here, away from the guns and the danger. I'll see what I can negotiate with the sheriff since I'm the one that got all of us in this mess."

"I still think I should come with you," Silas said with a frown. "Two of us are better than one. And I'm proof that you didn't murder at least one of the names he's trying to pin on you."

"You need to stay here to protect the house," Matt said. "Silas, please."

"I know, I know. I just ... Good luck, Matt." He offered his hand and the two men shook.

There was nothing else for Matt to do. No other way for him to procrastinate or delay the inevitable confrontation. He took a deep breath and opened the front door of the ranch house slowly, cautiously, only giving himself enough space to just barely slip through. Holding the white handkerchief in hand, he held it out and waved it as he exited the building.

"Hold your fire, boys," Sheriff Vance said when he spotted Matt. "You surrendering, Hawke?"

"I want to talk," he said.

He stayed with his feet squarely on the porch, not stepping any closer to the sheriff and his armed guards than necessary.

"You're armed. You expect me to believe you just want to talk?"

"Look, Sheriff. It's just me against all of you. The door behind me is closed. No one is coming to my aid. We both know that if I draw, I'll be dead before my finger hits the trigger."

Sheriff Vance looked him over, sighed and grunted his assent. "Fine. What is it you want, boy?"

Matt's pride smarted at being addressed so, but he was in no position to argue. He took a cautious look around the yard in front of the Conways' ranch house, trying to take in every detail and feature to better plan the defense of the ranch. He knew his chance of getting out of this 'talk' with what he wanted was slim to none, and he still had to figure out how to emerge from this disaster victorious.

The circle of toughs that the sheriff had brought with him seemed to go all the way around the house. Each one of the men was watching him carefully. And each one of the men could fire on the house with just a flick of the wrist. From where he stood, Matt couldn't see where the circle ended, only that he was surrounded.

Still with his hands in the air, one hand holding the white handkerchief, Matt counted eight men that he could see. Sheriff Vance was the only one still on his horse, and the rest of the group's animals seemed to be contentedly waiting near the edge of the pasture in the distance, hopefully out of any line of fire.

Matt was somewhat surprised to realize that the sheriff's group hadn't set up any kind of defense. They hadn't brought anything with them, no wagon or other barricade to position themselves behind. All they had was the single spruce tree and the stone wall around the well. Both of those barriers were relatively close to the house, each only a couple feet across and neither offered the kind of protection the men would need.

Either the sheriff wasn't taking him seriously as a threat, or he wasn't much of a strategist. Though Matt could count himself lucky at this realization, he knew there were plenty of other reasons why he should still worry.

Matt had hoped that Curtis would get word to the marshal in Cheyenne quickly enough to keep him from having to do this, but it had been nearly eighteen hours and there was still no sign of him.

"Hawke?" Sheriff Vance called to him. "Did you or did you not have something to say to me?"

Matt forced himself to focus. He couldn't do anything about the circle of men surrounding him. Now was not the time. He was not here to fight his way out. He could only hope to reason with the sheriff all the while keeping his hands in the air.

"Yeah, I just ... We seem to be at an impasse, Sheriff."

The older man smirked. "An impasse? Well, that's a big word for a boy like you, ain't it?"

"What I mean is," Matt continued, "let's talk about this. Find a solution."

"Sure we'll talk about it. When you come over to the jail. There's even a cot in your cell where you can have a nice long sit. We'll talk as long as you want, once you're behind bars for what you've done."

"Come on, now," Matt sighed, exasperated. "You know I didn't do anything. You *know* it. You're wasting everyone's time."

"I've got at least four people say they saw you shoot Bud Humphrey and Silas Denbow. I got reason to believe you were the last person to have seen Richard Conway alive. I'd say that's plenty to make an arrest with. Then we'll talk."

"Sheriff Vance." Matt's heart beat faster as his temper started to rise. "Silas Denbow isn't dead. I didn't do anything to him. Or, I mean, yes, I did shoot him. But it was an accident, and he's fine now. He's inside the house, in fact." He gestured behind him, without taking his eyes off the other man.

Sheriff Vance shrugged, unconcerned. "If that's true, he can come down to the jail once we've got you in custody. You're allowed a witness, I think. We'll have to ask the judge."

"He can also testify to seeing Bud Humphrey murder Mr. Conway."

"So you've said." The sheriff was maddeningly calm. "Isn't it convenient for you that Humphrey is dead, too?"

Matt took a deep breath to try to calm himself

down. Of all the times in his life, this was the moment he needed to learn to control his temper. He was already in plenty of trouble. So much trouble, in fact, that he couldn't see any way out. He was considering letting himself be taken in and trusting the law to do its job. He had always heard that the western frontier was lawless and uncertain, but maybe it was worth putting his faith in justice.

"Well..." he began slowly. "What happens if you do take me in to jail?"

The sheriff smirked again. "Starting to see reason, are you, Hawke? Once you surrender, you spend your days in a six-foot-square cell. You'll be fed and all, but you can forget about seeing daylight every again. The circuit judge'll be here in a month and can decide your fate then."

"But, what about ... a lawyer? Evidence? What will the judge use to decide?"

All around Matt, the men listening snickered.

"Sure, Hawke," the sheriff said indulgently. "We'll let Mr. O'Connor know about your case and he can decide if he wants to help. My understanding is he was disbarred in Ohio, and that's why he's out here, but he can't be completely useless."

"Isn't it in the Constitution?"

"Might be." He shrugged. "I dunno. But Wyoming Territory isn't one of the States yet, is it?"

"So ... I just ..." Matt felt deflated. He had nothing to go off of. No leverage or bargaining chip with which to defend himself legally. It was merely going to be his word against the sheriff's. Matt had been in town all of a week, while Sheriff Vance had been the town's appointed lawman for several years. Who would the judge really believe?

With all legal and above-board options taken off the table, Matt was floundering. He couldn't see any way of getting out of this without making an utter mess.

"All right, I have another proposal for you, then."

Sheriff Vance sighed and looked bored. "Get on with it, Hawke. We've been here already almost sixteen hours and I'm sure these men are growing impatient."

"Okay okay. What if you all stand down so the Conways can leave? We're talking about women and children here, Sheriff. They don't deserve to be caught up in this."

"We're talking about three individuals—four if I am to believe Silas Denbow is here as well—that are harboring a fugitive from the law."

"Well, maybe, but—"

"Face it, Hawke. You've been cornered. Like a rat in a hole." He grinned malevolently. "Whatever rigamarole you come up with is not going to work for me or for these men. Just surrender now to save all of us time and risk. Giving yourself up is the right thing to do."

Before Matt could respond any further, he heard the familiar clopping of horse hooves approaching. Whoever was riding toward the group seemed to be alone. Matt was elated. Maybe this was his break. It must be the marshal coming to rescue him and put the sheriff in his place. Maybe Curtis had come through after all. Matt kept his hands in the air, but watched down the path expectantly. Any second now the new arrival would emerge through the trees near the ranch's gate.

When he saw who it was, all the breath left his body.

Matt had been wrong in his guess. It wasn't the marshal. It wasn't anyone who would be able or willing to help Matt in the slightest.

Addison, the mastermind behind seizing the ranch away from the Conways, was the face that appeared through the trees. His black hat was pulled down low over his face, but Matt would recognize that grizzled hair and broad shoulders anywhere. His eyes flashed angrily as he took in the scene in front of him.

When Addison was still almost ten yards away, he yelled.

"Vance!" he shouted. "What are you doing? Just jawing with a murderer? Seize him!"

Matt froze; his hand went to his holster, but he knew the moment that he drew his weapon he would have a couple dozen holes blasted in him. He watched the sheriff's reaction to such a command. The lawman seemed resentful of being ordered around like this, but that irritated expression only flitted across his face for a moment.

Sheriff Vance turned around to assess Addison as he approached, then turned back toward Matt. All of the dozen or so men he had brought for muscle were watching him just as intently. If Matt moved an inch in any direction he'd be set upon.

"I'm raising the bounty to three hundred dollars," Vance shouted to the group surrounding Matt.

His stomach dropped as he heard the sounds of a dozen guns surrounding him being drawn.

CHAPTER TWENTY-SEVEN

All around him shots rang out. Matt couldn't escape it. He stood on the porch of a house that was surrounded by a group of men who not only wanted to kill or capture him, but who had also just been promised three hundred dollars if they could do so.

Matt rushed toward the door, trying to zig-zag toward it quickly to avoid presenting himself as an easy target.

The door was open when he reached it. Only barely, only enough for him to squeeze through. As his right armed snaked behind him through the tiny gap, Matt's luck ran out. A bullet tore through his forearm and lodged itself in the heavy wood. He grunted in pain, but kept moving.

"Everyone get down," he called to the house.

But they didn't need the instruction. To a person, each member of the Conway family acted instinctively for their own survival. Matt crouched low, trying to stay close to the ground. Bullets continued to fire all around them. Matt heard glass shatter in the bedroom and hoped Mrs. Conway was away from the window.

"Matt!" Violet exclaimed as he stumbled inside. "You're hurt! What happened?"

She rushed around the small kitchen to find a cloth and a tiny bit of the water that was left to clean the wound.

"Addison," he said breathlessly. "Addison's here. You've got to get down, Violet."

Violet squatted down on the floor next to him, working faster than Matt had ever seen her, wiping away the blood on Matt's arm and quickly wrapping it with a strip of towel she had cut off from somewhere. She pulled the knot tight, stopping any further blood flow. Matt clenched a fist in that hand, and then relaxed his fingers. The injury didn't seem too bad. He should still be able to shoot with that hand. He hoped.

"Matt!" Michael wailed. "Violet! They're shooting at us."

Matt turned to see the boy curled up in a ball in the corner of the big room. He held his rifle between his knees, the barrel pointed at the ceiling, and his arms over his head. Matt counted it lucky the boy was away from the window and the outside wall. Maybe he could avoid injury if he stayed put.

Matt crawled over to where Michael was cowering, which was difficult as he tried to keep from putting weight on his right arm. When he reached the boy, he put his hand on Michael's arm.

"Michael? It's okay. It'll be okay. I promise."

"How do you know?" he mumbled, still hiding his face in his arms.

"Because…" Matt trailed off. He was at a bit of a loss for how to explain to the boy. It was a deep faith, after all. Not necessarily logical, but based on what he knew about himself, and what he knew about this family he was with. "Because we're together," he concluded. "We're going to figure this out and everything will be all right."

Michael looked up at him finally, his face flushed and tear streaked. "You're sure?"

"I'm sure. But that means I need something from you."

Michael nodded. "Okay."

"I think you sitting here is a great plan. I'm glad you thought of it."

Michael smiled.

"Now, what I also need," Matt continued, "is for you to keep watch from here. Can you do that for me?"

He nodded. "The door?"

Matt nodded in return. "Yes. The door and that window. Think you can do that? Watch both of them? You can see them both from right where you're sitting. You're a good shot, right? If someone tries to come in either of those spots you think you can fend them off without hitting any of us?"

The boy swallowed, but nodded and grinned. "Sure I can, Matt. Sure."

"Great. That's what we need you to do. In the meantime just stay here, low like you are, and watch."

The gunshots continued outside the house, though Matt couldn't imagine they had any line of sight on anyone within. He heard chaotic shouting; some disagreement, maybe, between Vance and Addison. Some harried commands or directions. Matt couldn't focus enough to understand what they were saying. All he knew was that he had four other people he needed to keep alive all while being shot at.

Matt looked around the room again, and spotted Violet in place by the window. She was crouched down, under the windowsill, but held a small pistol in her hand ready to shoot. As Matt watched, the glass above her head shattered. Violet ducked, protecting her face with her arms. He had been wondering when they would finally hit the window. Now, at least, they had a space to shoot out of the house too.

"Violet," he called. "Are you okay?"

She looked at him quickly, nodded, and returned her attention to the shooting outside.

What a remarkable woman, he thought.

Next, Matt crawled across the floor, staying low and seeking out Silas and Mrs. Conway. The bedroom where the two had last been stationed wasn't too far, and Matt was able to reach them without injuring his arm much further.

"Are you both all right?" he asked from the doorway.

They were crouching on the floor, Silas by the window next to where the bed frame was propped up, and Mrs. Conway on his other side. She held two additional guns, and it looked as though she was ready to pass them to her nephew the moment he ran out of ammunition.

Silas only glanced at him grimly, before lifting his revolver back up to the windowsill and taking aim.

"We're just fine, Matt," Mrs. Conway said cheerfully. "We'll lick 'em in no time."

Matt almost laughed out loud, grateful for her positive attitude, even as he knew it was not realistic.

With every member of the family settled and as safe as possible, Matt returned to the main room of the ranch house to go over what other assets he had at his disposal. The manpower, the guns, his ability to reason with the sheriff, and ... No, that was about it. They had the walls of this house to protect them, but otherwise there was nothing else Matt, Silas or the Conways could do.

But he had to do something, because if they didn't make the mortgage payment by that evening, the entire property, all two-hundred-plus acres and the house and other improvements, would be forfeited back to the bank. And Matt couldn't allow that to happen.

He looked around the house again, certain there was something he was missing. There must be. While he looked, he moved the table and chairs back to fortify the door. He wasn't going back out there any time soon, not with a whole crowd of guns trained on the opening.

After Matt finished moving it by himself, he crouched down again backed up a few steps still looking around and at a loss for what his next move should be. With his next step, he felt an unevenness underneath him. When he looked down, he realized he was on top of the knot of rope that served as a handle for the Conways' root cellar. So far, no one had been very hungry that day—far too worried about living through the day to think about food—and he wasn't sure when anyone had been down there. Was there something, anything, hidden in the root cellar he could use?

Matt felt like he was grasping at straws, but was determined.

Using his uninjured arm, Matt wrapped his fingers around the rope and pulled up on the trapdoor. The comforting scent of cool earth greeted him, along with the louder sounds of gunshots. He looked down into the hole cautiously. There was still about a foot and a half of space between the floorboards of the house and the ground. Matt recalled being down in the crawl space with Silas a couple days earlier. He would need to remove another wooden door to get down into the root cellar.

Lying flat on his stomach in the house, Matt reached through the hole in the floor. His arm was just long enough to reach the edge of the wooden pallet covering the entrance of the root cellar.

But, as he struggled to move the wooden door from this distance, Matt realized he had another option.

He scooted his body forward a few more inches and hung his head down into the space under the house. Everything was upside down, but from this angle he could see all around the house. There was plenty of daylight to illuminate the space and he realized he was looking at the legs, ankles and feet of all of their attackers.

All of them.

If he could be quick enough, if his aim was true enough, Matt could shoot every single one of the men that were currently shooting at this house.

He pulled himself back up into the house to

consider. He would have to be lightning fast, faster than he had ever shot anything in his life. When he stopped to realize he had never even pointed a gun at another human being a few days ago, he was overcome with doubt. Could he actually do this? He didn't think he could get off more than three or four shots before one of the men realized where he was and fired back. Could he manage it in time?

Matt's thoughts were interrupted by a scream of pain. He looked around frantically, and realized it had come from the other room. Staying low, hopefully out of range of any bullets flying into the house, Matt crawled to the bedroom.

"Mother!" Violet called. She was just behind Matt, having also heard the cry.

"Mrs. Conway, Silas!"

Matt reached the doorway to the bedroom and grimaced. Mrs. Conway lay flat on her back across the floor of the room, right where the bed used to be. Silas had set aside his weapons and was working over her frantically. At first, Matt didn't see where she had been injured, but as Silas moved from one side of her to the other the growing patch of blood on her chest was apparent. Matt felt a chill wash over him at the sight. What had he done?

"No," he whispered. "No no no ... Silas what happened?"

Violet gasped from right behind Matt and then pushed past him to crawl across the room to her mother. "Mother!"

She looked frantically around the room for yet another piece of fabric she could repurpose into a bandage. Within arm's reach was one of the pillows that had been resting on the Conways' bed but now waited on the floor. Violet seized it, yanked the pillow out of the casing and ripped the fabric down the seam.

"I know, Mother, I know. This was a wedding gift. You've told me every time I washed it."

Matt was relieved to hear the teasing tone in Violet's voice. At least she wasn't panicking or desperate.

"What can I do?" he asked as he crawled closer.

Once he was at Mrs. Conway's side, he was relieved to see that while the bullet had pierced her chest, it was on the right side. Away from her heart at the very least, and low enough to not break her collar bone.

"Is this your first gunshot?" he asked her, trying to keep the mood light. "It had to happen sometime, I guess."

"Oh, please, Matthew," she wheezed. "Who do you think guarded the back of our wagon on the trip west to move here?" She started chuckling at the memory.

"Don't laugh, Mother," Violet scolded, as she leaned forward, pressing all her weight against the folded fabric. "We've got to stop the bleeding. We don't know when we're going to be able to get out of here to see Dr. Gilpin."

Silas had turned his attention back through the window, back toward the gang holding them hostage within the house.

He shook his head. "That's just the first. If we don't do something soon, we're all bound to get shot. Probably killed."

"I don't want to hear any of that talk, Silas Denbow," Mrs. Conway said shallowly. She struggled to get breath;

the bullet must have pierced a lung. "You think positive now. We have Matthew with us and things are not as dire as you're making out."

"He is right, though," Matt insisted. "We do need to do something soon, and I have an idea."

CHAPTER TWENTY-EIGHT

"What's your idea?" Michael asked from the doorway. "I wanna help!"

Matt turned, surprised to see that the boy had been listening. "Didn't I ask you to stand guard?"

"Well, yeah, but then, I heard ... I mean, Mother... And then, I was all alone."

Matt sighed. The boy was only twelve. "It's okay, Michael. You're right. It wasn't fair of us to leave you all alone in there."

"What was your idea?" Violet prompted, still focused on her mother's wound.

Matt glanced at Mrs. Conway and was relieved to see she already seemed to be getting stronger. Violet must have been able to staunch the bleeding.

"Well, the main problem here seems to be that we're surrounded, right? Weapons on all sides of us, so we have no hope of escape or even fighting back without being gunned down immediately."

"Cheerful," Silas muttered.

"But, I think if I go down into the crawl space below the house, I will be able to get some, or most of them. Probably not all. Even if I shot the fastest I ever have, someone will realize where I'm attacking from and I'll get hit. But I should be able to clear the way for you all to escape."

The other four looked at him in silence for a moment. Matt felt uneasy. What were they thinking about his idea?

"What?" he said suddenly unsure of himself. "I thought it was a good idea."

"It is. That's really smart," Violet said quietly. "Going under the house where you can get at all directions. I'm glad you thought of it, Matt."

She glanced at Silas who nodded.

"What?" Matt said, wondering what was being communicated silently. "What do you think?"

"Well, it just seems like you're taking a big risk all on your own," Silas said.

Matt sighed. "You're right. And, truthfully, I'll just be grateful if I'm able to come out of there alive."

"You can't shoot in all directions at once, Matt," Silas said.

"I know," he admitted. "Like I said, as long as you all can escape, I'll be happy. I'll start with the men in front of the house, just to be sure."

"No, that won't work," Silas said, shaking his head.

"You're not doing this on your own. We're coming with you," Violet said in a tone that rejected all contradiction. "We can do this together, Matt. It will be safer and more effective if all of us do this. Together."

"Wait," Matt protested.

"That is what you told me, Matt," Michael said. "That we'd be okay because we're together. Remember?"

"But, I can't let you—"

"Matt, please," Silas said, interrupting him. "They're both good shots. Fact is, they probably have just as much experience with a gun as you do, city boy. They both want to help. Are you really going to try to stop them? What are you going to do? Tie them up?"

"I—"

"All of us. Together," Violet said, slipping her small, soft hand into his.

Matt took a deep breath and looked at her. Looked at all of them. Looked at this new family he had found and would do anything to keep from losing. Even if that meant letting them put themselves in danger. Silas was right. They were all right. Together they would conquer this.

Without responding verbally, Matt lifted the trapdoor and pushed it all the way open. He took one final look at his allies, nodded, then dropped down through the hole. With the narrow space between the ground and the floorboards, Matt had a heck of a time twisting his body in the correct angles to maneuver himself. He needed to be on his belly, aiming his weapon out toward the circle of attackers, but going down feet first made that difficult.

After a few minutes of painful bending and turning, he finally got into position the way he wanted. Matt turned slightly to watch over his shoulder and saw Violet come down gracefully through the trapdoor next. The difference was she had thought ahead and dove down to the crawl space headfirst.

Matt smiled to himself. Smart woman.

Violet pulled herself through the dirt using her arms, crawling to where Matt was already situated.

"The second they start shooting back, I want you going back up through that trapdoor," he whispered to her.

She smiled and shook her head at him. "Back inside where my mother just got shot? Can't imagine it's much safer there, you know. I'm here to help, Matt. I'll be staying just as long as you do."

Their conversation was further interrupted by Silas and then Michael coming down through the trapdoor. The boy left it open behind them, so they could return quickly, and each of the four chose a position and a direction to guard. They negotiated in whispers. Matt insisted on being the one to shoot toward the sheriff and Addison.

"Fire on my signal," Matt said. "Fire quickly and try to hit as many of the men as you can. Once they start returning fire, go back. Don't argue. Don't hesitate."

He looked each one of them in the eyes, waiting to see that they nodded in agreement. Matt wanted this to end as quickly as possible, so Violet and Michael weren't in any more danger than they absolutely had to be. If Matt had an extra four arms to shoot with himself, he'd insist they stay inside.

But they wanted to defend their home, and who was he to stop them.

He nodded, pointing silently directing each of them to watch the feet of their designated targets. Matt faced forward again, watching the men in front of him. It only took him a few moments to recognize who was who.

Those mud-caked boots of Sheriff Vance were unmistakable.

Addison still was on his horse. Matt needed him to dismount. He didn't want to shoot the horse, but neither could he risk Addison getting away once the firefight began.

He waited and watched a moment longer. Silas cleared his throat. When Matt turned to look at him, the ranch hand nodded his head as though telling Matt to get on with it.

Matt had to do something.

"Wait here," he whispered to them. "I'll be right back."

Violet looked bewildered, but didn't question him as Matt crawled back through the dirt to the trapdoor, and then climbed up into the house. He tried brushing off some of the dust, but that seemed futile. He was covered with it and, besides, the floor of the ranch house was already soaked through with blood in places, and covered with broken glass and wood in others.

Matt was running out of time.

Still staying low, hopefully safe from more flying bullets, he hurried into the bedroom where Mrs. Conway was now doing so much better she was sitting up against the wall.

"Mrs. Conway, how are you feeling?"

"Matthew Hawke," she said teasingly. "You need to ask me something, don't you? You 'bout getting ready to propose to my Violet right now?"

Matt was surprised into an awkward chuckle. "Ah … No, no. No. Nothing like that. Not now, at least, no," he stammered. "I, uh…" Matt paused. He had completely lost his train of thought when she mentioned proposing to Violet.

"Because, you know, that's fine with me. I'm happy to have you as a son-in-law."

"Mrs. Conway, I … uh…" Matt blinked. Shook his head. Tried to recover his focus. He realized he still had his gun in his hand, which brought him back to the immediate situation. He laughed awkwardly. "Thank you, of course, but actually I was wondering if you'd be up for some light intrigue."

"If I can manage it, I'm happy to. What did you have in mind?"

Matt described the layout of the gang outside the house, and what he needed done.

"I'm sorry to even ask this. You should be resting and if the wound starts to bleed again—"

"Oh, hush, now," she said, interrupting him. "I can take care of this for you. I want to. They're not going to shoot at me, old and injured as I am."

"You're not old, ma'am," Matt said with a smile.

"Sweet boy." She moved to sit up. "Help me up now."

He gently, slowly took her hands in his and helped her to her feet. She gasped and had to stop several times in her walk to the front door, and Matt was there every step of the way. Once she reached front of the house, hand on the door handle, she turned back to Matt.

"Okay, son. Let me do my part. I heard what you said to my boy. We'll get through this together. This is my turn. You go back to your station. And God bless you."

He offered her a small, tight smile, as she kissed his cheek. This could all fall apart spectacularly, but he had done all he could do. Matt had swallowed his pride and accepted help from those he wanted to protect, but in doing so allowed all of them to become stronger.

And now he needed to get back into position.

This time through the trapdoor in the floor, Matt used Violet's wisdom and lowered himself down head-first, crawling forward as quickly and as quietly as he could. Once he was in place again, he made eye contact with Silas, Violet and Michael each in turn. They nodded to him and then turned back to face the men they were aiming at.

Above his head, Matt heard the front door of the ranch house open.

"Sheriff Vance?" Mrs. Conway called weakly. "Mr. Addison, thank goodness you're here. I've been shot, and I want to ... That is, I'm not sure I can ... Could you— I'm sorry, Mr. Addison, but do you think you could...?"

"Oh. Certainly, ma'am," Addison said.

Matt held his breath and listened. She had performed her part perfectly. She implied she was surrendering and needing help without actually saying so. She had managed to take advantage of the small piece of Addison that was still a gentleman. How could he refuse to help an injured woman?

This was the moment. With his eyes trained on the ground near Addison's horse, Matt took aim and rested his finger on the pistol's trigger.

There was a tiny creak of leather, as Addison shifted his weight to one side, and then a light thump as one foot landed in the dirt. Matt's heart raced. He didn't want to hit the horse. He had mere seconds. Addison's second foot landed on the ground and he took one step toward the house.

Matt closed one eye, looked down the barrel of his gun and squeezed the trigger. The resulting crack echoed under the house and against the boards, but it was quickly drowned out by the sounds of gunshots all around him. He took aim again, this time at what he knew to be Sheriff Vance's ankle, and squeezed the trigger. Matt was vaguely aware of his first two targets stumbling around, falling to the ground, holding their hands to the new wounds in their legs but he still had more targets.

He fired, again and again at the feet and legs of all the men in his line of sight. Though clouds of dust burst where he had shot the ground, he hit his targets more often than not. He reloaded his gun as quickly as he could and continued to fire. Around him he heard Silas, Michael and Violet each doing the same. He tried to keep one eye on the gang of thugs surrounding them, to be sure none had yet drawn their weapons and figured out where to fire back.

Bullet after bullet tore through the muscles of the men that had been attacking him. One after another the attackers fell to the ground, holding their wounds, cursing and yelling. Matt kept shooting. It was only a matter of time before one of the men looked under the house and realized where they were. He squeezed the trigger until all the bullets were fired and all the men were on the ground.

Quickly, he backed up toward the trap door again.

"Keep shooting," he called to his team. "Cover me, until they start firing back. Keep shooting!"

Matt pulled himself up through the trapdoor into the house, quickly grabbed more ammunition and reloaded his gun again all while making his way to the front door. He had mere moments to take control of the situation.

He opened the door and slipped out onto the porch, where Mrs. Conway was still standing. Only a short minute had passed since she had requested Addison's help. She had hidden one of the rifles in the folds of her skirt. Though she had to lean against the wall of the house to conserve her strength, she still had power enough to aim the weapon at Sheriff Vance.

Matt drew his own, yelling, "We've got you, Sheriff."

A flurry of cursing greeted him.

"You had your chance to do this reasonably. I won't ask again. Surrender," Matt commanded, training his gun on Addison. "Don't make me end this more violently than I already have."

CHAPTER TWENTY-NINE

With Matt's command for the men to surrender, all firing stopped. The injured men that were littered about the yard continued to groan and curse, but fortuitously, not one tried to fire back. Some had drawn their weapons, but dropped them in the dirt when they were hit. Some hadn't even gotten far enough to draw a weapon. Matt wondered how many of these men were hard and ruthless, like the sheriff, and how many were more reluctant participants like Curtis Bullock.

One, at least, who seemed to want to go down fighting, was the mastermind of this entire operation. Even with Matt's gun trained on him, Addison moved to draw his own weapon, as though attempting to call his bluff. Both Matt and Mrs. Conway reacted, each firing in Addison's direction. Matt's bullet hit the older man's thigh, while Mrs. Conway's landed in the dirt immediately to the man's right, and mere inches from his hand.

Addison yelped in surprise and put his hand to his new wound instead of the gun.

"I told you; I don't want to have to get more violent. Don't force my hand, Addison. You've been callous and cruel about all of this. I would feel no guilt whatsoever in shooting you again. This poor family doesn't need any more trouble from you."

"And what precisely are you going to do now, Hawke?" Sheriff Vance said with a condescending sneer. "You can't possibly hold all of us by yourself."

"He's not by himself," a sweet, feminine voice said from behind Matt. "He's got me."

"And me."

"And me."

"And me."

Matt didn't even have to look to recognize those voices. Every one of the remaining members of the Conway family was there backing him up. It had been brave of him to even attempt to take the sheriff into custody, to try to fight off a gang of muscle that had surrounded the house, but every step of the way these people that loved him were there to help. He could not have done it without the support of all of them. Together.

He felt a grin spread over his face. He had done it. He had reversed their fortunes and bested the corrupt sheriff, saving their lives.

Silas and Michael both stepped off the porch, to go see to the men on the far side of the house. Just because they had been injured and temporarily stopped didn't mean they would stay down. Matt and Violet set to work collecting the weapons of the men on this side of the ranch house. It took time to claim each gun, ensure they were safely disarmed and hidden away, but Matt hadn't gotten this far only to miss his chance.

As they slowly gained control of the group, Matt heard the approach of horses for the third time in twenty-four hours. This time when he looked up, past the trees to identify who was coming, what he saw made his chest feel near to bursting with relief.

"What do we have here?" the lead rider called in a droll voice.

He was about the age of Mr. Conway, grizzled short-cropped hair barely visible under his hat. His face was haggard and wrinkled, evidence of his weeks and months of work outdoors hunting down outlaws. The man's gray-blond mustache drooped low on each side, giving him an air of command and authority. He sat straight on his powerful mahogany-brown horse proudly.

There was no doubt who this man was. Especially since Matt noticed Curtis Bullock riding just behind him.

"You there," the marshal called to Matt. "You seem to be in charge of this mess. What is going on?"

"Are you the marshal?"

"That's right." The man reined in his horse and dismounted. He wrapped the reins lightly around a branch of the big spruce tree, and closed the final ten feet to stand in front of Matt. "Marshal Hollis. District of Wyoming Territory. This man here sent me a telegram saying you have a bit of a situation on your hands. You're Matthew Hawke?"

"I am, sir. Thank you for coming. This here," he said, gesturing to the angry man at his feet, "is Sheriff Vance. Did Curtis tell you about him?"

Marshal Hollis folded his arms across his chest and looked down at the sheriff. "Why don't you start from the beginning?"

As Matt began to explain the full extent of the sheriff's deceit, manipulations and crimes, the rest of the Conway family was taking care of all the other loose ends. Violet finished collecting the gang's guns into a pile she stacked on the porch. Michael went into the house to get his mother a chair, and then drew water from the well for them all. Silas saddled his horse and left for town to fetch Dr. Gilpin. Mrs. Conway needed to see a doctor sooner rather than later, and they also didn't want all the men to suffer anything worse than a leg wound.

Matt continued to talk, offering details and circling back to other parts of the story to fill in gaps he had forgotten. The marshal interrupted with questions periodically, but for the most part he just nodded and watched the injured men in the dirt.

"So, you say the man that just left," he pointed over his shoulder toward the gate, "is the same man that the sheriff here is accusing you of killing?"

"Yes, sir."

Marshal Hollis nudged the sheriff solidly in the side, enough to show him who was in charge, but not enough to injure him.

"Is that true, Mr. Vance?"

The sheriff almost didn't meet his eye, until the marshal poked him with his boot again.

"Well, I suppose that might have been Denbow," he admitted sullenly. "Of course, I can't say for sure, seeing as he's gone, but—"

"That's enough," the marshal said before turning to Matt. "Mr. Hawke, you have done a remarkable job here. I've heard complaints about this sheriff over the last few months, but never had enough evidence to do anything about it. Now that we have your testimony, we can get this sorted out as the law requires."

"So, then, can you lift the bounty on me?"

"Bounty?" He frowned. "Of course. With such flimsy evidence I can't believe this man even risked putting a bounty on you. Help me get this man up."

Matt and the marshal each took one of Sheriff Vance's arms and hauled him to his feet. In moments, he was handcuffed and tied with a lead rope to the marshal's horse. Matt next helped the marshal take custody of Addison.

In the chaos and explanations, Matt completely missed the next rider that came barreling through the gate. It wasn't until he heard someone call for "Susan Conway" that Matt looked up to see Mr. Bullock, the banker, riding up to the ranch house.

"I found it," he said, breathlessly. "I—" He stopped and looked around at the scene. His quick gaze recognized both Sheriff Vance and Mr. Addison taken into custody by a man not local to Juniper Falls. He frowned, but was not deterred from his original aim.

He came over to the porch of the ranch house, where Mrs. Conway was seated.

"Mrs. Conway," he said, waving a small stack of paper. "I found it. Your husband's life insurance policy. He had entrusted it to the bank for safe-keeping, though we hadn't yet had a chance to set up a safe deposit box for him when he passed. This form was," he flushed red, "it was in my office, ma'am. I'm so sorry."

"Why, Mr. Bullock, are you ... Are you certain?" She stood, still clutching one hand to the wound on her chest. Matt worried about her withstanding any excitement in her condition, but he knew better than to try to tell her that.

Mr. Bullock nodded. "I'm certain. This paperwork entitles you to several thousand dollars. Plenty to pay off the whole mortgage, not just the single payment owed."

"Several thous—?" she began wonderingly.

"Mr. Bullock," Matt said, interrupting. "Sir, the payment is due today, though. And I don't think that Mrs. Conway will be able to claim the insurance money and make her payment by the end of the day. There's only a few hours left, after all."

"Yes, yes. I thought of that, too. That's what this is." He thumbed through the stack of papers and pulled out one near the bottom. "I prepared it this morning just before riding out here. This is an addendum to the mortgage agreement that allows for one temporary extension. The life insurance policy is adequate collateral for the extension. Mrs. Conway, you just need to sign here and you will be legally protected for another couple months until the insurance comes through."

"Oh, heavens, Mr. Bullock. How can I thank you enough? You've thought of everything. You're too kind."

She sat back into her chair, looking bewildered.

"Are you all right, Mrs. Conway? Can you wait until Silas comes back with the doctor?"

She smiled at him. "You're such a sweet boy, Matthew. Yes, I'm sure I'll be fine. I'm just a little ...

flummoxed. This is a lot to happen to an old lady, you know."

"You're not old," he said with a grin. He had a feeling this might be a recurring protestation between the two of them.

"You," she said, shaking her head in amazement.

Violet moved away from them, but Matt could see the amusement in her smile.

"You," Mrs. Conway said again, putting a hand on either side of Matt's face and forcing him to look directly at her. "I'm not sure I will ever get over poor Richard's death, but you've done your part to make this whole mess easier."

"I didn't do anything special."

She didn't even acknowledge him. "Circle C Ranch is your home as long as you need one."

She held his hand in one of hers and squeezed it, directing her gaze to the ranch, the pasture and the sun lowering in the sky in the distance.

As Matt stood on the porch of the ranch house with Mrs. Conway, he watched the marshal ride away with several men walking behind the horse, tied to him and trailing.

Michael had gone off somewhere—maybe getting some sleep—and Violet was now the one drawing water from the well. There was plenty to clean, and Lord knew they hadn't had enough to drink over the previous day. Matt crossed the yard to help her.

Violet beamed at him when she noticed him approaching.

"Mr. Hawke," she said. "Can I offer you a cool drink? A little thank you for your service?"

Chained to the side of the well was a wooden dipper, perfect for drinking out of. She lifted a dipperful of well water and held it out to him, some of the water dripping down her wrist and onto the ground as she did. He took the dipper from her, his large hand closing over her small one briefly.

His long swallow went a long way to reenergize him. Water truly was God's miracle. Violet helped him to another drought without his having to ask. When he had drunk his fill, he returned the dipper to the bucket of water and asked Violet to take a walk with him.

There was so much going on close to the ranch house, and so much he wanted to say to her. After the chaos of the morning, Matt could now only think about this peaceful, calming presence at his side. He offered her his arm and led her through the yard, through the pasture, to the stand of cottonwood trees by the creek where they had had their intimate conversation just a few days previously.

"How are you?" he asked. "I'm so grateful you weren't injured, but I know it was a harrowing situation. I'm so sorry I had any part in putting you through that."

She walked forward a few steps to the wide tree with low branches that reached across the water. Turning to lean her back against one of the branches, Violet looked up at Matt with a serene expression.

"I'll be fine, Matt. I'm sure. My parents raised me to be strong in the face of adversity. This last twenty-four hours may be an extreme example, but I know myself. I can handle it."

He took several steps toward her.

"In fact," she continued, "I wanted to thank you for

not … for not treating me as though I would break. For respecting what I am able to do. I appreciate everything you have done for me and my family, but I also appreciate that you see me as I am."

"You've never struck me as a delicate flower," he said with a smile.

She shook her head. "In spite of my name."

He laughed. "I'm glad you were here through all of this."

"You did this," she said in a quiet voice, meant only for Matt to hear. "Not me. Not Mother. You did. You did this for us. I don't know what we would do without you."

He turned to her. There was a delicate curl that had escaped her hairpin and framed one side of her face. He wanted so badly to reach up and touch it, to feel the soft strands between his fingers, to tuck it back for her, caring and protective. Instead, he just took a step closer to her, close enough that he could smell the clean scent of her.

"You know, that's just what your mother said," he teased her. "She told me Circle C was my home as long as I wanted it."

"Oh?" she seemed to be feigning disinterest as she looked down at her hands. "And what did you say?"

"I didn't say anything." Matt's heart began beating faster as he realized what he needed to say next. "I thought I might want to speak to you about it first."

"Me? Really? Why?"

The teasing look on her face told Matt she knew exactly why.

"Violet," he said as he took her hand. "Violet

Conway. These last few days with you have been better than I could have hoped. Even though we only just met, I feel as though I have known you my whole life, that every step along the way led me to this very spot in Wyoming. I had no idea when I left Boston that you were who I was looking for."

"Oh, Matthew..." She blushed and looked down.

"Can I hope that you feel the same way?" he said, leaning closer to her.

He watched her shoulders raise and lower and she took a deep breath. She looked up at him, love shining in her eyes, and nodded.

"I love your family like it is my own. I love this ranch as though it were my own. I want to spend every day for the rest of my life working side by side with you, caring for the ones we love and building a life that we can be proud of. Violet Conway, will you marry me?"

"Yes, Matt. Of course, yes," she said breathlessly.

He leaned down to kiss her gently. Her soft warm mouth welcomed his and he knew in that instant that he had never been happier in his entire life. Everything was starting now.

They broke apart; he wrapped his strong arm around her shoulders and they both looked out toward the horizon, the ranch and the afternoon sun. This was the rest of their life. They belonged to each other and to this home they would build together.

I am so grateful you're here, that you've read my story. This book—*Hawke's Revenge*—represents a turning point in my writing career. It has always been dear to me, but I'm prouder of it than ever now. I started publishing western adventures as an experiment, and found I enjoyed them even more than I expected. A year into it, I had a handful of novellas released, was still learning how to market the books and research at the same time. This book was my first full-length novel in this genre, as well as my first book that included a romance subplot.

Those two things made all the difference, and *Hawke's Revenge* sold significantly better than my previous stories.

But it wasn't part of a series. It wasn't easy to advertise. As much as I enjoyed this book, I set it aside as I focused on other books and worlds to create stories for. But I always wanted to go back to *Hawke's Revenge*.

When I reached a point in my schedule that I could revisit the book, I decided to show it a little more love than I had time to do when it first launched four years ago. I did a final (final) proofread, while revising and adding almost 10% to the text. It is now in print and audio formats for the first time, with a custom cover designed specifically for this story.

As I did my revision, so much of the research and plotting came back to me.

Hawke's Revenge is set in the countryside of the Wyoming Territory, because I had recently read *Cattle Kingdom* by Christopher Knowlton. It is a history book that looks at the cattle boom of the late nineteenth century, and much of it takes place in Wyoming. I had been to that part of the country, and it seemed like the perfect setting for my story.

My personal memories of visiting Wyoming date back to when I was maybe thirteen or so. My family took a vacation to Yellowstone National Park, staying just outside the park boundaries for a week. Inside the national park, of course, were scores of meadows, mountains and forests, all of which would have been around in the late 1800s when this book takes place. But even outside the park, that part of the country is still used for grazing and ranches. It's incredibly easy to imagine what it might have looked like more than a century ago.

But also, as I read through the original version of the book, I was struck by how many details just never made it to the page. I mentioned that the characters are on a ranch, for example, but never follow-up with the sounds of the chickens, or the smell of cut grass or the feel of the well water splashed on the character's face after a long day of work.

I like to think my writing has improved in the four years since this book was written; I've changed and evolved the way I plan out stories and characters. I've gotten better at filling out the setting. There were certainly plenty of changes I saw to make as I made my revisions. Even so, I was surprised by how much I enjoyed Matthew Hawke, his backstory, his struggles and his hopes.

There's a sweet naiveté about the character that mimics my own knowledge of historical westerns when I was starting out. It's not a coincidence that this character is from a big city and doesn't know the first thing about ranching.

There are a lot more action scenes in this book than in the other books I write. A lot more gunshots. A lot more horse riding and injuries and blood-soaked bandages. A lot of remembering that the main character has a limp and I have to account for that in all the running he does. Revising the text gave me the chance to include more of those details, to hopefully make for a richer reading experience.

Juniper Falls is a fictional town, a few miles north-ish of Cheyenne and very roughly the location of Laramie, Wyoming, today. This was intentional so I could both not have to spend too much time researching specifics of an existing town, but also build it out to whatever I needed it to be. If the hotel needed to be across the street from the saloon, for whatever reason, I decided it was.

Cheyenne, of course, and the Wyoming Territory are both historically real. The US Marshal's office was historically located in Cheyenne, though the name of the marshal stationed there in the early 1880s has been changed.

The first railroad tracks were laid in Cheyenne in 1867. Cattle was brought to the area in 1880, and then a harsh winter of 1886-87 greatly setback the booming cattle business. For all these reasons, *Hawke's Revenge* is set in the spring of 1882, over the course of just a handful of days.

Other small changes include replacing some words that were not in use in the year when this book takes place. That's a simple consistency choice that I made for all my books only after *Hawke's Revenge* originally was released in 2019. The revision is minor, and likely unnoticeable, but it gives the book a more authentic air.

As with all of my books, I just want to live in this town with these characters forever. Chipper Mr. Demijon and steadfast Silas Denbow and the unnamed octogenarian couple living out on the frontier. Each person, even with only a few lines, is so clear to me. Though as of this writing I haven't decided to make Juniper Falls a series, the idea is always there in the back of my mind.

But for now, I'm just happy to finally give this book the attention it deserves and hopefully get it in the hands of more readers. I hope you loved it as much as I do.

A. T. Butler

(November 2022)

ACKNOWLEDGMENTS

If you are reading this far, I want to thank you first. Your time is valuable and I am so grateful.

Thank you to Alyssa, who introduced me to the possibilities in this genre. I'm not sure I would have ever ended up here without you.

Thank you to Spencer, who graciously listened to me talk about this book all through the original writing and for months afterward as I lamented not being able to give it attention. Your support helped me believe in myself when I would not have otherwise.

Thank you to OneMind, my mastermind friends who have watched my flailing and focusing and figuring out how to best support these books and my readers.

Thank you to readers who took a chance on the original version of the book, buying, reading, reviewing and telling other people about it. Without your reception back then, I would not have been revisiting the book now.

Thank you to my parents, who took me all throughout the American West when I was growing up, and for modeling a love of travel, outdoors, and self-sufficiency that now permeates my life.

ALSO BY A.T. BUTLER

Juniper Falls: Short Stories from the Western Frontier

Courage On The Oregon Trail Series:
Westward Courage
Faithful Trail
Frontier Sisters
Unyielding Heart
Wild Promise
Fierce Dreams
Seeking Home
Trouble and Grace (2024)

Oregon At Last Series:
Journey's End
Christmas in Oregon
Snowbound Promises
The Pastor's Baby
Frontier Fortune (2024)
Reluctant Spring (2024)

Jacob Payne, Bounty Hunter Series:
Trouble By Any Name
Danger in the Canyon

Justice for Jasper

Blood on the Mountain

Outlaw Country

Death By Grit

Desert Rage

Arizona Legend

Fool's Demise

Silent Night

Bountiful Justice Series:

Loyalty's Price

Riding for Justice

Trail of Redemption

ABOUT THE AUTHOR

I grew up in the southwest—California Missions, snakes and constant threat of drought weaving the backdrop of my childhood.

But it wasn't until I moved to Texas a few years ago that the magic and mythology of the American West began to seep into my soul.

I'd love to write about western adventures, strong women and noble men for a long time.

If you enjoyed this book, a review on your favorite retailer would be greatly appreciated.

- A

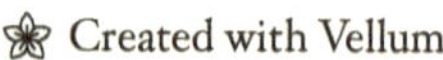 Created with Vellum

www.ingramcontent.com/pod-product-compliance
Lightning Source LLC
Chambersburg PA
CBHW061103190726
48286CB00006B/1856